A Convenient Wife

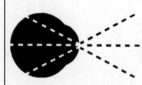

This Large Print Book carries the
Seal of Approval of N.A.V.H.

A CONVENIENT WIFE

ANNA SCHMIDT

THORNDIKE PRESS

A part of Gale, Cengage Learning

Detroit • New York • San Francisco • New Haven, Conn • Waterville, Maine • London

GALE
CENGAGE Learning"

LIBRARY OF CONGRESS CATALOGING-IN-PUBLICATION DATA

Schmidt, Anna, 1943–
    A convenient wife / by Anna Schmidt.
      p. cm. — (Thorndike Press large print Christian historical fiction)
    ISBN-13: 978-1-4104-3557-6 (hardcover)
    ISBN-10: 1-4104-3557-1 (hardcover)
    1. Widowers—Fiction. 2. Women teachers—Fiction. 3. Nantucket Island (Mass.)—Fiction. 4. Large type books. I. Title.
PS3569.C51527C66 2011
813'.54—dc22   2010048757

Published in 2011 by arrangement with Harlequin Books S.A.

Printed in Mexico
1 2 3 4 5 6 7 15 14 13 12 11

But if it were I, I would appeal to God;
I would lay my cause before Him.
He performs wonders that
cannot be fathomed,
miracles that cannot be counted.
— *Job* 5:8–9

To all those who have suffered
loss after loss in
spite of their honesty, decency
and devotion and
have not lost faith.

Chapter One

Sherburne, Nantucket
Late summer, 1850

The one thing that Caroline Hudson could not abide was a suffering child. Now she was looking at three of them, apparently all from a single family. The tall and lanky boy was dressed in pants two sizes too small and a shirt that hung from his bony shoulders like a nightshirt. Both garments were patched, frayed and smudged with dirt. Caroline judged him to be about twelve years old, although the way he kept his eyes focused on the toes of his scuffed shoes, it was hard to say for sure.

Then there were the girls. One was no more than six. A petite dark-haired china doll, she blinked up at Caroline from under thick black lashes and smiled. The other was clearly the eldest of the group. She was tall and thin like her brother, her strawberry-blond hair haphazardly braided without attention to brushing through the tangles, her clothing the fashion of a woman, rather than a girl of no more than fourteen. She faced Caroline directly, one hand protectively on her sister's shoulder as she peered up from under the brim of her bonnet and made her announcement.

"We've come for schooling, miss."

"I see," Caroline replied, looking beyond the children standing on her front porch. "And where are your parents?"

The girl glanced down and her brother looked up for the first time, his eyes darting about as if seeking the nearest escape.

"We've come for schooling," she repeated. "This is a school and my brother and I have come for lessons." She motioned toward the small brass sign on the gate that announced the entrance to Miss Hudson's School for Young Ladies and Gentlemen.

"The new session does not begin for another two weeks," Caroline replied. "Did your parents send you here alone?" Surely the parents were aware that Caroline's school was private and accommodated a maximum of twelve students whose parents paid tuition that it did not appear these children could afford.

"We come on our own," the boy muttered.

"Came," his elder sister hissed.

Caroline racked her brain for some adult she might connect with them. The entire island of Nantucket was a small and close-knit community and the town itself even more so. Caroline had lived on Nantucket her entire life. True, she did not personally know every citizen, especially those who lived in the more remote areas, but surely . . .

"My name is Eliza Justice," the eldest girl said, dropping into an awkward curtsey. "I'll be fifteen in November. This is my brother, Jerome. He's thirteen. And my sister, Hannah, is five, but I know that you only accept older children for your school so Hannah's just here to . . ." Eliza's confidence appeared to falter for the first time.

"And who are your parents?" Caroline asked.

"Tyrone and Sarah Justice," the girl replied.

"Your family is new to the community?"

Hannah piped up for the first time. "No, ma'am. We've been living here my whole life. Our house burned down and Mama . . ."

Eliza silenced her sister with a squeeze to the shoulder. "Will you teach us or not?" she asked.

"Won't you please step inside?" Caroline

11

could not believe she was asking these little ragamuffins to enter her home. Of all the homes on India Street, the Hudson house had been considered the finest. Of course, those had been the days before the great fire, the days before the whaling industry that sustained the island had begun to falter, before Caroline's husband of barely six months had decided to seek new wealth in the gold fields of California. Those were the days before he'd gotten himself killed in a saloon fight and she had been left with nothing but this enormous house that he had insisted they buy.

"It's important to keep up appearances, my dear," he'd pontificated when she'd protested they could hardly afford such a mansion. Now the house was hers alone, or more precisely, hers and the bank's. Caroline had opened the school in order to pay off the house and keep a roof over her head.

"Oh, my," Eliza whispered as she stood just inside the door and took in the spiral stairway winding all the way up to the third floor. Her gaze flickered over the large elegantly furnished rooms on either side of the expansive foyer and the gleaming chandelier that caught sunshine filtering through the fanlight over the front door.

"This way," Caroline instructed, leading

12

them into the cozy parlor she used for interviewing prospective students and their parents. She indicated the damask-covered sofa, one piece of a suite of furnishings her parents had sent as a housewarming gift. They resided in Washington, where her father served in the president's cabinet. Caroline was far too proud to let them know that Percy had left her deeply in debt. "Please sit down," she invited the children.

"No, ma'am, that's too fine," Eliza said, just as her brother started to perch on the edge of the sofa. He bounded back to his feet. "We'll stand."

"Very well," Caroline said. "Now then, Eliza, am I correct in guessing that your parents know nothing of this visit?"

Eliza flushed and for the first time she refused to meet Caroline's eyes directly. "Papa wouldn't care," she said, "and Mama always said that learning was the key to the future."

"I see. Well, certainly there is the public school where you and your siblings could go and learn for free. The Quaker school would be another option and . . ."

"They don't teach all the things you teach — manners, how to be a proper lady or gentleman and that. Mama said —"

The brass knocker on the front door

slammed repeatedly against the plate in a measured pounding that Caroline always associated with bad news. "Please excuse me," she murmured.

She peered through the narrow glass beside of the door and saw a man. He was dressed in a thick turtleneck sweater that was fraying some at the edges of the neck and sleeves, trousers that were patched at the knees and a seaman's cap pulled low over his forehead. He was tall, and the broadness of his shoulders and muscles in his arms were clearly evident through the knit of his sweater. His face — what she could see of it — was weathered by wind and sun. And his hair was copper in color with thick side-whiskers, while his face was clean-shaven. At the edges of his sideburns, his skin was discolored and an angry scar ran from his cheekbone through one sideburn. It disappeared beneath the high rolled collar of his sweater. She watched as he lifted his hand to the knocker again and she saw that the skin on his hand was also mottled and scarred.

Her heart went out to him. So many men had tried in vain to save people and possessions during the fire, and so many of them wore just such badges of their courage. Caroline pulled the door open before he could knock again.

The man snatched off his hat and squinted down at her. "Morning, ma'am," he said. "I believe my children have come here uninvited. I'll just see them home and beg your pardon for your trouble."

"And you are?" Caroline asked, aware that the three children had once again banded together in the sheltering protection of Eliza's arms.

"Tyrone Justice, ma'am."

"I am pleased to meet you, Mr. Justice. I am Caroline Hudson and your children have come to me to see about the older ones attending the school I offer here in my home."

The man looked away for a minute and it seemed to Caroline as if he was trying hard to control some force of anger within himself. "We'll just be going, ma'am," he repeated, as he tried to look beyond her to where they waited in the foyer. "Liza, come now."

Caroline lowered her voice and positioned herself more firmly in the doorway. "Your daughter's intentions were quite laudable, if misguided, in coming here today."

He glared at her. His eyes were as black as September storm clouds over the Nantucket Sound. "Misguided? You mean because I can't pay for your lessons?" It was more a challenge than a question.

Caroline sighed. Her late husband had suffered from that same kind of pride. What was it about men who, faced with hard times, insisted on clinging to their vanity?

"On the contrary, Mr. Justice, the children and I were just about to discuss why Mrs. Justice thought sending them to inquire about lessons was a good idea. Perhaps she failed to discuss the matter with you because she hoped to have it come as a surprise."

"There is no Mrs. Justice," he muttered. "Liza, Jerome, Hannah, let's go."

The children filed past Caroline. Bringing up the rear, Hannah gave Caroline's flounced skirt a slight tug. "Mama died in the fire," she whispered. "I was just a baby." And then she was gone, hurrying to catch up to her sister and brother and the man who marched ahead of them down the front walk, obviously confident that they would follow.

"Mr. Justice," Caroline called and was relieved to see him turn, then say something to Eliza, who kept walking back toward town with her siblings. When he looked back at Caroline this time he did not remove his hat.

"Mr. Justice," Caroline continued as she

16

stood just inside her closed wrought-iron gate and faced him through the bars. "Perhaps we can work something out. It's rare to see children who are so determined to learn." She laughed, trying to disarm his scowl. "Actually, most of my pupils come under duress. Perhaps Eliza could —"

He took half a step closer, grasped the bars and growled, "Don't you think I want my children to learn more than just the basics? Don't you think I try to see that they are in school as many days as possible? Don't you understand that there's little work to be had and what work there is keeps me away from dawn till after sunset? If Liza comes to your school, then who'll watch over Hannah?"

"Then send Jerome," Caroline heard herself reply and wondered at her determination to win a battle begun by three children in tattered clothing who'd had the audacity to knock at her door.

"Jerome can work."

"He's a boy," Caroline replied.

"He's big and strong and age doesn't always matter." He turned away, then immediately turned back. "Look, ma'am, I appreciate your concern, I really do. But people like you —" He glanced toward the house, gleaming under a cloudless blue sky and bright August sun. "— People like you don't understand. I pray you never have to. Good day, ma'am."

"People like me?" Caroline said in a low tone that made him pause and look back. "How dare you judge and label me, Mr. Justice? How dare you assume I have never known pain and suffering? You have lost your wife? I have lost my husband. You are struggling to find work? I have turned my home into a school just so that I can pay my bills and feed myself. Do not presume to think you know me, sir."

And with that Caroline turned on her heel and marched up one side of the dual stairway that led to her open front door. Without so much as a glance back to see if he had gone, she went inside and closed the heavy cypress door with a slam that rattled the glass on both sides of it.

Ty Justice stood outside the gate for a long moment after the teacher had disappeared back inside her grand mansion. He gazed up at the three stories of the house and realized that, first impressions aside, it was badly in need of painting and repair. He allowed his attention to wander on to the gardens — wild and overgrown — and then he suppressed the ridiculous idea that sprang full-blown into his mind. Shoving his hands into his pockets, hunching his shoulders as if the day were blustery instead of calm, he stalked off down the street.

By the time Ty reached the dilapidated fishing shack near the docks where he had settled with his children after the fire, Eliza was chopping potatoes and onions for soup. She did not glance up when Ty entered.

"Where's your brother?" he asked.

"I sent him for water. Hannah went with him."

Ty sat down in the lone wooden chair, which along with an old warped table and two wobbly benches furnished their one-room shack. He watched his daughter expertly dice the few vegetables into the smallest pieces so that everyone would be sure to have bits in their bowl of soup. Of his three children she was the one who most favored her mother. At least in looks. But she got her hair-trigger personality from him.

"Mrs. Hudson seems like a nice lady," he ventured.

"It's Miss Hudson," Eliza informed him. "After her husband left for California and no one sent word until he got killed, she went back to using her maiden name."

Ty was surprised at his daughter's knowledge of the woman. "And how do you know that?"

Eliza shrugged. "People talk and when you're a child, they assume you aren't paying attention. I know a lot of things." She set the knife aside and dumped the vegetables into the heavy iron pot, then wrapped her apron around the handle to lift it onto the stove.

"I've got it," Ty said, taking the pot from her. He waited until she was adding salt and pepper to the soup and added, "What's wrong with the public school, Liza?"

"We can't learn how to be proper ladies and gentlemen there." Eliza sipped the soup, added more seasoning along with a small piece of bacon fat and set the pot back on the little cookstove in the corner. "Mama always said . . ."

"Mama isn't here, is she?" Ty replied quietly. "Things have changed, Liza. I'm sorry for that, but it's a fact we have to accept."

When she said nothing and refused to meet his gaze, Ty got up and left the dark, close room. Outside, he headed to the far end of the wharf where he could take a moment and get hold of his emotions. They ran the gamut from sadness and grief to anger and guilt. Ever since the fire, he'd

20

been determined that his children know they could rely on him. And nothing aroused Ty's temper faster than a reminder that his late wife had come from a high-society Boston family. Sarah had assured him that, regardless of how much money he made, the children would be educated. Up until the fire, she had often talked about supplementing their public schooling with lessons in music and art.

But Sarah's parents had blamed Ty for her death after he had left her and the children alone to go and help fight the fire. After her death, they'd tried taking his children away from him, but the children — even as young as they were — had repeatedly run away, finding shelter on the docks of Boston in hopes of finding someone who would carry them back to Nantucket, back to Ty. Eventually his in-laws had given up, salving their consciences by declaring that the children were too much like Tyrone and nothing at all like their precious daughter.

Ah, sweet Sarah, he thought as he stared out at the harbor, only a tenth as busy as it had once been. *What am I to do? What's to become of them?*

There had been a time when Ty would have gone to church and on bended knee sought God's guidance for his troubles. But

Ty was no longer a praying man. He had given up his faith in anything greater than himself that night when the fire had raged through town, searing buildings and people without distinguishing as to one from the other. It had been Sarah who had insisted he go help put the fire out, assuring him it would never reach their little cottage near the bay.

But the fire had spread faster than any of the men who fought it could fathom, and when Ty had realized that his house — his family — lay directly in its path, he had run just ahead of the flames to the cottage. The first floor was already engulfed in flames and he saw Sarah at their upstairs bedroom window with their children. Eliza was holding the baby while Jerome helped Sarah tie bedsheets together and lowered them out the window like a rope. Then at Sarah's urging Jerome swung over the sill and shinnied down the sheets, testing their hold as he came. Next came Eliza, the baby tied to her chest in a sling Sarah had devised from one of her shawls.

Ty had pulled each child away from the house and given them over to the caring arms of his neighbors. Then he'd glanced up and seen Sarah frozen in the window, her eyes huge with panic. The sheets had come loose from the window and crumpled to the ground.

"Jump!" Ty had shouted.

"I can't," she mouthed and Ty understood that her lifelong fear of falling held her back.

"I'll catch you," he had promised. "Come on now, Sarah." Neighbors took up the cry.

But she had stood there, her hands riveted to the sill of the window. Ty had wrapped his mouth and nose in a water-soaked rag and dashed into the house. Blinded by smoke, he felt his way to the staircase and grasped the railing. It pulled free as it seared his palm. He stumbled up the stairs and into the bedroom in time to watch as his wife dived from the window, her nightgown aflame, her screams echoing against the crackling and burning of the house. He had stumbled to the window and leaned against its smoldering frame as he saw his wife lying below. It was hours before he realized how that hot wood had seared its imprint into his cheek and neck.

"Papa?" Ty glanced down now and saw Hannah staring up at him. "Liza says come and eat."

Ty shut away the vision of that horrible night and released a shuddering breath.

"Don't be mad at Liza, Papa," she said, "about going to the schoolteacher's house."

Ty bent and scooped his youngest daughter into his arms. "Oh, Hannah, Papa's not mad at Liza. I'm just sad."

Hannah sighed and wrapped her short stubby arms tight around his neck. "Oh, then I'll be sad with you, Papa, so you won't be alone."

Stricken with guilt that this baby was consoling him, Ty squeezed her hard, then released her and grinned. "All better," he announced. "How about you?"

Hannah considered this for a moment. "Still sad," she replied.

"Well, now, that won't do," Ty said, furrowing his brow. Then he started making goofy faces and Hannah tried hard not to laugh, but the giggles broke through as they always did. When Ty carried her back inside the shack, Jerome and Eliza looked up, trying to read his mood.

"You know, we just might be able to work out something with Miss Hudson and this schooling thing," Ty announced, after they'd eaten the soup and he'd exclaimed over what a good cook Liza was.

His eldest daughter gave no sign she had even heard him, other than her shoulders stiffening slightly. As usual Jerome looked to his sister for guidance and, not getting any, stared down at the table. It was Hannah who responded.

"Oh, Papa, do you promise?"

Ty hesitated long enough that Eliza turned to stare at him, and in her eyes he read her doubt. He glanced at Jerome, who was still focused on tracing a carving on the old table, then met Eliza's gaze directly.

"I promise."

CHAPTER TWO

The last thing Caroline might have imagined was that she would ever see Tyrone Justice again and certainly not twice in one day. But late that same afternoon, there he was, hat in hand, this time at her back door.

"Mr. Justice," she said, eyeing him cautiously as she debated whether or not to invite him inside.

"Miss Hudson." He bowed his head slightly, then stared up at the side of her house. "I couldn't help noticing that you've got some loose shutters up there on the upper floors. With winter coming on and all, I could fix those."

Caroline was well aware that her house needed work and she had hoped the influx of cash from the new term would allow her to attend to those very matters. But this was August and it was hard to imagine the cold, blustery winds that might come in a few months. "I'm afraid I can't afford repairs until after the new term begins — and perhaps not even then."

"I thought we might work out some kind of a trade." Unlike his son, Tyrone Justice met her eyes directly, and Caroline found she could not look away.

"What sort of a trade, Mr. Justice?"

"I could fix those shutters in exchange for lessons for my children."

It was hardly an even trade. Repairing the shutters would barely cover the cost of a few lessons for just one of his children. Caroline searched for the words to tell this proud man that she could not afford to offer charity. "Please step inside, Mr. Justice. That sun is still quite warm."

"Thank you." He wiped his work boots on the mat outside her back door and stepped into the kitchen.

"I was just about to make myself some tea. Would you care to join me?"

"Please don't trouble yourself."

"It's no trouble at all. Please have a seat, Mr. Justice."

Perched on the edge of one of her kitchen chairs, he did remind her of his son. She recalled Jerome seated on the edge of the sofa in her parlor earlier that day. The image made Tyrone Justice seem a bit less of a potential problem.

"Of course, I know fixing a couple of shutters is hardly a fair trade," he said as he watched her moving around the kitchen. "But it seems to me that there might be other chores you could use a hand with," he said. "Liza is an exceptional housekeeper, keeps our place spotless and she knows how to mend and sew. And Jerome? That boy loves growing things. He found an old oil barrel and cleaned it out and planted some potato eyes and onions in it. Why, we had potato soup this noon," he told her, pride evident in the way his eyes flashed and his voice rose with every bit of information he offered.

"It's late in the season for starting a garden," Caroline reminded him.

"But not so late that it wouldn't be good timing to prepare for next spring," he countered.

Caroline considered that fact along with the realization that it had taken a great deal for such a proud man to come back to her home. She placed sugar cubes and a saucer of lemon slices on the table and stepped to the stove to quiet the whistling kettle. "As I reminded the children earlier, there are free schools, Mr. Justice."

"Aye," he admitted. "I'd like to think of them here."

"Why?" She poured the water over the tea leaves, and set the pot on the table to steep while she got two cups and saucers from the shelf and set one in front of him.

For once Tyrone Justice was not watching her. He was fingering a patch on the knee of his trousers. "My late wife came from a family of high social standing in Boston," he said. "Eliza was right in saying that education was very important to her."

"Admirable, but why my school?"

He waited for her to pour the tea and pass it to him. She offered him lemon and sugar and he refused the lemon but dropped three cubes of sugar into the hot liquid. He sipped his tea, blowing on it to cool it. He was silent for so long that she thought he was ignoring her question.

"Mr. Justice, I'm afraid that —"

"I was set to leave on a voyage — this time as the ship's captain, when the fire broke out. That fire took it all — my wife, my home, my livelihood. I didn't want to lose my children, as well. I tried to do what was best for them and I let my wife's parents take them to Boston. Wanting to keep them here with me seemed like I was maybe just being selfish."

Caroline stirred sugar into her tea. *How could anyone think it selfish for him to need his children, after all he had suffered?* "I'm quite sure your in-laws must have appreciated . . ."

He stirred his remaining half cup of tea with a vengeance. "My wife's parents believed that I was to blame for the loss of their only child, and they hoped they might replace her by taking our children from me. 'For their own good,' they said, as if I would ever harm a hair on their heads."

"But you have them now."

Tyrone put down his spoon and, for the first time since Caroline had met him, the man smiled. That smile transformed his features, softening them, revealing dimples on either side of his mouth and taking ten years off the haggard lines of his countenance.

"They ran away," he admitted. "Not once but three separate times. Every time I would take them back to their grandparents, explaining to them how this was what their mother would have wanted, explaining that I was doing it because I loved them so."

"I take it the last time they ran away you decided not to return them?" Caroline was beginning to wonder if she could become embroiled in a legal issue, should she decide to teach the Justice children.

"No, ma'am. I took them back to Boston

each and every time, but that last time my in-laws refused to receive us. They had their butler meet us at the door with a note. In effect the note said they washed their hands of us, that they could see now that I had poisoned the children's minds against them and clearly nothing they could do would change that. They could only hope that someday the children would realize what they had given up."

Caroline sipped her tea and allowed the silence to stretch between them as she attempted to look at the situation from all sides. "Once again, Mr. Justice, I would ask, why my school?"

He cradled the teacup in his large hands, holding it as gently as someone might a delicate blossom. "Eliza is a great deal like me, ma'am. And I think maybe she wants to go back to that house in Boston someday and present herself to her grandparents. I think she wants them to see that she is indeed her mother's daughter — graceful, intelligent and refined. But she needs guidance and that kind of guidance won't come in a public school."

"And Jerome?"

Tyrone set the cup down and ran his fingers through his thick, curly hair. "I want my son to have every opportunity and it's

31

likely he'll need to leave this island to have that chance in life."

"Surely you could teach your son your trade."

"As I believe I mentioned, my trade was that of a whaler, Miss Hudson. It's hardly a viable career for a youth today. No, Jerome needs to learn his figures and his reading and how to conduct himself in the world of business."

Caroline hesitated, knowing she was on the brink of agreeing to the ludicrous idea of exchanging lessons for his repairs, and chores performed by his two eldest children. She tried to imagine the three scruffy children she had seen that morning sitting among the finely dressed children of Nantucket's wealthier families.

"I cannot," she said finally.

Tyrone stood up and frowned as he picked up his hat and headed for the door. "You mean you won't."

"I mean exactly what I said, Mr. Justice," Caroline replied as she too stood and moved to halt his progress toward leaving. "To place your children in the midst of my current roster of children would be cruel. The boys and girls that I teach are . . . well, frankly, the situation would put your children at risk for teasing and ridicule, and I will not be responsible for such a thing."

Tyrone blinked. "Because of the way they dress or because of me and where we have to live?"

"Children do not tolerate differences," she tried to explain. "Yes, the clothing would catch the attention of the others."

"And if they come here properly dressed . . ."

"And groomed," Caroline added firmly, seeing where he was headed. "Yes, then we could perhaps give the matter further consideration."

And again came that smile, like the sun breaking through the morning fog. Tyrone Justice thrust out his hand and Caroline took it, unable to look away from the unexpected warmth of his smile. He pumped her arm as if trying to fill a bucket with water from the public well, all the while babbling on. "And I'll see to those shutters first thing tomorrow and send Jerome to get started on clearing out those flower beds and Liza can help you with the inside work. You must have a list of chores to be done to get this place ready for opening."

"And Hannah?" Caroline couldn't resist teasing the man a little.

He frowned, then grinned down at her. "Why, Miss Hudson, did I fail to mention that with Eliza, you also get Hannah? Not one, but two helpers."

Caroline wasn't at all sure that this would work. In fact it was beginning to sound more and more as if she might be doing double duty herself — overseeing the children at their chores and then teaching them, as well. "You do understand that this — arrangement — is for a trial period only, Mr. Justice? I will allow them to come here for two weeks before school opens. In that time I will test their current aptitude in order to further evaluate where they might be placed in the program."

"Yes, ma'am." His tone was solemn but the way his eyes sparkled she was quite sure that he thought he had won her over.

"If for any reason I deem it inappropriate to continue our arrangement, then it will come to an immediate halt. I would be sorry to disappoint the children but I do have a loyalty to my . . . to . . ."

"Those who can pay," he finished for her. "There will be no cause for changing our bargain, Miss Hudson. My children know how to work hard. That's a lesson they've learned from me."

"Very well. They have two weeks from Monday before I'll need to determine if Eliza and Jerome — if there will be a place

34

for them in my class. Be very sure that both children understand that nothing has yet been decided, Mr. Justice."

"Yes, ma'am. And we'll start on those repairs and chores first thing tomorrow. You can start testing them tomorrow, as well."

But when the morning came, it was Eliza and Hannah who presented themselves at Caroline's back door, their curls covered in mop caps and their clean if patched dresses covered in aprons.

"My brother will be along later," Eliza stated as soon as Caroline answered the door.

"And good morning to you, Miss Eliza and Miss Hannah," Caroline replied. If she was going to teach these children, she may as well start right away.

"Morning," Hannah chirped, her usual sunny smile firmly in place in spite of the fog and drizzle. "Papa says we're to do whatever you say and no arguing." This last seemed more directed at her sister as a warning.

"Is Jerome not well?" Caroline asked as she ushered the two girls into the kitchen.

"Papa got a paying job cutting hay. He said that . . ."

Eliza cast her sister a glance that immediately silenced Hannah. "My brother will be along later," she repeated.

"I see," Caroline said, but she was thinking that Ty Justice needed to be reminded that there was little differentiation between a job that paid hard cash and one that traded service for service. After all he was the one who had practically pleaded with her to agree to this arrangement in spite of her reservations. She turned her attention to the girls. "May I please see your hands?"

Eliza held hers out, palms up, and Hannah mimicked her sister. Then she turned them palms down so that Caroline could inspect her nails. And all the while she stared boldly, even defiantly, at her inspector.

"Very nice," Caroline murmured. "Have you had your breakfast?" The girls were painfully thin, their skin sallow and their hair dull under their mop caps.

"Yes, ma'am," Eliza said as her sister chorused, "No, miss."

"Which is it?" Caroline asked.

Eliza's cheeks turned a speckled red as Hannah explained. "We had our tea like always but Liza had no time for making a proper breakfast. She had to get me dressed, pack lunches for Papa and Jerome, wash up herself and walk all the way here with me holding her back 'cause I'm slow."

With each word out of Hannah's mouth, Eliza's fists tightened and her eyes remained fastened on the kitchen floor.

"You have shorter legs than your sister," Caroline replied. "They'll grow and one day perhaps it will be you calling for Eliza to hurry up." She moved around the kitchen gathering eggs, milk and cheese, then slid an iron skillet onto the stove. "As it happens I have not yet had my breakfast and, since your father has complimented your culinary skills, Eliza, please prepare something simple for the three of us to share while I go over the schedule for the day."

Hannah was blinking up at Eliza with confusion.

"She wants me to cook us a proper breakfast," Eliza explained as she retied her apron and approached the stove. "How would you like your eggs prepared, Miss Hudson?"

"Surprise me," Caroline replied. "Now, Hannah, do you know how to set a table?"

"Yes, ma'am," Hannah said. "I do that all the time." She glanced around the large kitchen and her smile faded as she saw the stacks of clean dishes stored above the counter in glass-front cabinets. "I'm gonna need a stool," she murmured.

"I'll reach the dishes you need," Caroline

assured her. "You set the table." She saw that Eliza had carefully broken two eggs into a bowl and was now grating only a small handful of cheese onto a plate.

"I find that I'm quite hungry this morning, Eliza. Perhaps if you would double your usual recipe?"

"Yes, miss," Eliza murmured as she reluctantly added two more eggs to the mixture.

"We need three plates," Hannah announced proudly. "I can count to fifty," she added. "Papa taught me."

Caroline placed three plates in a stack on the table and very carefully Hannah distributed them.

"Now here are your napkins and flatware." Caroline laid out three linen napkins and three each of forks, knives and spoons, then turned to get the glasses. "And since you've already had your tea, perhaps a nice glass of milk would be good with our repast."

She turned to set the glasses on the table and found Hannah staring up at her, two little fists planted on her hips and a frown furrowing her brow. "You talk funny and we don't use nothing but spoons."

Caroline heard Eliza suck in her breath.

"But if all we have are spoons, how will we slice the bread?" Caroline asked calmly as she placed a loaf of wheat bread on the table.

"We don't need to slice it. See?" Hannah clamored up on a chair and reached for the loaf. "You just tear off a hunk — not too big though — and . . ."

"Hannah!"

The little girl froze at her sister's command. She looked from Eliza to Caroline and back again and burst into tears. At the same moment, Eliza stopped stirring the eggs she had poured into the hot skillet and ran to her sister's aid. By the time Caroline had rescued the loaf of bread that had tumbled to the floor, a thin trail of black smoke was rising from the skillet and the scent of burning food permeated the kitchen.

But before Caroline could think how best to address the situation, Eliza had already scooped her sister onto her hip, returned to the stove and used her apron to grasp the skillet handle and slide it to one side. She glanced around, then grabbed a pitcher of water and poured it over the burnt food.

"There. The fire's out and there's been no real harm," she murmured to her whimpering sister. She allowed Hannah to slide down her side until the little girl was standing next to her, clinging to her skirt, and then Eliza turned to face Caroline. "We'll go now, miss," she said. "Papa will see that you're paid for the ruined food." She wrapped her arm around Hannah and guided her toward the back door.

"Just a minute," Caroline said sternly. "You came for lessons and there's a lesson in this. Lessons can be difficult. Are you willing to give up so easily?"

Eliza turned and surveyed the mess they'd left in their wake. "You want us to clean up?"

Caroline sighed. "I still want to have my breakfast and, yes, I want you to help me clean this up."

"We can't cook in the skillet until it's been scrubbed," Eliza pointed out. "And we'll have to use more eggs, and . . ."

"Suppose we didn't have more eggs, Eliza. Suppose all we had were the bread, the milk and the cheese?"

Hannah was observing this exchange with interest, her tears forgotten. "We could have that for breakfast," she announced triumphantly.

"So we could," Caroline replied. "And now, Miss Hannah, if you would finish setting the table using all the utensils, your sister can put the skillet in to soak while I slice us some bread and cheese." She waited, knowing that Eliza was not nearly as ready as Hannah to accept this plan. "You want to learn to be a proper lady, and that includes knowing how to manage a household with all of the large and small tragedies and mishaps that might be involved," Caroline reminded her.

Eliza loosened her hold on Hannah and gave her sister a gentle push toward the table. "Set the napkins with the fork on top on the right side of the plate," she instructed, holding up her right hand as a clue. Then with a look that mirrored the fierce pride that Caroline had noticed on Ty Justice's face the day before, Eliza returned to the stove and began cleaning up the mess.

CHAPTER THREE

Several days passed before Caroline saw Tyrone Justice again. Jerome arrived each day late in the afternoon and spent an hour raking the yard and trimming the shrubbery, until darkness set in. Eliza and Hannah continued to arrive early enough each morning for Eliza to prepare breakfast and Hannah to set the table. On the third morning, however, Hannah had set only a place for one.

"What's this?" Caroline had asked.

"Papa says we're not to propose," Hannah announced.

"Impose," Eliza corrected. "We have our breakfast before we come," she told Caroline.

"Well, perhaps if you explained to your father that this is our time to go over your duties for the day," Caroline replied.

"Yes, miss, he knows."

Given the fact that the man had yet to

show up to perform the promised repairs, Caroline was disinclined to permit Ty Justice to decide how she should run her household. "Well, Eliza, I am uncomfortable eating while the two of you sit here, and we have far too much to accomplish for me to eat and then meet with you, so you'll just tell your father that . . ."

The look that crossed Eliza's face spoke volumes. She wasn't afraid of her father. Rather, she had too much respect for him as the head of their little family to oppose him, and Caroline realized that it was unfair to expect such a thing. "On second thought, I'll write your father and request a meeting so the two of us can decide the best course going forward."

"Yes, miss," Eliza murmured, relief evident in both her tone and posture.

That morning Caroline sent the girls upstairs to dust and at noon she called for them to wash their hands and join her in the dining room. There she had set three places with her best china and crystal and her grandmother's sterling silverware.

"Now then, ladies, our lesson for today is how to behave at afternoon tea," she announced. Eliza and Hannah stood just inside the entrance to the dining room and stared at the spread of fresh berries, bite-size sandwiches and tea cakes that Caroline had set on the sideboard. "Please remove your mop caps and aprons. You can leave them on the hall table. Then put these on." She handed each girl one of her hats and a pair of gloves.

Hannah giggled with delight. "We're going to play dress-up," she crowed.

"Shhh," Caroline heard Eliza advise. "Just do what she says and don't say anything."

When the girls returned wearing the hats and gloves, Caroline was waiting to greet them. "Good afternoon, ladies. How lovely of you to come," she said. "Please have a seat."

Hannah immediately took the chair at the head of the table. "You're not wearing a hat or gloves," she commented, as Caroline waited for Eliza to sit and then took the place across from her.

"That's quite observant, Miss Hannah," she said. "I am the hostess. This is my house and one does not wear hat or gloves in that situation."

"Oh. Does one eat?"

"Hannah!" Eliza looked as if she might happily crawl beneath the large table.

"That hat is so very becoming on you, Miss Eliza," Caroline continued as she poured a cup of tea for each of them.

44

"Thank you?"

Caroline nodded her approval and saw Eliza relax slightly. She passed the plate of sandwiches and quietly stopped Hannah after she'd taken three. "Eliza?"

"No, thank you?"

Caroline frowned.

"Perhaps one," Eliza added, quickly realizing her mistake.

"If Jerome was sitting here, he'd eat the whole lot of them," Hannah commented as she stuffed an entire sandwich into her mouth.

"All right," Caroline said, "let's take a moment here to reflect. Eliza, do you see anything amiss?"

Eliza appeared to swallow her own sandwich whole and then looked over at Caroline's empty plate.

"We didn't wait for you?"

"Very good. Shall we try again?" Caroline offered Eliza the platter of sandwiches and the girl took one, placed it on her plate and waited. Hannah, vigilant as always to everything going on around her, finished chewing the sandwich she'd crammed in her mouth and copied her sister's actions.

"Excellent," Caroline said and beamed at the two girls. They really were quick to learn and eager, as well. She had accomplished far more than either of them had realized. For when they had refused breakfast and yet could not help but look longingly at the food Caroline had had little appetite for, she had become determined to feed them before she let them go for the day. Combining a meal and a lesson had seemed an inspired idea and one that even Tyrone Justice could surely find no fault with.

At first Ty thought his daughters' sudden loss of appetite was the product of exhaustion after the long hours they spent working at the school every day. He suspected that Miss Hudson was less than pleased that he had not fully lived up to his end of their bargain. But the opportunity to earn some real money bringing in old man Hatter's hay crop was not something Ty could afford to let pass. Surely the woman could appreciate that. Surely she wouldn't take out her irritation on his girls, making them do extra work to make up for the absence of him and his son.

"You girls had better eat," he muttered as he chewed a piece of the hard, stale bread he'd managed to save from the loaf Mrs. Hatter had brought out to the fields at noon that day.

"Papa, do not speak with your mouth

full," Hannah advised. "Miss Hudson says to wait until you chew and swallow, and then speak."

Hannah seemed not to notice the sudden silence that fell over the table. Instead she proceeded to demonstrate her lesson by chewing a tiny morsel of potato and then swallowing in an exaggerated way. Jerome, unsure of whether he should laugh or remain silent, glanced over at his father.

Ty had turned his attention to Eliza. "What's that woman teaching you?" he asked.

"Table manners," Eliza replied.

"Table manners? What about the reading and arithmetic? What about teaching you lessons that will do you some good?" He fought to control the temper that, though never far from the surface these days, he had always refused to show in the presence of his children.

"She gave us a book," Hannah announced, clamoring down from the wooden bench to retrieve three slim volumes from the bed she shared with Eliza. "She sent along one for you, Jerome, but you have to return it and pass a test," she added, her voice filled with awe. "And Eliza has a note from teacher for you, Papa, and we did so good today that she sent along the rest of the cakes for us to share with you and Jerome."

"Cakes?" Ty's pride roiled within him. His children did not need charity.

"And the most hugest blueberries I ever saw," Hannah continued.

Ty stood. "Give me the note, Liza."

His daughter fished in her apron pocket and produced a small cream-colored envelope with his name written on the outside. "Now, wrap up the cakes and berries," he said and left the shack.

From inside he could hear his two younger children protesting the loss of the treats. Liza calmed them, although her own voice sounded wistful.

He slid his thumb under the sealed flap of the envelope and pulled out the folded paper.

Dear Mr. Justice,
Please be so kind as to call at my home at your earliest convenience so we may discuss the arrangement we seem to have agreed to in principle if not practice.

Yours truly,
Caroline Hudson

What was that supposed to mean? Ty wondered as he mimicked her words under his breath. He tried to envision the petite

48

blond woman with the startling green eyes sitting at her desk penning the note. He read it again, searching for some underlying message.

"Here," Eliza had come outside, too, and she thrust a basket at him. "Can we keep the books? They're only borrowed. She didn't give them to us."

Ty considered that and nodded. Without a word, Liza turned back to the shack. "Has she given you anything else?" Ty asked.

"No, sir." Liza paused. "But that first day we went I burnt up some eggs — four of them — and she had to throw them out."

"Did she ask you to pay for them or replace them?"

"No, sir." She waited for him to say something more and when he didn't she asked, "Can we still go there — Hannah and me? And Jerome when you can spare him?"

Ty realized she was almost holding her breath waiting for his answer. He picked up the basket and then pulled Liza to him and kissed her forehead. "Let me go visit her and see if we can work it all out. But, Liza, no more eating there. You pack a lunch for you and Hannah, same as you do for me and Jerome."

■ ■ ■ ■

Caroline was sitting in her garden, enjoying a book of poetry and the evening breeze when she heard the creak of her front gate.

"Why, Mr. Justice," she said as she marked her place in the book and laid it aside. "Won't you join me for a glass of lemonade?"

"I've already eaten," he said as he set the basket on the table and removed his seaman's cap. "Your note said come at my earliest convenience, so here I am."

"I appreciate that, although there was no need to bring a gift."

"Cakes and berries you gave my girls. I don't need your charity, miss, and neither do they."

Caroline frowned. "And do you approve of waste, sir?"

He looked directly at her for the first time. "Waste?"

"Precisely. Those cakes are a day old, as are the berries. Such delicacies do not last. My choice was to throw them out or give them to someone I thought might enjoy them while they were still reasonably fresh."

"Or you could eat them yourself," Ty reminded her.

Caroline laughed. "And so we move on to the sin of gluttony, Mr. Justice. I could hardly consume all of those treats myself. Eliza and Hannah were so pleased with the idea of sharing them with you and your son, especially when the two of you spent this dreadfully hot day in the fields. Consider them a gift from your children, who love you dearly, not as a gesture of charity from me."

"I don't want you feeding my girls," he said. "I understand there's eggs to be repaid and . . ."

This time Caroline felt annoyance override her usual good humor. "I have not asked for eggs and I have fed your daughters in the course of providing them with the lessons you requested. I do not understand your objection."

"My objection is that —"

"Perhaps you are feeling some guilt in that you elected to accept the job in the hay fields and take your son there as well, rather than attend to your promise to —"

"That's a paying job, miss. There's rent to be paid and food to be bought and —"

They were talking over one another, their voices rising enough that Caroline was aware of attracting the notice of a passing neighbor.

"Please sit down, Mr. Justice," she said, indicating the scrolled wrought-iron chair opposite her.

As usual, he barely occupied the space of the small chair, choosing instead to sit on the edge as he rolled his hat in his hands.

Caroline sat across from him and took a deep, calming breath. "Now then, perhaps we should begin again. Are you still interested in having your children receive their schooling with me?"

"Yes, but —"

Caroline held up her hand. "Very well. Shall we renegotiate the terms of that arrangement, since your original plan does not seem a practical one?"

"I'll get to the shutters and repairs as I promised," he growled, refusing to meet her eyes.

"Please look at me when you address me, Mr. Justice. You are not some indentured servant in this. We are agreeing to terms. We are equals, in that each of us can offer something the other one needs and wants. Now, then —"

His head shot up and Caroline had a moment's pause once his eyes met hers. He leaned slightly forward and placed one hand on the small table that was all that separated them. "I am not your equal, Miss Hudson.

You have this house, you have a paying job, you can meet your obligations."

Caroline swallowed and met his eyes directly. "And you have those children, sir. In terms of personal fortunes, I would say you are the far richer of the two of us."

The silence stretched between them. Ty was the first to break it. "I'll be finished at Mr. Hatter's the day after tomorrow. Monday I can start the work here."

"Unless some other paying opportunity arises?"

"I'll be here."

"And Jerome as well?"

"Yes."

"Very well." She stood up and Ty got quickly to his feet, as well. She held out the basket of cakes and berries. "In the meantime, please do not insult me by refusing a gift that was meant only as a gesture of appreciation for the excellent help your children have provided these last several days. You have taught them the lesson of responsibility, sir, and whether or not you continue to allow them to come here, that is perhaps the most valuable lesson they could possibly learn at such a tender age."

"Thank you." He glanced over at the garden. "I'll still need Jerome tomorrow for most of the day, but he'll be here first thing on Saturday."

Caroline nodded. "Excellent. Then it will be the same schedule as I have set with Eliza. For every two hours he works, we will spend half an hour on lessons, and I will send him home with a book or exercise to complete before our next session."

"What about Hannah?"

"I teach children much older than Hannah, Mr. Justice. My students are on the brink of adulthood. However, I see no reason why Hannah could not come here with her siblings, at least until we can determine whether or not the older children will attend my school."

Ty took hold of the basket, his fingers brushing hers in the transfer. "And if I start Monday, I should be able to finish work on those shutters by the end of the week. Then if you'll make up a list, we can . . ."

"Mr. Justice, I do appreciate that a paying job must come ahead of our barter. Perhaps it's best if we see how things go up to the opening of the semester before I make such a list. Now, won't you please stay and join me for a glass of lemonade?"

"No, thank you, miss," he said. "I'd like to share this rare and special treat with my family. You have a good evening, now."

Caroline did not miss the emphasis he

54

placed on *rare* and understood that making a regular habit of giving the children food to share with him would not be appreciated — or tolerated.

"And a good evening to you and the children, Mr. Justice," she replied, wondering why it felt as if it was she who had received the greater treat. Tomorrow the delightful Hannah and the intriguing Eliza would return, challenging Caroline without a word to come up with ways to expand their horizons. And by week's end, Jerome would be there regularly, as well.

Caroline picked up her empty glass and the book of poetry. Down the street she was quite sure that she heard Tyrone Justice whistling a sea tune as he reached the end of her block and turned the corner toward town. She envied him the evening he would spend with his children as she walked inside her empty house and closed the doors for the night.

As promised, Tyrone Justice came to her house late on Monday afternoon and went to work until it was no longer light enough for him to see. While he repaired the shutters and parts of the roofing that had come loose over the last winter, Jerome worked in the garden.

Ty had been right to give Jerome responsibility for the yard work. Caroline had gone outside one afternoon to point out some perennials she hoped to save, and Jerome had simply nodded and continued pulling out vines and brush that had covered over the more desirable plants. The following morning when she'd gone out to inspect his work, she had fully prepared herself to find those plants she had hoped to save gone with everything else.

Instead each plant, along with some she had quite honestly forgotten had once blossomed there, had been carefully pruned and mulched, and the earth around it had been cultivated to allow room for the plant to grow properly in the spring. If this one bed was any example of Jerome's work as a gardener, then he was every bit the treasure his father had promised.

She walked past the long wooden ladder still resting against the side of the house and looked up.

"Mr. Justice?"

No response, and she wondered at her disappointment that she had missed him. Tomorrow she would compliment the boy in his father's presence.

Saturday morning, before the term was officially scheduled to begin on Monday, the rain was relentless and the island was covered in a thick, gray fog. The Justice children arrived at Caroline's door soaked and bedraggled.

She had avoided dealing with the decision of whether or not to permit them to enroll in her school, but now time was growing short and it would be only fair to let them know her decision one way or the other.

They had all certainly lived up to their end of the bargain, and yet she leaned more and more toward facing the difficult task of telling Tyrone Justice that she could not accept Eliza and Jerome in her classroom. It was hardly a matter of their scholastic ability. Both Eliza and Jerome were bright children who caught on easily to the exercises she had used to test their aptitude. Eliza was gifted in expressing her ideas through the written word, even poetry, while Jerome had a greater gift for numbers and science. Even the irrepressible Hannah was a quick study, delighting most in what she considered the games Caroline used to teach them proper manners.

There was little doubt that Jerome and Eliza could shine in the classroom. But as Caroline watched them gather round the kitchen stove to warm themselves and as they stripped off frayed mittens and scarves and slid their stocking feet out of scruffy shoes, she knew that she had to face facts.

The first fact was that she was fully booked for the semester. And even if she had the space, Tyrone Justice's children had no proper clothes. The other students would see their obvious poverty as a sign of weakness. They would make assumptions about Eliza and Jerome — testing their abilities, their ambitions, their worthiness.

Not that her students were intentionally mean or petty, but they had all been raised to attach high value to a person's social upbringing and genealogy. Some of her pupils could trace their ancestry back to the *Mayflower,* and all could claim kinship to one or more of the founding families of Nantucket. No, it would never do. It would be unfair to the Justice children to subject them to the possibility of ridicule.

"Is your father coming today?" she asked.

"Yes, ma'am."

"He went to borrow some tools he needs," Hannah announced.

The three children took their places around the kitchen table and waited for Caroline to give them their chore assignments for the day.

"Our work today will be concentrated in the classroom," she said, focusing on her list rather than the eager faces of the children. "We need to wax the desktops, fill the inkwells, distribute the readers and slates and . . ."

"You get your own slate," Hannah whispered excitedly to her siblings.

Eliza shushed her and gave Caroline a look of apology.

"Girls, everything will need dusting, and please pay special attention to the railings and corners. Jerome, please concentrate on making the entrance as presentable as possible."

"Yes, ma'am."

It struck Caroline that Eliza had been especially quiet since arriving. Her long hair hung dank and limp around her face and she seemed distracted.

"Eliza? Are you not well?"

Her eyes widened. "Oh, no, ma'am. I mean, yes, ma'am. I mean, quite well, thank you." But Caroline saw a heartwrenching sadness shutter the girl's eyes, which were so much like her father's. Her heart beat an irregular staccato. Something was clearly wrong. Had some new misfortune befallen the family? Was Tyrone hurt or ill or . . .

"Jerome, why don't you and Hannah get started? You can unpack those boxes in the classroom. Go along, now," she urged, when both children glanced at their elder sister for approval.

When they had gone Caroline poured a cup of tea and set it in front of Eliza. "What's happened?" she asked.

Chapter Four

Eliza hesitated but then wrapped her palms around the teacup to warm them. "A man came to the cottage late yesterday. He was there when we got home and Papa was upset. I know I shouldn't eavesdrop, Miss Hudson, but Papa seemed so worried."

"And what did the man want?"

"He works for a woman in town who owns the whole row of fishing shacks and warehouses that survived the fire along the wharf, and I think she's going to tear them down and build something else."

"But where will you and the others who live there go?"

Eliza shrugged. "Papa asked the same thing. The man said it wasn't his problem."

"Did he say how much time the owner was giving you to find other accommodations?" Ordinarily Caroline would not encourage the girl to report a conversation she should not have heard, but this was serious.

"No, ma'am, but Papa didn't go to borrow tools. That's what I told Jerome and Hannah. It was a lie, but sometimes . . ."

"Where did he go?"

"I think he went to see the woman." Her eyes filled with tears. "Oh, Miss Hudson, if we have no place to live, how will we be able to come to school here?"

Caroline felt a flush of guilt. Hadn't she spent a good part of the previous hour trying to come up with a way to let the children know she could not take them on as pupils? "I'm quite certain your father will come to some solution," she assured Eliza. "Now, finish your tea and go join the others. We have a great deal of work to do today."

"Yes, ma'am." Eliza swallowed the last of her tea and took her cup and saucer to the dry sink. "Miss Hudson?"

"Yes."

"Thank you for everything you've done for us. I mean, even if we can't come to school here, we've already learned so much."

Caroline tried to find her voice around the lump that seemed to block her throat. In the short time she'd known them she'd come to care so much for these precious children. "You've earned everything you've gotten since coming here," she said and meant it.

"I was thinking maybe I could keep working for you, even if we can't come to school?" The girl's question was spoken barely above a whisper and was as much a plea as an inquiry.

"Let's not get ahead of ourselves here, Eliza. We must assume that nothing has changed until we know differently."

"Yes, ma'am."

But things had changed already. Caroline's determination to let the children know they could not possibly enroll as regular pupils now seemed unusually cruel. Surely there was another way.

The scraping of heavy boots outside the back door interrupted Caroline's thoughts. She opened the door to Ty and saw in his ravaged features the answer to her unspoken query. Whatever had transpired between him and his landlady, the outcome was clear. He and the children were to be evicted. And yet Caroline would not betray Eliza's confidence by revealing that she knew the real reason he was late.

"Come in at once," she said and saw that her sharpness had left him with the impression that her concern was for the wind and rain blowing into the kitchen, rather than for him. That was her intent, for Ty Justice was a proud man and would not accept pity from anyone — least of all her, a veritable stranger.

Without a word of greeting, he pulled off his slicker and hung it on a hook by the back door. In seconds a puddle had formed on the floor below. He glanced around and spied an empty pail, which he placed under his coat to catch the water. "I'll be working indoors today unless the weather lets up, if that's all right. I can check the chimneys," he mumbled as he headed for the hallway.

"You'll need to remove those wet shoes," she said absently. Her attention was focused on the sudden realization that the children might well have been better off if she had never agreed to give them even a taste of her world.

Ty glanced down at his shoes, mumbled an apology and bent to untie the laces.

"Here, sit a moment." Caroline pushed a kitchen chair in his direction. "Do you want a cup of tea? It will rid you of some of the dampness."

To her surprise he nodded. "Tea would be nice." He finished removing his boots, set them by the door and took a place at the table. Caroline could not help noticing that one sock needed darning.

"We have to discuss your children, Mr. Justice," she said as she set the tea in front of him and took a place across from him.

Ty took his time adding three sugars — same as Hannah did. "I know you're thinking they can't stay," he said. "I know we've been fooling ourselves and I should have put an end to it a week ago. And now . . ."

His voice trailed off as he concentrated on stirring his tea.

"And now?"

"It's out of my hands," he said. "We'll be finishing up whatever is needed to get you open on Monday and that'll be the end of it."

"What about the children?"

"They are my children, miss. They are not your concern."

"Please, Mr. Justice, do not deny them this opportunity."

Suddenly he was on his feet, pacing from the table to the window and back again. "I would deny them nothing if it were in my power to give it to them, but we do not live in that world. My children and I live in a world where we are dependent on others, Miss Hudson. I doubt you can fathom what that can do to a man . . . to a father."

He was such a devoted father, Caroline

cast about for something — anything — that might ease the pain that marred his handsome face. "Perhaps if you prayed on the matter —"

The bark of his laughter seemed to rattle through a body devoid of humor. "And exactly where would I direct such a prayer, Miss Hudson? To the God who took my wife, my children's mother? To the God who left me with no way of earning a proper living so I could care for my children? To —"

"Stop that this instant," Caroline ordered. "I will not permit you to blame God in this house or in my presence." Her reprimand was born of pure frustration. She was a woman used to solving problems, but there seemed to be nothing she could do for the children — or for Ty.

The two of them locked eyes across the table. Then without a word, Ty grabbed his slicker and his boots and went back out into the rain, slamming the kitchen door behind him.

Ty jerked the laces of his boots tight and knotted them, then rammed his arms into the sleeves of his slicker before crossing the yard. He'd left his hat back there in the kitchen. No matter. There was no way he was going back to claim it. The schoolteacher could have it. More likely she'd send it with Eliza later.

He walked without thought of direction, up one block and down the next, oblivious to the fine houses he passed and grateful that the weather had kept most other people off the street and out of his way.

He wished Sarah were with him. She had been the antidote to his quick temper.

"Oh, Sarah darling, why didn't you jump while I was there to catch you?" he muttered aloud.

A man in a black frock coat and stovepipe hat approached Ty. From beneath a large black umbrella he looked at Ty strangely and then crossed over to the other side of the street.

"Wandering around in the rain talking to myself. That's going to sit well with the locals." He jammed his fists into his pockets and hunched his shoulders against the downpour.

"Mr. Justice!"

The voice was muffled by the rain and wind but that uppercrust lilt was unmistakable. Ty kept walking. He'd seen the pity in Caroline Hudson's eyes when she'd sat across the table from him. He didn't need pity. He needed a job and a roof over the heads of his children. He stalked on, ignoring the repeated call of his name, and then stopped in his tracks when he heard his youngest shout, "Papa, wait!"

What could the woman be thinking, bringing a child out in weather like this? Furious, he turned and started back toward the tall form and smaller one barely visible through the downpour.

Hannah catapulted herself into his arms. "Oh, Papa," she chastised as she ran stubby fingers through his wet hair, "you are soaked to the skin."

It was impossible not to feel a slight flicker of humor at this child's adult reprimand. Caroline offered him the shelter of her large black umbrella and he held it over them. Their eyes met and held. Flustered, Ty turned his attention back to his child.

"And what, may I ask, brings you out on such a day, Lady Hannah?"

Hannah giggled. "You forgot your hat and Miss Hudson was coming to bring it to you and I . . ." She cast a wary eye at the teacher, then looked abashed and said, "I ran after her, even though she told me not to come."

"You must learn to mind your elders, Hannah," Ty said, but he was looking at Caroline, noticing for the first time that she'd come out without her bonnet.

In spite of the umbrella, her hair was covered with fine beads of moisture and instead of weighing down her curls, the dampness seemed only to encourage them to curl more. The overall effect softened her features, and he realized that Caroline Hudson was beautiful. She was wearing a cape of navy-blue wool and he could smell the mustiness of the wet fiber mingling with the lavender soap she seemed to favor. She'd given Eliza a cake of that soap and the girl had treasured it as if it were frankincense and myrrh. So caught up was he in his discovery that behind the façade of the stern schoolmarm lay a vulnerable and caring woman that it took a moment for him to realize that she was offering him his cap.

"Too late for that to be much protection," he said and stuffed it into his hip pocket. He hitched Hannah more firmly onto his hip and lifted the umbrella higher to cover the three of them. "Take my arm, Miss Hudson."

She hesitated.

"It's better to keep the three of us close enough to fit under your umbrella."

She nodded and slid her fingers around his crooked elbow. "You know, Mr. Justice," she said in a voice pitched higher than usual, "The fireplace in the classroom was repaired last spring. However, please do check the fireplaces in all the other rooms, including the upstairs bedrooms, to be sure they are working properly."

So this was the tactic she had chosen — to simply act as if their conversation about his children had never taken place. Sarah had done that, as well. Was it a trait of the oh-so-polite blue-blooded society both women came from? Or was it just something women did? And what did the source matter? It was the result that counted and, to his way of thinking, the result was that somehow the woman had seen the error of her ways in bringing up something that was none of her business. "I'll take care of it, miss."

"Also," she continued as if he had not spoken, "I have an idea that we should discuss when you have a moment."

Caution signals swept through his brain like the rotation of a lighthouse lantern warning ships approaching the harbor.

"An idea concerning what matter?"

Caroline glanced up at Hannah, who was engrossed in this exchange between her father and teacher. "We can discuss it later. Now let's get this child inside and out of this relentless downpour."

"I have an idea to discuss with you, too, Papa."

"Truly? And what might that be?" Ty was glad of his child's interruption.

Hannah giggled. "I have an idea that we need to go shopping. Eliza and Jerome need new clothes for the start of school, and wouldn't it be fun to surprise them?"

Ty's spirits plummeted at the same time as he felt Caroline's fingers tighten around his arm.

"You know, Hannah," she said, "I was thinking the same thing. How would you like to go shopping with me while the others are busy this afternoon?"

Ty could not believe the woman would presume to . . .

"In my attic," she continued, "there are two whole trunks of clothing. One contains items my husband wore and the other is full of items I no longer have use for. Do you think we might shop there?"

Hannah frowned. "It's not the same as a real shop."

"That's true, but it's always fun to pretend, don't you think? And this is especially nice because we will be the only customers."

"Oh, yes. You'll be the shopkeeper and I'll buy things."

Ty could hold back no longer. He wanted to tell the woman to stop filling his child's head with impossible ideas. He wanted to shout at her to wake up and understand his situation. "I'll see to clothing for my children," he muttered, "but thank you."

"But, Papa —" Hannah started to object, took one look at her father's eyes and closed her mouth. As soon as they were back inside the warm kitchen, she took her time unbuttoning her coat, taking special care to spread it near the heat.

"I didn't mean —" Caroline began, still absorbing the fact that apparently she had decided to admit Eliza and Jerome to her school.

"I can provide for my children," Ty repeated.

"But it's already so late in the day and the shops will be closing and they'll be closed tomorrow. With school starting Monday, I had only thought to —"

Ty wheeled around to face her. "My children won't be going to your school, Miss Hudson. We'll be moving to the mainland so I can look for work." Then he brushed past her and headed down the hall, the scent of lavender and damp wool dogging his steps.

Ty had barely left the room when Hannah

burst into a tearful wail that brought both Eliza and Jerome on the run. Caroline lifted the sobbing child onto her lap.

"What's happened?" Jerome demanded. Caroline had noticed that every last bit of the boy's reserve disappeared the moment he thought his baby sister needed him.

"Papa won't let you and Liza come to school because I was bad," Hannah sobbed.

"Oh, no, child," Caroline rushed to assure her. "Your father isn't upset with you."

"He was real mad," Hannah told her sister.

Caroline hastened to reassure the older children. "He's upset with . . ." *Me.* ". . . the way things are right now."

Eliza sighed. "Did he really say we couldn't start classes on Monday?"

"His mind was on other matters. Right now it may seem to him that schooling for you is not possible, but I'm sure we can find a way through this," Caroline explained. "He just needs time, children. Now, did you finish polishing the desks as I asked?"

"Yes, miss," Eliza assured her. "Everything's dusted and polished, but Papa's in there now and —"

They heard the bang of metal on metal as Tyrone wrestled with opening the flue. Caroline could only imagine the dust he was creating with his insistence on checking a fireplace she had already told him was in good repair. It certainly would not do to point out that, letting in the soot and debris, he was undoing a morning's hard work by the children. "Perhaps your father misunderstood me," Caroline told the children, who were looking at her to signal how she might respond to their father's obvious irritation. "It's the one in the dining room that —"

"We can stay late and redo everything," Eliza said.

"Let's not get ahead of ourselves until we see how much damage there is. Now then, children, I need you to go up to the attic, where you will find two trunks. Eliza, here are the keys. Jerome, you take the lamp. It will be dark up there. Please open them and start bringing the contents down to the third-floor bedrooms. Spread everything out on the beds."

"Yes, miss." Eliza gave her brother a nudge toward the back stairway. "Come on, Hannah, you can help."

Her tears forgotten, the little girl ran up the stairs ahead of her siblings, announcing, "I get to unlock the trunks."

What could she be thinking? Those trunks were filled with clothes — hers and her late husband's. What was the point of unpacking them after all this time? Her purpose had been to distract the children, but surely a game or cooking lesson would have accomplished the same thing.

A metal tool clattered to the hearth in the classroom and Caroline started at the sound. Her instinct was to follow the children up to the attic and give their father time to calm down — or better yet, to leave. But what would that solve? Were all males such exasperating creatures, or was it just that Caroline seemed to attract such men?

She took a deep breath and blew it out as she closed her eyes on a prayer. *Father, give me strength and the words to help those precious children.*

Ty felt her presence more than heard it. He was clanging around with various tools, trying to release a flue door that she had assured him worked perfectly. Well, it was a good thing he'd decided to check for himself, because although the flue chain appeared to drop, signaling an opening, the door itself was jammed shut.

"You could have had a fire first thing," he said without looking up at her.

"Mr. Winslow was here in the spring and he assured me —"

"Winslow is a man who takes advantage. No doubt you paid him."

Caroline bristled. "Yes, for the work he did."

"For the work he said he did," Ty corrected. "Come over here and see for yourself." Now that he had found the problem and was well on his way to solving it, Ty was feeling more in control. This was something he could teach the teacher.

She crossed the room and gathered her skirts as she bent to peer up into the chimney. "I can't see anything."

"Look there," he instructed. "You see the chain appears to be in the open position?"

"It is in the open position," she argued, dropping to her knees now and pressing forward for a better look.

Ty hesitated. He hadn't been this close to a woman since Sarah died. He'd forgotten things. Warm breath when speaking close to his face. Hair coming undone with the exertion of trying to peer up into the dark fireplace. A dress — plain and yet perfectly accenting a slender waist.

Suddenly she sat back on her heels, her skirt billowing around her so that she looked for all the world like a flower in bloom. "Well?" she demanded and the moment passed.

"Now watch." Ty struck a match and held it well into the opening of the hearth. It burned without so much as a flicker.

He saw her glance toward the window, where tree branches swayed in the wind and the rain lashed at the glass. "With that wind, if the flue were open, the match would have gone out," he said.

"And if we had started a proper fire, the room would have eventually filled with smoke. Oh, Mr. Justice, you have done me such a service. Thank you."

Ty couldn't help feeling a rush of pleasure at her genuine appreciation. "I can fix it. It's just going to take some time. Eliza can see that the others get home and have their supper."

"The weather is still quite nasty, Mr. Justice. Why not let the children stay here while you work? We can all have supper together."

He started to protest, but she held up her finger like the schoolmarm she was. "Now Mr. Justice, you and the children have been such a help to me in getting things ready for Monday's opening. Surely you will not deny me the pleasure of preparing a meal to show my gratitude."

Ty studied her for any sign that she might be baiting him. "I know you mean well, miss, but —"

"It's just dinner."

But they both knew that wasn't true. "I heard Hannah take the blame," he said. "It wasn't her fault."

"I know." She seemed to be thinking of something more she wanted to say but pursed her lips instead.

"You think I'm being unfair to my children, but I ask you, what would you do?"

"I don't know the full details, so how can I offer advice?"

It would be such a relief to confide in someone. But Caroline Hudson was not just "someone." She was a woman of influence in the community. Her opinion of him could affect the future of his children. And how could she hold any esteem for him whatsoever? He'd had little formal education before he'd run off to join the crew of a whaling ship. Miss Hudson was someone who valued education.

"Tyrone, tell me, what's happened?"

It was the first time she had used his given name, and it was his undoing. He rubbed his hands over his face. "We are to be evicted."

"I'm so sorry. Surely there are other places."

"No. I've asked around. I thought perhaps

Mr. Hatter and his wife might take the children on the farm. Then I could go to the mainland and look for work and send for them once I was settled."

"I know Beatrice Hatter. I could speak with her at church tomorrow."

"They've already turned down the idea. They would take Eliza, but not the other two." He met her gaze. "I am not splitting them up."

"Of course not. Perhaps there are places in the city?"

He thought he would be physically ill at the thought of the slums and almshouses he'd seen when he was searching for the children those times they had run away from Sarah's parents. And yet, what choice did he have? There was no one locally to care for the children, and their mother's parents had rejected them. Both his parents had died when he was away at sea. His siblings had headed west after the great fire. There simply was no one.

His misery must have shown in his expression, for suddenly he felt Caroline Hudson's delicate, warm hand covering his. "Mr. Justice, I am so sorry for your troubles. Please, there must be something I can do to help."

He bought time by allowing his eyes to

roam over the high-ceilinged room. This room had been built as a ballroom. The chandelier in the center was a masterpiece of pewter and crystal. Even on a dreary day such as this one, it caught the light and sparkled. The wood floor was laid out in an intricate parquet design. The windows rose floor-to-ceiling and were dressed in brocaded drapes with gold rope tiebacks. This room on its own was a palace compared to anything he'd ever been able to offer his family.

He looked down at her fingers, long and perfectly manicured, still resting on the back of his weathered and discolored hand. Oh, how he hated asking anyone for help. She tightened her hold just slightly.

"Mr. Justice?"

"If you had a spare room," he began, the words nearly choking him as he forced them out. "They don't need much and they could continue with their chores to pay for the rent until I can send some money."

"And their schooling," she added as she released his hand.

"I thought you were all filled up for the semester."

"They have to attend school, and it will be far easier for me to manage that here than to get them off to public school before

I have to teach my own classes. They'll need clothes, of course, but —"

"A room," he countered as he stood up and brushed off his hands. "Nothing more." But even as he spoke the words, he knew there was more.

"They have to eat," Caroline reminded him, her tone closer to that of the school-marm.

"A room and two meals a day, then. Those are my terms," he agreed, as if he had any power at all to set such boundaries. "Liza can make do with the leftovers."

Now Caroline Hudson was on her feet, toe to toe with him as she looked up at him with those green eyes that had hardened into emeralds. "They will eat what I eat and when I eat, Mr. Justice. And they will attend classes. Those are my terms."

He headed for the door. "Then I'll make other arrangements."

"Mr. Justice!"

His hand was on the filigreed pewter doorknob, but her commanding tone stopped him from leaving. "I will not have my children embarrassed or used by you to teach those fancy pupils a lesson or —"

"The children are in the attic unpacking the clothing I mentioned earlier — clothing I once wore, as well as the clothing my late husband wore. He was a small man and I believe there are items there that will serve Jerome quite well."

Ty tightened his grip on the doorknob until his knuckles went white. Did the woman not understand? "I do not want your charity." He ground out each word as if it were physically painful to do so.

The room went absolutely still, except for the clock on the mantel tapping out each second. "Mr. Justice, this is not charity. You have already indicated that the children will work for whatever they are given. Now, please come here so we can discuss this reasonably."

Tyrone made the smallest concession to her request. He released the doorknob and half turned toward her.

"Better," she murmured. "Now then, although I deplore the entire idea of child labor, nevertheless for the purposes of our discussion, let us say they have taken positions on staff here in my school."

Ty watched her as she paced back and forth at the front of the rows of soot-dusted desks. He edged forward and leaned against a desk in the back of the ballroom-turned-classroom.

"What's doing their chores in exchange for room and board got to do with you giving them clothing?"

"I set high standards for myself and my pupils, Mr. Justice. Surely you can appreciate that anyone on staff here at the school needs to maintain a certain level of —"

"It's still charity, miss, and —"

"Think of it another way. Did the captains of the whaling ships you served on have servants back here in their Nantucket homes? A staff who helped the lady of the house maintain the household?"

"Sometimes."

"And did those workers wear uniforms when they were working at the captain's home?"

Ty shrugged. "Yes, but —"

Caroline stopped pacing and walked slowly up the aisle toward him. "Well, then, Mr. Justice, who provided those uniforms? The captain or the workers?"

"That's not the point."

"Well, I assure you that it was the captain who provided those uniforms — a cost of doing business. There is no difference here. Your children will be performing defined tasks for the school. Sometimes those tasks will require them to interact with the pupils. I have an image to preserve here, Mr. Justice."

Ty felt trapped. On the one hand, he had

agreed that the children would perform chores in order to pay for their room and board. But the thought of having them catering to a bunch of wealthy . . .

"Of course, there is another way of going about this," Caroline said. She had moved to one of the large windows and seemed to be engrossed in watching it rain.

"I'm listening," Ty muttered.

Her next words were spoken so softly that all he heard was ". . . guardian." He moved closer but she continued to stare out the window.

"I mean it would be a temporary arrangement, of course, while you get settled. But if the children were introduced to the community as my wards, then no one would dare to . . . to —"

"Think less of them?"

She turned then and he saw that her eyes had softened into pleading. "Oh, Tyrone, they are such wonderful and intelligent children. Why not give them a chance to blossom?"

"You would be their guardian?"

"Temporarily," she assured him, "and I would review every decision regarding their welfare with you before making it."

"I can't see how that changes anything."

"It changes everything. Tomorrow the

children could accompany me to church and meet some of the other children who attend my school. It would be good if you would come with us whenever you are in town."

He could feel himself beginning to come around to her way of thinking. "You'll not be making decisions without my approval?"

"Not in terms of their health or well-being. I certainly will not have my decisions regarding their dress, activities or deportment questioned while they are living here."

"I expect you'll still work them — expect them to earn their keep?"

"I shall expect them to perform the same household chores that other children perform in their homes. Don't you understand, Tyrone? I am offering your children my home. I am offering to assume the role of guardian until such time as you can once again resume your parenting duties."

Ty walked to the far end of the large room and back again. Caroline remained where she was, but she watched him steadily. The very idea of handing over his children to this woman was preposterous — a measure of his desperation, surely.

"And if it doesn't work? If they run away as they did before? If —"

"Then we — you and I — will discuss

85

those situations as they arise. I am not in the habit of anticipating problems, Mr. Justice. Life is challenging enough without foreshadowing."

He could hardly argue that point. Ty felt a smile break through the scowl he realized had almost become his permanent expression. "I thought you were now calling me by my given name, Miss Hudson."

The delicate skin across her cheekbones pinkened and she looked away. "I . . . that was a slip of the tongue, sir." She crossed the large room and stretched out her hand. "Do we have a bargain?"

He accepted her hand, but instead of shaking it as he might have in any other business venture, he simply held her hand between both of his. "I do have one condition."

Her eyes registered her recognition that any bargain between them was a tenuous thing. "And that is?"

"When it is just the two of us, you will call me Tyrone and I will call you Caroline, beginning now."

"Very well," she said, but her voice cracked slightly, and he saw that she was as taken as he was by the realization that their relationship had moved to a very different level.

CHAPTER FIVE

The older children were quiet when Caroline called them down from the attic so that Tyrone could tell them of the plan. Jerome scowled, looking more like his father than he usually did. Eliza's expression shifted from resignation to something that Caroline could only describe as hopeful.

Hannah, on the other hand, made no secret of her opinion of the news. "No," she said stamping one foot for emphasis. "I want to live with you, Papa."

Caroline glanced at Ty, saw that he was at a loss to comfort his youngest and knelt next to her. "But, Hannah, if you go with your father, how shall I manage without you?"

The little girl's eyes widened.

"You've been such a wonderful help to me in getting ready for the beginning of the new term. Of course, I shall simply have to make do unless —"

Hannah edged closer. "Unless what?"

"Unless you might agree to stay for a little while — just a few weeks." She glanced up at Ty, entreating him to join her in persuading the child.

"A few weeks gives me plenty of time to find work and a place for all of us to live," Ty assured his daughter.

"And Papa will visit us as often as possible, won't you, Papa?" Eliza joined the circle gathered around Hannah.

"I promise," Ty said.

"Jerome?" Caroline held out her hand to the boy and drew him into the circle.

"I can work, too," he said, turning to his father. "I could go with you and we could both —"

Ty ruffled the boy's hair. "Not this time, son. Your schooling is what's important and Miss Hudson is offering you that opportunity."

Jerome pulled away and assumed his usual posture of staring at the floor. "I'm not as smart as Liza is."

"Nonsense," Caroline said. "Eliza has her gifts and you do, as well. Your head for figures is really quite remarkable, Jerome."

"I've noticed that myself, son." Tyrone stood and placed his hand on Jerome's thin shoulder. "And I'm counting on you to watch out for your sisters — and Miss Hudson — while I'm away."

"Yes, sir."

"Well," Caroline said, "I think we've had quite enough unsettling news for one day. Mr. Justice, perhaps you and Jerome could go along and pack up the children's belongings to bring here while the girls and I prepare a light supper for us all to share."

She saw him hesitate a moment as he let go of the last vestiges of the pride that had for so long kept him from accepting help. *Trust me,* she wanted to say. And perhaps he saw that message in her eyes, for he nodded. "We won't be long," he said as he ushered Jerome toward the back door.

"Mr. Justice?"

He glanced back at her and she swallowed hard, hoping she wasn't about to put the man over the brink.

"You may as well take my horse and wagon to save time." *And it will spare you and Jerome the embarrassment of walking through the village streets with your worldly belongings.*

"There's not that much," Eliza rushed to say. "Shall I come too, Papa?"

"No, you stay here and help Miss Hudson. Jerome and I will be back shortly," Ty said.

He had neither accepted nor refused her

offer, but moments later she heard the jingle of harness and looked out to see Tyrone instructing Jerome in the proper way to hitch up the horse and wagon.

Thank you, God, she prayed, *for giving me the proper words to find my way around this man's fierce pride so that I can help these dear children.*

"Who wore all those clothes from the attic?" Hannah asked when the silence around the supper gathering threatened to suffocate them all.

"Hannah." Eliza's reprimand went unheard by the little girl. "The clothing belongs to Miss Hudson."

"But who wore the boy's clothes?"

"Hannah." There was no mistaking the warning in Ty's voice.

"That clothing belonged to my late husband," Caroline explained to Hannah.

"He was late? You mean for school?"

Jerome and Eliza exchanged horrified looks. Ty frowned but the corners of his mouth twitched slightly.

Caroline smiled at Hannah. "I can see why you would ask that. Sometimes grown-ups have a way of saying things that can be confusing."

"Why?"

"Sometimes it's difficult to say what we really mean," Caroline continued. She glanced at Ty and he nodded as if to encourage her. "So, grown-ups say things like 'my late husband' when they really mean the person has passed on — died."

"Like Mama?"

The shadow that passed over Ty's face nearly broke Caroline's heart. "Yes," she murmured.

The only sound for a moment was silver against china, then Hannah said softly, "Now I see. Someone you loved died. I'm sorry." She placed one chubby hand over Caroline's.

For a moment Caroline thought she had lost the ability to breathe. The child's gesture was so innocent and genuine. It had been so long since anyone had shown such concern for her. She blinked rapidly to stem the sudden danger of tears overflowing. "Shall we have some cake?" she asked, pushing back her chair and gathering dishes at the same time. "Eliza, would you help me clear, please?"

She hurried into the kitchen, but it wasn't Eliza who followed her. It was Ty.

He stood just inside the door, a plate in each hand. "Where do you want these?"

Caroline gestured toward the table and

busied herself collecting plates and forks for serving the cake.

"We don't need dessert, Caroline."

"It's a celebration. Of course, there should be dessert." She seemed incapable of keeping her voice steady and found it impossible to look at him.

"You loved him very much — your husband."

That gave her the control she thought she'd lost. "I was touched by Hannah's kindness. For one so young, her ability to see to the very heart of a situation is quite remarkable." She sliced cake and placed the pieces on small plates decorated with flowers. They had been a wedding gift.

"How long ago did your husband die?"

"Must we discuss this now? The children are waiting." She handed him two of the plates, placing a clean fork on each. She could feel him studying her and when she looked up at him she saw that he had taken her response for coldness. "Percy and I married when we were quite young. It soon became obvious that we had different ideas about what the institution of marriage should entail. Eventually he was seduced by the call of adventure in the gold fields of California."

"And you refused to leave Nantucket," Ty

guessed.

"He did not ask me to come and when I asked to do so, he refused. He left without me and I never heard from him again."

"There were no letters?"

"One day two years ago," she continued as if he had not spoken, "a dray pulled up to the kitchen door and two men unloaded a large steamer trunk. It was filled with his clothes and personal effects. There was also a letter from the doctor in a small town somewhere in California regretting to inform me that my husband had died in a mine explosion. Sadly, there were no remains."

"I'm sorry for your loss, Caroline."

"Thank you. Now please may we eat our cake? I still need to have the children try on clothes that might be appropriate when they accompany me to church in the morning."

"You could start taking them to church next week," he suggested.

"I suspect they have been too long without the blessings of entering God's house. And you, as well." She swept through the swinging door, announcing, "I have cake for good children." She was relieved when Ty seemed amenable to joining in her teasing.

"Are there any good children at this table?"

"Me, Papa," Hannah shouted.

"Ah, here's a proper young lady," Ty said, setting one plate in front of Eliza. Then he fixed his eyes on Jerome. "And you, young man, appear to be well behaved."

Jerome blushed and grinned but neither he nor Eliza touched their cake. They both sat with their hands in their laps as if waiting for a train. Caroline had never been more proud.

"I seem to have an extra plate here," Caroline said as she placed a slice in front of Tyrone and then another at her own place.

"It's for me, I'm sure," Hannah said in a whisper. "See? Everybody has a piece 'cept me."

"Why, Miss Hannah, I believe you are quite right. Please forgive me." Caroline set the final plate in front of the little girl, who immediately grabbed her fork and cut into the slice. But a look from Eliza stopped her cold and she put down her fork and folded her hands in her lap in perfect imitation of her sister.

Ty chewed the bite he'd taken as he looked at each of his children. "Aren't you hungry? Miss Hudson made you this —"

"We're waiting for Miss Hudson to be seated and to start her piece," Eliza said.

"Then we get to eat," Jerome added.

"That's good manners, Papa," Hannah said and then looked at Caroline for confirmation.

"Please eat your cake, children," Caroline said. As she took a small bite she could not help risking a look down the table to where Tyrone was leaning back in his chair, his own dessert abandoned. She tried to read his mood. Was he upset because the children had embarrassed him? Was he rethinking his decision to leave the children with her?

"It's getting late," he said, standing abruptly. "Thank you for your hospitality, Miss Hudson. Children, I expect you to do as you're told without any argument, understood?"

"Yes, Papa," three voices chorused.

He hesitated a second, then walked to each child, kissing Eliza's cheek, clutching Jerome's shoulder and lifting Hannah from her chair, high into his arms for a hug.

"I'll be back as soon as I can," he said as he kissed the child's forehead.

"Of course. Why don't you plan to —" Caroline said.

"As soon as I can," he said again as he returned Hannah to her chair, then headed for the front door.

"I'll see your father out," Caroline murmured as she placed her linen napkin on

95

the table and motioned for Eliza to tend to Hannah, who seemed about to burst into fresh tears.

He was already at the door. But something in the sag of his broad shoulders made her go to him and place her hand on his back.

"They'll be all right, Tyrone."

"Why are you doing this? Why would you do something like this when you barely know us?"

"I believe that it was God who brought your children to my door that morning. I don't fully understand His purpose, but I will not ignore the mission He has set before me. I can help your children, Tyrone, for however long they are with me. And more to the point, they can help me."

"With the chores," he said flatly.

"With the loneliness," she replied. "Every morning since they came to stay here I find myself awaking with a renewed spirit, a kind of anticipation of what the day might bring. So it is I who am indebted to you, Tyrone, and not for the repairs you've made that will hopefully see me through another winter."

"You're going to need to replace most of the roof, and there are some places around the windows and doors where the wood is beginning to rot."

"I know, but all of that will have to wait until spring."

"I'd stay and fix them if I could, but I think you'll be all right for one more winter." He touched a curl that had come free of her chignon, wrapping it round his finger. Caroline held her breath as their eyes met.

Ty was the first to look away, pulling his fingers free of her hair as if he'd suddenly realized he'd placed them too near fire. "Goodnight, Caroline."

"You'll come tomorrow to say goodbye?" Suddenly Caroline had the memory of her husband, leaving without so much as a look back at her. Leaving as if he couldn't wait to be free of her. Surely Ty had none of those feelings when it came to his children. And yet, might he not believe that he had done all he could for them in placing them with her? "It's important, Tyrone."

He hesitated. "Don't you think that might upset them more? Especially Hannah?"

"They need to know that they can count on your return. That you'll visit every chance you have. That this isn't like their mother dying and leaving them forever."

"I'll think on it."

"You could take the later steamer and come to church with us."

To her surprise, Tyrone smiled at her.

"Now, Miss Hudson, don't go pushing matters beyond what's reasonable to expect of me."

And just what's so unreasonable about suggesting to come into the sanctuary of God's house? She pressed her lips into a prim, hard line. "After church, then. Good night, Mr. Justice."

The next morning Ty could not have said why he found himself walking up the hill toward the small white church. The last vestiges of fog hung over the town but the spire of the church broke through the gloom, proving the day would be a clear one.

Although the church doors were open and he could hear the organist practicing, it was too early for the congregation to gather. Ty passed the entrance and walked around to the side of the white-frame building. The church cemetery was as deserted as the church itself. A lone mourner stood with head bowed next to a fresh grave near the entrance.

Ty stepped around her and followed the stone steps down the embankment until he came to another marker. Sarah's marker was a grand, ornate block of marble that her parents had insisted upon. Immediately after her death it had seemed as if Sarah's parents might be a true comfort to Ty and the children. They had arrived the day after the fire, moved Ty, the children and themselves into the home of a business associate of Sarah's father, helped Ty arrange everything, including a wake following the service in the borrowed house. They had cradled baby Hannah and made a fuss over Eliza and Jerome. They had visited with Sarah's dear friends and neighbors.

But as soon as the last mourner left the wake and Sarah's mother had excused herself to get the children settled for the night, Sarah's father had placed his hand firmly on Ty's shoulders and steered him out to the porch. "We need to talk, Justice."

There had been none of the warmth and comfort he'd heard in the man's voice throughout the day. Without giving Ty a moment's respite, Sarah's father had laid out his terms. The children would live in Boston with their grandparents. In return, Sarah's father would set Ty up in his own business on Nantucket. He could visit the children, of course, but those visits would take place in Boston, where the children would attend school and be far better clothed and fed than Ty could ever possibly afford.

By the way he turned back toward the

house, assuming the conversation was ended, it was obvious he had expected Ty to embrace this idea. When Ty stopped him with a protest, the older man laughed and then made it clear that he expected Ty to practically get down on his knees in gratitude. And so Ty went with his first instinct — a habit Sarah had repeatedly warned him about. He punched his father-in-law in the face, bloodying the older man's nose and getting himself locked out of the house for his action.

He had spent the rest of that night here in the cemetery, breathing the fresh earth of Sarah's grave, knowing his in-laws were right in saying they were far more capable of caring for the children than he was. What was he going to do with a baby?

And so he had returned the following morning, hat in hand, eyes fixed firmly on the tops of his boots, still coated with dirt from Sarah's grave. He had agreed to the terms his father-in-law had laid out, with one exception.

"My children are not for sale, sir. Keep your money. I'll find work myself and once I am reestablished I will come for my children to bring them home."

He could still call to mind the smirk on his father-in-law's face. "God willing, should that day ever come, they will have the good sense to refuse to go with you."

Now Ty ran his fingers over the lettering of Sarah's name. "Ah, sweet Sarah, have I made yet another blunder? This woman — this teacher . . ."

Caroline.

"She seems genuine enough and yet she comes of the same world as your parents. The fancy clothes, the proper manners. The money that might now be gone but was once the core of her world. She can give the children the schooling you wanted for them and she can give them passable clothes and meals, but why would she do such a thing?"

The loneliness, she had said.

"Is that it, Sarah? Is the woman realizing she might never have a child of her own and is she wanting our children to fill that gap?" He swallowed hard, closed his eyes and let the silence of the cemetery surround him.

"I'm doing the best I can, Sarah," he whispered. "But I have no home to shelter them. I have no work to buy them what they need. I just have Caroline Hudson's word that she'll treat them right and give them up when I come back for them."

He bent and on the grass-covered grave placed the small bouquet of heather he'd gathered. When he turned to leave the cemetery, the steeple bell started to peal, calling the locals to church. And coming up the hill was Caroline Hudson, followed by three children that he almost didn't recognize.

CHAPTER SIX

Caroline had never met a man as stubborn as Tyrone Justice. It was one thing to be determined to care for one's family. It was quite another to be so obstinate that to even consider accepting an offer of help was out of the question. On top of that she felt as if there were a kind of reverse snobbishness about the man — he was so certain that he and his children would be seen as lesser beings that he, in fact, was the one who labeled others.

And yet in spite of her irritation with the man, there was something enormously engaging about him. She sensed that underneath his many layers of worry and sadness, there lay a man of exceptional humor and intelligence. A man of character. A man of faith.

She turned her attention back to making sure the children were ready for their first foray into her world. She was frankly exhausted. She had stayed up most of the night altering one of her old dresses for Eliza and cutting down a pinafore to make a dress for Hannah. She'd also taken in the pants, shirt and jacket that had belonged to Percy so that Jerome would look less like the ragamuffin who had shown up on her doorstep just two weeks earlier. But when the children saw the clothes, clean, pressed and laid out for them, they were so delighted that Caroline forgot all about her lack of sleep.

Eliza had arranged her own hair into finger-rolled curls and found two matching pieces of ribbon to tie back Hannah's unruly locks. Meanwhile, Jerome ran a finger round the starched collar of his shirt, his Adam's apple bobbing convulsively.

"It's tight," he protested when Eliza gave him a warning look.

"It will ease as the starch softens," Caroline assured him. "Shall we go?"

"Where's Papa?" Hannah planted both feet and folded her chubby arms, making it clear she had no immediate plans to move.

"Your father will see you after church. Now, come along. We don't want to be late." Caroline opened the door and waited for the children to precede her. To her amazement there were no further protests.

As they approached the church, a movement in the cemetery caught her eye. Tyrone was waiting there, watching her and the children as they climbed the hill. For a moment she thought he had decided to join them in church after all, but then he stepped behind a large tree and she understood he did not want the children to see him.

Oh, please don't leave without saying goodbye. I have promised the children.

There was nothing to be done but take the children into the church and pray that when they emerged he would still be there, and that this time he would allow the children to see him.

Ty hadn't meant for her to see him, but the sight of her with his children had caught him off guard. It had been like going back in time. For an instant he'd envisioned his family all dressed up and on their way to church for Hannah's christening. It was the last time they'd all been there together. Tyrone had only entered the church once since that day. He'd attended his wife's funeral and afterward turned his back on anything to do with religion.

He knew that Eliza often came to the church and cemetery when she thought he wouldn't know. He'd said nothing. She was

105

old enough to make up her own mind about such things. He just hoped that whatever comfort she found in coming here, it wouldn't someday go up in flames as his faith had.

From his vantage point he watched Caroline pause as several curious neighbors approached her. He saw her place a gloved hand on Eliza's shoulder and then Jerome's as she obviously made introductions. He saw Hannah fairly dancing with excitement as she showed off her new clothes. And when the neighbors smiled and one lady bent to admire Hannah's hair ribbons, Ty breathed a sigh of relief.

He studied Caroline Hudson, heard her laughter and saw how Hannah pressed herself against the russet wool of Caroline's skirt. Instead of reprimanding the little girl for possibly mussing her Sunday best, Caroline laid her hand gently on his daughter's curls and seemed to draw her closer.

He watched his son assume a stance that Ty was well aware he himself often took when he was uneasy — weight shifting from one long leg to the other, hands clasped behind his back. He saw Caroline place her hand in the crook of Jerome's arm. Saw his son's startled smile as he escorted her and his sisters into the small church.

Perhaps it would be all right after all. He would leave for the mainland, stopping first in New Bedford, and if there was no work to be found there, moving on until he found something. Then he would come back for them. No matter how long it took.

Caroline barely heard the words of the sermon. Her attention drifted to the window. Was he still there? Would he be there after church? Would she be able to persuade him to come back to the house for Sunday dinner? Would he even give her the opportunity to make the invitation?

Hannah snuggled up next to her and yawned. Caroline drew her closer and in minutes the child was asleep. Next to Hannah, Jerome sat forward, his elbows resting on his thighs and hands dangling between his legs. He was frowning. Beyond him Eliza was hanging on every word the minister said.

And across the aisle young Thomas Woodstock watched Eliza with the kind of dreamy-eyed devotion only a teenaged boy struck by the vision of his first love could muster. Caroline smiled when Thomas's mother gave him a firm nudge directing his attention back to the pulpit.

The organist struck up the closing hymn

and Hannah roused and stretched. "We'll see Papa now?" she asked as the congregation stood for the hymn and benediction.

"If he can make it," Caroline promised, already preparing the children — and herself — for disappointment.

Outside, the churchyard and cemetery were deserted.

"Won't you and the children join us for dinner, Miss Hudson?" Matilda Woodstock had followed Caroline and the children up the aisle, pushing past other church members to stay close. She and her husband, John, sent all of their five children to Caroline's school.

"Thank you, but we are otherwise engaged," Hannah replied in a perfect imitation of the etiquette lessons Caroline had given them. But when all eyes turned to her, she hurried to add, "Our Papa is coming for lunch."

"I see," Matilda said. "And who is your father?"

"Tyrone Justice," Hannah reported proudly, back on firm ground once again.

"I don't believe I've had the pleasure, Miss Hudson. Is Mr. Justice . . ."

When Caroline realized Hannah was again about to speak up, she hurried to interrupt. "Mr. Justice is leaving this afternoon on business. The children will be staying with me and attending school while he is gone. Thank you so very much for your kind invitation, Mrs. Woodstock. Perhaps another time?"

"And Mrs. Justice?" Matilda Woodstock was known to be tenacious in ferreting out information.

Caroline saw Jerome's fists clench. "The children lost their mother in the fire," she said quietly. "Now, if you'll forgive us, I'm sure the children would like to pay their respects by visiting their mother's grave."

As Eliza led the way down the stone steps, Caroline was well aware that others had gathered around Matilda to hear what she had learned. Well, let them gossip. It was hardly the first time that Caroline's actions had been cause for comment in the small community. Matilda Woodstock and others had made no secret of their disapproval when Caroline had taken back her maiden name after receiving news of Percy's death.

"It's over here," Eliza directed when Caroline continued straight on the path of crushed clamshells. She led the way to an impressive marble marker and stopped. "Papa's been here," Eliza said as she bent to straighten the bouquet of heather. "He always brings Mama heather because she loved it so."

Caroline took a moment to read the deeply carved inscription on the marker.

Here lies
Sarah Copeland Justice
Beloved daughter
Loving mother
Devoted wife
1818–1846
Rest in peace

Hannah had busied herself gathering a second bouquet of colorful fall leaves, while Jerome had as usual gone off alone, walking among the graves.

"She was very young," Caroline said.

Eliza nodded. "Sometimes I wish . . ." She shook her head and swiped at her eyes with the backs of her hands.

"Look, Mama," Hannah said as she scattered the leaves over the grave. "Aren't they pretty?"

"She can't hear you," Jerome grumbled from his position two rows away.

"Can so," Hannah shouted. "Papa said so."

"Children," Caroline said sternly. "We should go. Your father . . ."

But would he come? And what if he

didn't? Caroline was suddenly so aware of the disappointments and tragedies these children had had to face in their young lives. For another child the disappointment of not seeing their father for perhaps weeks, if not months, might be bearable, but for these children? It could be devastating if Tyrone chose to leave without saying one last good-bye.

"Jerome, please escort your sisters back to the house. I have an errand I must run."

"Yes, ma'am." Jerome herded the girls up the path but Eliza turned back just before reaching the churchyard. "Shall I set a place for . . . ?"

"Yes," Caroline replied. "Your father will be there." *Even if I have to drag him there myself.*

Ty was resting on the canvas duffel that held what was left of his worldly belongings. He'd come straight to the docks from the cemetery, having decided that waiting around to say yet another farewell to his children was just plain cruel. He was leaving. They were in good hands. Why rub their noses in it?

Sunbeams danced across the light chop that rippled the waters of Nantucket Bay. He was so very tired. Tired of failing. Tired of losing. Tired of fighting. He had almost closed his eyes, but opened them and sat up when he caught a glimpse of a russet-colored skirt swaying along the wharf in his direction, like a ship homing in on its port.

"I believe we had an agreement, Mr. Justice," Caroline Hudson announced.

He squinted up at her but neither stood nor made any effort to sit up. "Good day to you as well, Miss Hudson." He could not help but take note of the sharp contrast between the near-squalid surrounding of the docks and her prim suit, its long embroidered jacket buttoned to her waist then flaring over her full skirt. Beneath the coat she wore a plain, high-collared blouse with a bow tie. Her yellow curls were tightly wound and half-hidden under a ridiculous little hat with ribbons trailing down the sides. He also took note that the pleated ruffle at the hem of her skirt was spattered with mud and debris from the wharf she had crossed to stand before him.

"I would appreciate the courtesy of speaking with you directly, Mr. Justice."

"I can't see that we can get much more direct, and I thought you had agreed to address me by my given name when we were alone."

She glanced around the crowded dock,

where men were busy organizing luggage and goods for the passage to the mainland and passengers were beginning to gather. "There are occasions that call for more formality, Mr. Justice. This is such an occasion. Now, please stand up."

Ty took his time getting to his feet. He brushed off his sweater and the front of his trousers.

"You're a mess," she said without any particular surprise. "What you need is a hot shower, a shave and haircut and a change of clothes. No one is going to hire you in this state."

She was right, but he was in no mood for her lecture. He'd been perfectly content wallowing in his own misery. Surely he'd earned it. Not that he had plans to give in to his melancholy, but surely after everything he'd been through, the woman could understand that . . .

"Come with me," she ordered.

To his shock, Ty picked up his duffel and fell into step alongside her. "I don't think I should —"

"That's your problem, Tyrone. You sometimes do not think things through. For example, you are in no condition to apply for even the most menial position. But more to the point, what kind of example is this to set for your children?"

"I don't believe my children are around."

She ignored this and kept walking. Heads were turning as she continued up the street into town, but Caroline seemed oblivious to the stares of others. Ty could hardly blame people for being curious. They must make quite a sight — the schoolmarm in her Sunday best and the rumpled sailor.

She made a sharp left turn and stepped through the side gate of a gray-shingled house with a painted wooden barber pole mounted next to the door.

"Hello, Martha?"

A woman of about sixty years came to the door. "Why, Henry, it's Caroline. Come in, dear. It's been a month of Sundays since —" Her eyes bypassed Caroline and settled on Ty.

"This is Tyrone Justice," Caroline said when Henry joined his wife at the door. "He is in desperate need of a shower, a haircut and a shave." She waited a beat, then added, "Mr. Justice, this is my uncle, Henry Wofford, and my Aunt Martha."

"It's Sunday." Martha had lowered her voice to almost a whisper as she spoke to Caroline. "The Lord's day."

"I am well aware of that and I pray He will forgive me, but Mr. Justice must leave

114

today to seek work on the mainland and he could be gone for several weeks. His three children lost their dear mother in the fire, and they are staying with me for the duration of their father's search for work and a proper dwelling for all of them."

Tyrone felt that he should protest, take the older woman's side. It was Sunday and shops were closed for business. He glanced at Henry Wofford, who shrugged his shoulders, leaned against the door frame and sucked on his pipe.

"Please, Aunt Martha, I know it's unusual but surely you can see for yourself . . ."

Mrs. Wofford sniffed the air and made a face. "I can smell for myself, that's for sure. Well, come on in," she ordered. "Henry, draw the shades. We don't need the whole town talking about us doing business on a Sunday."

Henry Wofford led the way into the front of the house where he had his shop and, following his wife's orders, pulled the shades. Mrs. Wofford busied herself gathering supplies, then looked up at Caroline. "You need to go home," she instructed. "I assume this young man knows the way to your house once we're done here."

"How long?" Caroline asked.

Mrs. Wofford walked around him, sizing

up the work to be done. "An hour." She glanced at the duffel he'd left at the door. "Have you clean clothes in there?"

"Some."

She compared his size to her husband's and muttered something about letting down hems. "We'll make do, then," she said as she once again turned to Caroline. "Go," she ordered. "He'll be along directly."

"I can't pay you," Tyrone told Henry Wofford.

"Did we ask to be paid?" Martha Wofford huffed. "It's bad enough we're doing this on the Lord's day, but perhaps for charity's sake we'll be forgiven. Keep your money, Mr. Justice."

If I had any, I would. But his heart swelled with gratitude that there were people like the Woffords — and Caroline — who saw in him a man worth helping.

Caroline wasn't the only one who had to look twice at the man who appeared at her front door a little over an hour later. The children seemed equally stunned at the transformation in Tyrone's appearance.

"Papa?" Eliza stared at him. "You look — taller."

Indeed he did, but that wasn't all. Uncle Henry had done wonders, trimming the man's sideburns to hide the angry burn mark branding one side of his face. And his hair — the unruly curls that Hannah had inherited — had been properly cut and tamed, making it evident that he had once been quite a handsome man.

No, not once, she thought as she stepped back to allow him to enter the house. *He still is.*

He was wearing black trousers and a gray sweater and carrying a felted wool jacket that she recognized as belonging to her uncle. His boots were not polished but the mud that had caked them was gone. He seemed far more intimidating than he ever had before, and Caroline had trouble finding her voice.

Thankfully, the children chattered on, their excitement evident in the way they clustered around their father. "Miss Hudson and I made a pie," Eliza said. "It's your favorite, Papa. Apple with raisins."

"You didn't come to church," Hannah chastised. "I fell asleep but I think it was a good sermon."

Jerome remained silent, watching the others as always to signal as to how he should behave. But Caroline saw the boy smile when Ty put his arm around his shoulders. "Looks like we both got new clothes, son."

"Yes, sir." Jerome ran his finger around his shirt collar. "Mine itch. Do yours?"

Ty laughed and the sound filled the usually empty rooms of the house. "No, son, mine are fine. Traveling clothes should be comfortable, according to Miss Hudson's aunt."

Smiles turned to frowns as the children were brought back to the true reason their father had come.

"You're still going?" Jerome asked.

"Have to, son. You know that. And, remember, I'm counting on you to look after your sisters."

"Liza's the eldest," Jerome muttered.

"But you are the man," Ty said softly. "Can I count on you?"

For the first time since she'd known them, Caroline saw Jerome meet his father's eyes without hesitation. "Yes, sir," he replied, as if taking a direct command from a beloved sea captain.

"But you'll come back, won't you?" Eliza asked.

"I'll come back when I can and that's the best I can promise. Will you trust that?" He directed this to all three children.

"Yes, sir," Jerome answered.

"I understand, Papa," Eliza whispered.

Hannah burst into tears and clung to Ty's leg.

He knelt and picked her up and without addressing her tears directly, he added, "And when I return I expect there might be a small present or two — at least for those children who are brave and mind Miss Hudson and tend to their chores."

Hannah swallowed her tears at once. "Presents?"

Ty shrugged. "Maybe. Some things we just have to wait and see." He glanced at Caroline and she wondered if this remark was meant for her, to remind her that this was a test, that he had no choice, but that it was not permanent.

She cleared her throat. "Children, please bring the serving dishes to the dining room while I have a word with your father."

As always Eliza took charge, handing out assignments to each sibling as they followed her to the kitchen.

Caroline glanced at the dining table, set with her best china and crystal and wondered if she shouldn't have served the meal in the kitchen using the everyday crockery. Tyrone might be uncomfortable and nervous around such fragile glassware. At least she had had the good sense to plan a cold meal of smoked fish, cheese and bread. A hearty fish soup simmered on the stove and there was fresh fruit for dessert.

"I . . . you look . . . I'm glad you came — for the children's sake." The wide skirt of her dress seemed to take up a great deal of space, making the large hallway seem suddenly quite close.

"You were right to make me come, Caroline. I see that now." He smiled. "And your aunt and uncle were far too generous and kind. I will find some way to make that right with them."

"They have been such a comfort and support to me. It's good to have family and friends one can count on in difficult times. Shall we?" She motioned toward the dining room and Ty stepped aside to allow her to lead the way.

Contrary to any fears Caroline might have harbored of awkwardness on his part, Ty seemed far more at ease than she was. He waited for her to indicate his place at the table, then followed her to her chair and held the chair until she was seated. He did the same for Eliza while indicating with a nod that Jerome should seat Hannah.

This display of manners and breeding was unnerving to Caroline. She realized that in so many ways she had been guilty of the very traits of prejudice that she anticipated in her regular pupils and their families.

"Are you going to be in Boston by tonight, Papa?" Eliza asked as she passed him the meat platter.

"My plan is to go first to New Bedford and see what I can find there."

"Why New Bedford?" Caroline asked, falling into the rhythm of polite table conversation. Though she had taught it to the children, she had needed Eliza to get it started on this occasion.

"The fishing and export trades are still strong there," he explained. "They never suffered the setbacks we had here on Nantucket."

"What are setbacks?" Hannah asked.

"Stuff that gets in the way," Jerome said, but Hannah still looked puzzled.

"Things you might not remember, Hannah," Ty said. "When you were just a baby I used to work on a ship and go on long trips to hunt for whales and bring things from other countries back here."

"You're going on a long trip now." Hannah's eyes narrowed suspiciously.

"Not nearly so long as back then," Caroline hastened to assure her.

"And the reason I'm going to look for work first in New Bedford is because it's not so far away."

"Could we come and visit?"

Caroline saw Ty glance her way. "Let's see what happens," she replied, "but yes, if your father finds work in New Bedford then we could all take the steamer over one day for a visit." She stretched out her hand to touch the little girl's arm.

"But if there's no work there, Hannah, I have to keep looking and that means I might have no choice but to go to sea once again. You understand that, don't you?" Ty also reached out to his child and Caroline saw that they were connected through their determination to reassure Hannah. They looked up at the same moment, their eyes meeting. His pleaded with her to make things all right.

"You'll be so busy with the start of school and helping me here, Hannah, that the time will go by before you know it. As a matter of fact, I don't know how we'll get everything done in time."

"Could I help?" Ty asked.

Caroline was surprised. Was this not the same man who just that morning had been determined to be on his way as soon as possible?

As if he'd read her thoughts, he grinned. "There's a later ship. I have some time."

"Then you should spend it with your

children," she said softly as she stood to clear the table. "Eliza, why don't you show your father your rooms while I clear? Then perhaps, Jerome, you could give him a tour of the classroom and, Hannah, you can show him how you take care of the erasers and chalk for me."

Ty's children gathered around him, pulling him in three different directions in their excitement to show off their new surroundings. He followed them to the front hall and then said, "I won't be missing out on that pie, will I, Miss Hudson?"

Their eyes met. His filled with unspoken appreciation for all she was doing to help him and the children. Hers clouded with unshed tears at the realization that he had given her his trust.

"No, Mr. Justice. There will still be time for pie."

CHAPTER SEVEN

Ty followed the children up the stairway to the second floor. "Hannah and I are here just across the hall from Miss Hudson," Eliza explained as she opened the door to a large, sunny room that overlooked the back garden. The room itself was like a garden, with frilly floral coverlets over two iron beds, ruffled sheer curtains and a large oval floral rug.

"It's a nice room, isn't it, Papa?" Eliza seemed anxious to have him approve.

It was larger by half than the cottage from which they'd just been evicted. "It's a nice room," he said, clenching his fists against his guilt that he had never been able to offer his children such fine quarters.

"My room is down this way," Jerome said. "I don't have to share."

"Ours is bigger and prettier," Hannah reminded him.

Jerome ignored that as he pushed open

the door to a room only slightly less grand than the girls' room. There was a full-size bed, a matching dresser and a desk. The room was darker because of a smaller window and bulkier furnishings, but it was certainly as inviting.

Ty walked around the room, running his fingers over the desk and chair. "You'll be using this when you study, son. I'm going to be thinking about you sitting here."

"Where are we going to study?" Hannah asked. "We don't have a desk in our room."

"Yes, we do," Eliza said, leading the party back down the hall and pointing to a small round table with two chairs. "That's our desk and when we read, we can use the window seat."

Hannah looked to Ty for approval and he nodded. "Looks perfect to me. And speaking of studying, how about showing me the classroom? I haven't seen it since you finished setting things up there."

Jerome ran down the front stairs, his heavy step sounding like thunder as the others followed. "I polished every desk," he said proudly.

"Looks good, son." Ty allowed his eyes to roam around the unused ballroom completely transformed now into this classroom. Twelve desks of varying sizes were lined up like sailors on deck. Everything faced the fireplace he had repaired. On one side of that was a larger desk — Caroline's desk. On the other side stood an American flag, and mounted on the wall above the mantel was a colorful map of the world.

Ty moved closer to study the map, thinking of all the places he had traveled when he'd gone whaling. The things he had seen. The adventures he had known. But he had been younger then and filled with the promise of tomorrow. Now he dreaded the danger and work of being on a ship's crew, and he couldn't help but wonder how far he would have to travel now to make good on his promise to provide a secure future for his children.

"Children, there's pie for you in the kitchen," Caroline said. "Go ahead. Your father and I will have our dessert in here." She set two plates with napkins and forks on her desk. "Go, before your pie gets cold," she said, and the children hurried off to the kitchen.

Ignoring the pie, Ty walked the perimeter of the room, touching the erasers in the blackboard tray and smiling as he imagined Hannah pounding them to shake free the accumulated chalk dust. He paused at the bookshelf and examined the titles. And all the while he kept his back to Miss Caroline Hudson, the woman he was trusting to care for his children.

"They'll be all right, Tyrone," she said, and when he turned she had taken her place at her desk, but not yet touched her pie.

"I know. Thank you — for everything. There is no way I can ever repay your kindness, Caroline."

"Kindness should never come with a price tag. You have raised three wonderful children, Tyrone. You should take comfort and not a small measure of pride in that accomplishment."

"Hardly raised them. They're so young. Still plenty of time for one or more of them to go astray."

"That's unlikely."

"How can you know that? You never . . ." He stopped himself short of insulting her.

"Had children?" She got up and brought him his dessert. "True. But I have spent these last several years working with children. Children who have been given every advantage. Some turn out to be quite remarkable, most are merely ordinary and a few have the power to spoil the whole barrel."

"Sarah's responsible for the way our three have come up."

"I don't wish to wound you, Tyrone, but their mother has been dead four years now. It is you who have been there during these very formative years. It is you they have watched and taken cues from in how to behave and interact with others. It is you who have kept alive the memory of who their mother was and what she might expect of them."

He stalled for time by taking a bite of his dessert. It was possibly the best pie he'd ever had. "Eliza made this?"

Caroline smiled. "It's my recipe but yes, she put it together. She's incredibly quick, Tyrone. And Hannah, nothing gets past her curiosity. She'll be reading by the time you come back, mark my words."

"And Jerome?"

"Jerome feels things more deeply than you may realize, Tyrone. And he holds them inside. He's a little like you in that way."

Tyrone felt his defenses rise. "I've kept very little from you, Caroline. If you think it's easy for any man to admit that he has failed his children, his wife, himself, then . . ."

"I am not blaming you, Tyrone. I am simply saying that Jerome may be less will-ing to ask for help than the girls are."

"He's a boy," Tyrone said as if that explained everything. He took the last bite of pie and set the plate on the desk. "Why are we having dessert away from the children, Caroline? What was it you needed to talk to me about?"

"I wanted to assure you that the children will have a place here for as long as necessary. With that in mind I hope that you will not feel pressured to settle for whatever position may come along."

"You mean, take something that to you would be beneath me." He saw immediately that he had riled her.

She placed both palms flat on her desk and glared at him. "All work has meaning and value. That is one thing I teach these pupils every day. God has given each of us certain skills and talents. You appear to have been given intelligence, as well as an ability to work with your hands building and repairing things. But that combination can also be used to create new things — new ideas, new ways of making your way in the world. I am simply suggesting that you consider every possibility."

It had been a very long time since anyone other than his children had shown the slightest faith in his ability to succeed. Now this teacher was actually giving him a lecture on the subject. "Why do you care what I can and cannot do?" he asked.

He had meant to throw the words at her, to take back control of a conversation that was uncomfortable for him. But she remained where she was, daring him to look away.

"The question is, why don't you care more?" And with that she picked up her untouched pie and began to eat. But he couldn't help noticing that her hand shook as she guided the fork to her lips.

The man was watching her and fighting hard to hide a smile. She had tried to talk seriously to him, to encourage him, and this was the result. She set down her fork and indicated his empty plate. "If you're finished . . ."

"With dessert, yes. Our conversation is another matter."

She refused to look at him. She expected that he had found some great source of amusement in all of this. So she was surprised when he came around the desk, relieved her of the plates and then tilted her chin to look up at him.

"I am not one of your pupils, Caroline, so save your words of praise and encouragement for Jerome or Eliza or Hannah."

She forced her eyes to remain fastened on

his. "Tyrone Justice, one day your insufferable pride will be your downfall. I only hope your children do not suffer as a result." She pulled free of his touch and left the room.

The children had finished their dessert but remained at the kitchen table, and she could hear the low murmur of their voices as she came down the hallway.

"Don't talk foolish," she heard Eliza say just as she entered the kitchen.

"Your father will need to leave soon," Caroline told them. "If you promise there will be no inappropriate behavior and to mind Eliza you could all go and see him off at the docks."

"What's in-pro-prate?" Hannah asked.

"No crying," Jerome translated.

"So go and get your coats and hats and then meet us in the foyer."

"Yes, ma'am."

The two older children started up the back stairway but Hannah tugged on Caroline's skirt. "Don't worry, Miss Hudson," she whispered. "Papa will come back to us. He promised and he always keeps his promise."

Caroline's heart was so full of sympathy for these children that she bent and kissed Hannah's cheek, fighting back tears of her own as she did.

"Will you come see me off, Caroline?" He was standing in the doorway still holding the plates and his voice was gentle, forgiving.

Do you really want me to?

"Of course," she replied briskly. "That's the best idea, in case Hannah —"

He took hold of her arm and gently turned her to face him. "Hannah will be fine. I'd like you to be there."

The flight her heart took at that moment was such a new and unfamiliar yet exhilarating feeling that she thought she might faint. To steady herself she looked down and drew in a deep breath. "Just let me get my coat," she said.

By the time everyone was dressed and out the door they could hear the ship's bell calling passengers to board. Ty lifted Hannah in his arms. "We're going to have to walk fast," he told Eliza and Jerome.

"We should have hitched the wagon," Caroline said, knowing it was too late and that would only delay them further. "Mr. Justice, why don't you and Jerome and Hannah go ahead. In case you have to board before we can get there, Jerome can watch Hannah."

"If you're sure," he said.

"Go."

He and Jerome took off at a trot, Hannah's curly head bobbing up and down over Tyrone's shoulder.

Caroline took Eliza's arm and set off after them, but the shoes they wore, coupled with the cobbled street, hampered their progress. By the time they reached the dock, Jerome was holding Hannah's hand while Ty made a leap onto the ship as it pulled away from the dock.

She stood with her arms around the children as Ty found a space at the railing and waved. Jerome waved his hat while Eliza waved her handkerchief, and Caroline realized that this was not the first time the two older children had watched their father leave.

"Miss Hudson?"

"Yes, Hannah."

"Would it be in-pro-prate to cry now?"

"Not at all," she said as she felt her own tears well.

Hannah nodded but instead of wailing as she had before, she simply stood there watching the ship get smaller and smaller as silent tears rolled down her chubby cheeks.

"Why Caroline Hudson, I never thought to see you here. Are you seeing someone off?"

Matilda Woodstock was the last person Caroline had expected to see at the docks. "Hello, Mrs. Woodstock. The children were just seeing their father off. And you?"

"John is off to New York. Business, you know." She looked closer at Ty's children. "Am I to understand that you are taking on guardianship of these dear orphans?"

"They are not orphans. Their father is still living."

"But . . ." Matilda looked at the departing ship. ". . . he is leaving them."

Caroline was aware that the children were listening. "Mr. Justice has left the children in my care while he attends to some business in New Bedford. Our situations are quite similar, in that you will be preparing your children to start the term tomorrow and I will do the same with Mr. Justice's two older children."

Matilda's lips moved but no words came out.

"And now if you'll excuse me, it's time for the little one to nap. Come along, children."

Caroline settled Hannah for her nap and returned downstairs to find Eliza and Jerome waiting for her. "What shall we do?" Eliza asked.

"I'm not sure," Caroline replied. "What do you usually do on Sunday afternoons and evenings?"

Jerome shrugged. "Liza usually tends to the mending and watches over Hannah. Sometimes Papa and I go fishing or clamming — for our supper."

"I see."

"What do you usually do?" Eliza asked.

"It varies. Sometimes I go calling, but it's past the time for that today. Sometimes I read or play the harpsichord." *Or pace the rooms of the house and wonder how I'm going to keep the school going for one more year.*

"Mama played the violin," Eliza said. "She promised to teach me, but . . ."

Would the losses these dear children were forced to endure ever stop coming? Caroline wondered. How often had Eliza thought about music lessons before Caroline had mentioned the harpsichord?

"I could teach you the harpsichord. In fact, Jerome, go upstairs and look in the compartments of my late husband's trunk. He played harmonica and perhaps his is there. If you like, my uncle plays the instrument and I'm quite sure he would . . ."

The smile that split Jerome's normally somber expression was so like his father's smile that Caroline felt her breath quicken.

"A shipmate of Papa's plays. He has his own fishing boat now and Papa says he's a first-rate cooper. He lives on his boat down at the wharf. Roscoe would teach me," Jerome said. Before Caroline could comment he had taken off up the stairs.

"Does Roscoe have a last name?" Caroline asked Eliza.

"I'm sure he does, ma'am. But we don't know what it is. He's just always been Roscoe."

Caroline tried to envision herself at the docks inquiring after a Mr. Roscoe, last name unknown. Running a school had given her the idea that caring for three children would be little different from managing the multiplicity of learning levels of her pupils. But she was beginning to realize that it was one thing to have charge of children for a finite period of the day and quite another to have charge of them around the clock.

It was at that very moment that Caroline began to doubt her sanity in taking on the task of caring for Ty's children. Then a sleepy-eyed Hannah came down the stairs and burst into a grin when she saw Caroline.

"That was a very short nap, Hannah."

"But I had the best dream," she announced as she flung herself into Caroline's lap. "We were all at the docks again. Only this time Papa was coming home and we were all so happy." She wrapped one of Caroline's side curls around her forefinger. "Do you think that dream could come true, Miss Hudson?"

"I do," Caroline said. "We just have to be patient."

An out-of-tune blast on the harmonica told Caroline that Jerome had been successful in his search. Perhaps music would be a way of connecting with the children until Ty came home.

For Ty, arriving in New Bedford was in many ways like stepping back to a time when work on Nantucket had been plentiful, when he'd had a home to shelter his children and when Sarah had been alive. But even before the fire, the whaling industry had already begun to desert the island for the deeper harbor of New Bedford. There were still some ships that sailed from Nantucket, but he knew those captains and there wasn't one he wanted to work for unless he had no other choice.

No, here in New Bedford he might start fresh, find a good job at a decent wage. Even late on a Sunday afternoon, New Bedford's harbor was crowded with ships and small craft of every description. Many flew the flags of faraway countries as the hum of foreign speech mingled with the clanging of rigging, and the rumble of carts and drays rolled alongside the docked ships, loading and unloading according to whether a ship had just come in or would soon be leaving.

Ty followed the crowd down the gangplank to the dock. He could start by calling on the several ships he passed that were clearly preparing to set sail. Some might be gone as soon as the following day. But serving on a ship's crew could take him away for months — even years — depending on the ship's destination and purpose. He could not simply leave without letting the children know. Without letting Caroline know.

Instead he turned away from the familiar bustle of the docks and set off toward town. On the passage over he'd discovered the bread and cheese that Eliza must have tucked inside his duffel for him, and he was glad to know he would not have to spend any of the few coins he had on food. At least not right away.

He hitched his duffel higher and turned down a street lined with horse chestnut trees. On either side there were fine well-kept houses with gardens that featured plantings he recognized from ports as far away as Asia. The wrought-iron gates and fences featured replicas of whales and harpoons and whaling ships — testament to the occupant's probable status as a sea captain or perhaps the owner of a shipping business.

Aimlessly he walked until he turned a corner and found himself back on the main commercial street of town. He passed closed shops without registering their wares, all the while thinking that if he did not join a crew then what choices would he have for employment. Fishing — most especially whaling — was what he knew. What he had done since he'd sailed away on his first voyage as a cabin boy of thirteen.

Those voyages had been his classroom. A captain had taught him the basics — how to read and write and keep the necessary numerical logs. His mates taught him, as well. Their lessons were often of a more practical nature — survival skills that had served him well when storms had threatened to overpower them and the resourcefulness to repair a battered ship when it limped into port far from home. And just before the fire, everything he had learned on those voyages had prepared him for the one opportunity he had longed for — to captain his own ship.

And then the fire had destroyed everything in its path, including Ty's dreams and the future for his family. All he had left of those days were his memories and his gift for the seaman's craft of scrimshaw. There had been a time when he had whiled away the dreary weeks and months of a long voyage by crafting some intricate design on a piece of walrus tooth or whalebone to impress a shipmate's sweetheart back home. Now he found himself standing in front of a shop window showcasing a variety of wares decorated in scrimshaw. A small oval brooch caught his eye. The shopkeeper displayed it against a pale green blouse. The color of the blouse made him think of Caroline Hudson's eyes, and the scrimshaw brooch make him think that one day, he would carve something finer for her. But for now . . . He turned the handle of the shop door and a bell jangled merrily. For reasons he couldn't fathom, that merry jingle made him think of Caroline's laugh — and that made him smile.

CHAPTER EIGHT

The storm rolled across the island just after Caroline had made sure all three children were in bed for the night. She had made herself a cup of tea and set the oil lamp on the kitchen table so she could read her Bible. This was a part of her Sunday routine, but it felt different tonight. The house felt different and, although the children had fallen asleep almost as soon as their heads touched the pillows, the quiet was different.

Tonight the house felt truly occupied, as if somehow all the time she had spent here alone, she had been waiting for someone to come along. Even when her school was in session, her pupils went home at the end of each day, and on Sunday nights the house had always felt especially bereft.

But today had been different. The children had been so excited as they had donned their new clothes and followed her to church. Then there had been the time they had shared here with their father. It wasn't just Tyrone's physical size that seemed to fill whatever room or space he entered. The man had a presence about him that dared one to look away or ignore him. Instinct told her that he would have made an exceptional sea captain. She could only hope that presence would serve him well in his search for employment.

Thunder cracked with a blinding flash of lightning close on its heels. Caroline heard whispers and then footsteps and seconds later all three children were standing barefoot in the doorway to the kitchen. She closed her Bible. "Come, sit," she invited. "I'll heat some milk to help you get back to sleep."

The two girls curled themselves into chairs, tugging at the hem of their nightgowns to cover their feet. Jerome sat bolt upright in his chair, his eyes darting to the window with every new flash of lightning.

"The storm will pass," she assured them. "It always does."

"Yes, ma'am," Eliza said. "It seems louder and brighter here."

Ah, not just the storm but the new surroundings — the larger rooms.

"But think of this. My house is far sturdier than the place you lived in on the docks.

The storm may rattle the windows and even bang at the doors, but it cannot come in unless we let it."

Hannah giggled nervously. "Bang on the doors," she repeated as she glanced at Jerome and Eliza.

Both older children grinned sheepishly. "We were never afraid before," Eliza admitted.

"Because your father was there," Caroline guessed, then added, "Well, I have lived in this house all alone for several years now. I have to tell you that I'm very glad for your company. It always makes a storm seem less threatening when you share it with someone."

She poured milk from a pan into three crockery mugs and set one in front of each child, then took the last chair at the table. "I was reading my Bible. I do that every night just before I go to sleep. Shall I read to you?"

Three heads nodded as the children leaned closer and blew on their milk to cool it.

Caroline read them the passage that told the story of Daniel in the den of lions.

"He must have been so frightened," Eliza said when Caroline finished the story.

"I'm sure he was, but God was with him."

"Do you think Papa is frightened?" Jerome asked.

Three sets of eyes were suddenly riveted on Caroline. "Your father is very brave, as Daniel was," she said, choosing her words carefully.

"But Papa doesn't pray or go to church — not since Mama died," Eliza said.

"God is still with him," Caroline said. "Have you children ever seen the sheep that Mr. Olsen raises on his farm?"

They nodded. "And have you seen that sometimes a lamb or sheep will stray away from the rest of the flock?"

Again their heads bobbed. "And Mr. Olsen has a dog who chases that one and brings it back," Jerome said.

"Exactly."

"So even though Papa has strayed, God will find him and bring him back?" Eliza guessed.

Caroline nodded. "Now go to bed. We have a very busy day tomorrow."

The children drained the last of their milk and carried their cups to the dry sink. "Good night, Miss Hudson," Eliza said.

"G'night," Jerome mumbled.

But Hannah wrapped her arms around Caroline's waist and hugged her. "I love you, Miss Hudson."

Caroline felt as if her heart was so full that it might actually overflow. She caressed Hannah's sweet uplifted face. "Children, perhaps since we are all to share this house, you might call me Miss Caroline when the other pupils are not around."

"That would be nice," Eliza said. "Good night, Miss Caroline."

"Sleep well, children."

And as they went up the stairs she heard Eliza assure the others, "See, God is like Mr. Olsen's dog."

Caroline smiled at the oversimplification and then stood at the kitchen window, gazing at the storm as it moved out across the bay. "Watch over him," she prayed, "and bring him back to the fold soon."

Tyrone Justice never expected to spend his first night in New Bedford in the chapel known locally as Seamen's Bethel. But when the storm had come up suddenly with gusting winds and drenching rains he'd ducked inside the nearest shelter. Here and there a few souls knelt before one of the marble memorial tablets that lined the walls. Each tablet named a man or boy lost at sea. The memorials were donated by family members — the man's widow or siblings or, in the case of a cabin boy, his parents.

Ty sat down in the last pew. As the storm settled into a steady downpour and dusk turned into night, one by one the mourners left. Ty was alone with the monuments to those lost at sea and the candles lighted in their memory. He set his duffel under the pew and rubbed his face with his rough hands. He was so tired, but the last place he wanted to be was a house of worship.

What use could God possibly have for a man like him? A man who had failed to save his own wife. Who had fallen so low that he had turned the care of his children over to a relative stranger?

He got up to leave but the rain stopped him at the door. He could not afford to ruin the new clothes that Caroline's aunt and uncle had given him. The chapel was a place to spend the night and tomorrow he would begin the search for work in earnest.

Tomorrow I'll start to turn it all around for us. I'll pay back all that I owe — to Henry and Martha Wofford, to Roscoe, who offered me a place to stay after the eviction, and certainly to Caroline.

He had never been comfortable accepting gifts from others. Sarah had once said that he was the most difficult person she'd ever known when it came to choosing something for Christmas or his birthday. He'd accepted her gifts because he'd known what they'd meant to her, known the care and trouble she'd taken to choose a present he would like.

But keeping a gift from strangers like Henry and Martha Wofford was beyond his ability. He was well aware that they had provided the clothing as a practical gesture. He was going in search of a job. His own clothes were beyond help. But he had assured them that he would return the clothing as soon as he could. What he didn't say was that he fully intended to give some token of appreciation to each of them, as well as Caroline, in the bargain.

He thought again about the scrimshaw brooch he'd seen earlier in the shop window. Perhaps once he'd found steady work he could buy that for her. And if there was no work to be had on land, then the months he would spend at sea would allow plenty of time to create gifts for everyone.

His head bobbed. He was so very tired. As his eyes drifted closed he imagined Caroline wearing the brooch he'd seen. It would suit her, for she always smelled of lavender.

In the two years since Caroline had opened the school, this term had been the worst start of a new year by far. Of the five Woodstock children she was expecting, only Thomas arrived on the first morning. In response to her question about his siblings, he handed Caroline a sealed envelope and then took his usual place near a window.

Caroline slid her thumbnail under the flap and pulled out a sheet of stationery engraved with Mr. Woodstock's business address. She scanned the contents quickly. The Woodstocks had decided to place their children in the public school for the time being. They wished her well in the new school year.

"Thomas?"

"I'm not going there, Miss Hudson. I told them so. They think I'll come around but I won't. I like it here just fine."

Thomas was a daydreamer. Bright but unfocused. To Caroline's way of thinking he had made a good choice. At least here he would get the individual attention and prodding he often needed to complete his work. Still, defying his parents . . .

"I'll call on your parents after school today," Caroline said. "We'll work things out."

"They aren't home. Mother left this morning for New York. She and Father are going to Europe for six weeks."

"I see." But she really didn't see how she

was going to manage when four of her paying enrollees had elected to attend another school.

It had not ended there. Over the summer Noah Johnstone had grown several inches and even the largest desk would not do. On top of that he had changed from an outgoing charmer to a sullen, angry young man. His twin sister, Helen, had always been a bit of an elitist, but that trait had blossomed over the summer into full-blown snobbery.

Helen took one look at Eliza and smirked. "Who's this? The maid?"

Caroline was halfway across the room, her finger pointed directly at Helen, when Hannah backed into the curio cabinet. Caroline kept the cabinet in the classroom to display items she used to illustrate various lessons. But when Hannah bumped the case, the top glass fell and sent all the contents clattering into a pile.

Hannah burst into tears. Helen flounced away to a seat close to Thomas. Her brother, Noah, lounged against the mantel, studying Jerome while their younger sister, Laura, ran to comfort Hannah. The rest of the class stuck close to their desks, watching the scene play out.

That was just the first day. By the end of

the week things had only gotten worse. Caroline was used to having the late afternoons and evenings to prepare for the next day's lessons. Instead she was cooking for the four of them, mending Hannah's ripped apron and scrubbing Jerome's soup-stained shirt. Eliza offered to help, but Caroline could not forget Helen Johnstone's comment about Eliza being hired help. And while Eliza appeared to have taken the slight in stride, Caroline was determined to show the other children that Jerome and Eliza had every right to be in class and were to be treated with the same respect as any paying student.

Late into the night she sat at the kitchen table grading the exercises the children had completed and setting up lessons for the following day. By the second week of classes, twice Eliza had come down to start breakfast — the one weekday chore she was assigned — and found Caroline sound asleep at the table.

And there had been no word from Tyrone. The first week the children had asked daily if there had been a letter. Then only Hannah asked, growing crankier with each day that passed with no word.

"He promised."

"Yes, he did. But promises are not clocks,

Hannah," Caroline explained. "You cannot tell time by a promise."

"But how long?" Hannah demanded, and Caroline could not help wondering herself as she watched the children grow more ill-humored by the day.

Caroline was kneading dough for bread one Saturday morning in early October when she heard the metallic click of the gate latch. She had sent the children to town to visit her aunt and uncle, hoping that the fresh air and change of scene would lift their spirits. The weather had been damp and gray for days now and the promise of an early winter hung in the air. There was always so much work to be done that there had been little time for her to take the children out. The week before she had even missed church for the first time in years.

She wiped her hands on her apron, half expecting her visitor to be the minister, come to be sure she and the children would be at church the next morning.

The caller tapped the front door knocker and Caroline pulled off her apron and left it on the kitchen chair. As she hurried down the hall, she pinched her cheeks. It would not do for anyone to see her looking tired and pale.

"Coming," she called, forcing a lilt into her voice.

She steadied her breath, planted a smile on her lips and pulled open the door.

Ty dropped his duffel, spread his arms as if to embrace her and then lowered them to his sides when he saw it was Caroline and not the children who greeted him. "Hello, Caroline."

It took all of Caroline's willpower not to fling herself against the man. She could practically feel the solidity of his chest, the strength of his embrace and the promise of solace she was sure she would find there.

"Hello, Tyrone," she said. "Please come in. The children have gone into town to visit my aunt and uncle for the morning. They've been indoors for days. The weather has been quite raw here — well, I imagine it's been that way in New Bedford, as well. How are things in New Bedford?"

"Fine, last time I was there. I came from Boston."

"Boston? Oh, my." *Did you find work? And if so will you be taking the children there? I've gotten so accustomed to their company. It would be so quiet — so lonely without them.*

"Caroline, I could use a cup of your tea," he said.

They were still standing in the foyer, the

front door wide open, the wind blowing dried leaves into the hall.

"Of course." Caroline hurried to close the door. "I'll sweep that up later," she added with a nod toward the leaves.

"I'll take care of it." He set his bag to one side of the hall, then gathered the pieces of leaves and stems in one large hand. He carried them into the parlor and threw them into the fire as if he knew the house, had lived here all his life.

As if he's come home.

"Sit here, and I'll bring the tea. The fire is nice," Caroline said. "Let me hang up your coat." She bustled around him, fussing over him as she would a long lost family member.

"You look tired, Caroline."

"It's been a busy time. The first several weeks of a new term are always more stressful, but soon everything will settle into a routine and . . ."

"Running the school and caring for my brood — it's been too much."

"No." Her protest was sharp and left no room for debate. She softened it with a smile. "It's been such a joy having the children here. Although they have missed you desperately. Did you get their letters?"

"Yes."

Yet you did not write them.

"Hannah has asked for you several times a day."

"And Eliza and Jerome?"

"They understand time better than Hannah does." She knew he wasn't fooled. He expected they had given up on him, and certainly the older children would be as stunned to see him as she had been.

"I'll get our tea and then you can tell me everything."

When she returned with the tray, he was across the hall studying the posted papers and drawings the class had made. Whenever he came across something of Eliza's or Jerome's, he paused and leaned in closer as if wanting to memorize every word.

"You can have those if you like," she said.

"Are they good students, then?"

"Top of their class," she assured him. She would not tell him how their excellence in the classroom had only worsened the way the other students treated them when they thought she wasn't looking. Helen and her friend Rose Dalton whispered and giggled, casting sidelong looks at Eliza while Noah baited Jerome, spoiling for a fight.

"Come, have your tea before it gets cold," she said.

Ty followed her back to the parlor and slid the door closed to keep the heat in the smaller room.

"Did you find work?" Caroline asked, meaning to make casual conversation but leading with the one thing uppermost in her mind.

"Some. Several ships were loading and unloading when I got to New Bedford. So there was plenty of work there that first week and I was able to take a room in a local boarding house. I got two meals there as well, so that helped. At night I was always tired. I'd start a letter and then fall asleep."

"If there was a lot of work in New Bedford, why go to Boston?"

"The work in New Bedford isn't steady."

"And in Boston?" Caroline felt bands of fear tighten around her chest with each word out of his mouth. He was going away again and this time he would take the children with him.

"There were some possibilities. I was offered a position as foreman at one of the mills. But then when I was walking the factory floor with the owner, I looked at the girls working the machines. Caroline, they were younger than Eliza. I couldn't do that — couldn't go there day after day and be responsible for seeing that those children put in their ten or twelve hours."

"Were there other opportunities?"

155

"I didn't look. Boston is a long way from here and it's a city. It's crowded and dirty and there are people around who make their way in the world by preying on others. At least here the children are safe."

"So you've come back."

"Not for good. Just to keep my promise."

"Then it's a visit, not —"

"I have to work to support my children, Caroline, and with winter coming on there are fewer and fewer opportunities to be had here."

They drank their tea. The clock on the mantel seemed to hack away at the seconds, each movement a pronounced thud in the sudden silence.

"I brought you this," Ty said, setting down his cup and pulling an envelope from his pocket. "It's not enough but it's a start."

Caroline did not have to open it to know that it was money. She felt insulted. She had not taken in his children for money. She had done so because they needed her — and she now realized that in so many ways she had needed them. Needed their laughter and their curiosity.

"It's for the tuition," he explained. "I asked around. I know what the other parents are paying."

She saw him set his jaw and knew that

156

refusing the money would embarrass him. "I'll apply it to your account. Thank you."

"Are the children keeping up with their chores? Giving you the help you need?"

"Yes."

He nodded and she began to see that he had come with a kind of mental checklist. Pay the tuition. Be sure the children are doing well in school and tending to their chores. And then what?

"I made one more stop while I was in Boston," he said, his voice barely audible. "I went to see Sarah's parents."

Caroline could not have been more surprised if he had suddenly announced that he had returned to church. "Why?"

He ran his long fingers through his thick hair and released a bark of a laugh that held no humor. "I thought if I could tell them about the children being here with you, enrolled in your school, getting the education they had wanted for them, then maybe they would forgive me. I thought that maybe enough time had passed so that the pain of Sarah's death might have lessened and the possibility of spending time with their grandchildren might outweigh the hurts of the past."

"What happened?"

He got up, pacing restlessly. "Nothing

157

happened. They refused to see me. How can they do that, Caroline? How can they turn their backs on their daughter's children? I can understand them blaming me, but blaming the children?"

"I'm sure they don't. They lost their daughter, Tyrone, and then you told me their grandchildren kept running away. That must have been so very hard for them."

"But to not want anything to do with your own flesh and blood." He turned away, his voice breaking.

Caroline went to him and took his arm. "Why did you go there, Ty? The true reason."

"As I mentioned, the best-paying job is with a ship. Working on a crew I could make enough to pay back what I owe you and your aunt and uncle and provide everything the children need — clothes, books, food. But I'd have to sign on for the whole voyage, and who would be there to take care of the children for the months I'd be gone? I had no place else to turn, Caroline."

You have me! She had to press her lips together to keep from shouting at him. "Tyrone, the children are welcome to stay with me for as long as necessary. As you can see from their work, Eliza and Jerome are doing quite well, and truly they are no trouble at all. In fact they are a great help to me."

"Why would you do that? It's one thing for you to take them in for a few weeks, but this would be months — perhaps as long as two years. Why would you take on the care of three children you barely know?"

Just then Caroline heard the kitchen door open and the familiar hum of the children's voices. "We'll discuss this further at a later time," she said. "Go greet your children. They've missed you terribly."

She stayed in the parlor listening to Hannah's shriek of pure delight, Eliza's softer but no less pleased greeting and Jerome's manly, "Hello, Papa."

Her emotions roiled, a mixture of thankfulness that he had come and envy of the unconditional love he shared with his children. She realized that in the few weeks they had been with her, she had begun to know them as individuals and she had come to treasure the quirks of their personalities. Jerome's dry sense of humor. Eliza's gift for finding the good in any situation. Hannah's glee over the simplest things — a scarlet leaf, a caterpillar.

She stood at the window and closed her eyes, blocking out the children's excited chatter as she silently prayed.

Forgive me, Father, for my jealousy. Help me know if my motives are pure in offering to take the children while Tyrone is away. And if it be Your will, perhaps there is work that would not take Tyrone away from the children. Away from Nantucket. Away from me.

As this last thought crossed her mind, her eyes flew open. What should it matter to her if he stayed or went? Their only real association was the children. It was the children she meant to pray for — wasn't it?

"Miss Caroline?" Hannah's excited cry echoed down the hallway, accompanied by the patter of her feet as she ran toward the parlor.

Caroline met her at the door. "What is it, Hannah?"

"Oh, Miss Caroline, Papa's come home just like you said he would. I thought he would never come back. It's been days and days."

Weeks, Caroline thought. She smiled at Hannah. "Yes, isn't it wonderful?"

"Come on," Hannah ordered as she grabbed Caroline's hand and pulled her toward the kitchen. "Papa brought presents just as he said he would."

In the kitchen Jerome and Eliza were seated at the table while Tyrone lifted his duffel onto a chair and pulled out a pack-

160

age wrapped in brown paper and string. Hannah climbed onto the remaining chair and craned her neck to see what her father might have brought her.

"This is for Eliza," he said, handing his eldest a pie crimper, its wooden handle shaped like an apple tree, "who makes a fine apple pie."

"Oh, thank you, Papa," Eliza said. "Miss Caroline, could we try it? Could we make a pie for tonight's supper?"

"I think that's a lovely way to celebrate your father's homecoming, Eliza."

"This package is for . . ." Tyrone pretended to hand the package to Jerome but then turned and gave it to Hannah instead.

"It's a ribbon — no, three ribbons," she shouted. "See, Liza? A pink one, a green and a purple."

"Let's tie up your hair," Eliza said.

"Jerome, I had some trouble finding anything to buy for you."

Caroline watched Jerome shutter his eyes to hide his disappointment. Then Tyrone pulled something from his pocket and handed it to the boy.

"It's your boatswain's knife," Jerome murmured as if he'd just been handed a treasure beyond imagining.

"Aye."

The father and son looked at each other for a long moment while the two girls ran to find a mirror so Hannah could admire herself. "Thank you, sir," Jerome said, his voice cracking.

Caroline swallowed around the lump that blocked her breathing. "Well, now," she began as Jerome raced off to show his knife to the girls.

"There's something for you as well," Tyrone said, handing her the last package, wrapped in green paper and tied with ribbon, rather than string.

"Tyrone, you really should not . . ." Caroline saw the look he gave her and did not add the rest — that he should not be spending his money on presents for her. "Thank you."

"Open it."

"Shall I wait for the children?"

He shrugged.

Caroline smiled and untied the ribbon. "They can see it later," she said, her excitement evident in the flush she felt color her cheeks. "Oh, Tyrone, it's far too dear." She cradled the brooch, examining the intricacy of the carving. "It's a branch of lavender — my favorite."

"I know. I mean, I figured as much. You like it, then?"

"It's beautiful," she said. "And every time I wear it I'll think of you and the children. Thank you, Tyrone."

"No, Caroline. It is I who must thank you. You could have closed the door on us that very first day, but instead you made a place for my children. No gift can ever repay you for what you've done for my children — and for me."

He raised his hand and seemed about to caress her cheek when all three children came rushing back into the kitchen. Hannah catapulted herself into her father's arms. "I love my ribbons, Papa."

As the older children added to the chorus of gratitude and excitement that their father was back, Caroline slipped away, into the hall. She stood before the mirror and studied her face, trying to imagine what Ty saw when he looked at her. She touched her cheek. What if he had touched her, cradled her face in those large hands? She closed her eyes, savoring the vision. Then she pinned the brooch on her blouse, and ran her finger over the grooves of the engraving as she listened to the music of Tyrone's laughter rolling down the hall like the surf breaking on the beach on a calm summer's day.

CHAPTER NINE

Caroline sent Jerome to invite Henry and
Martha to join them for supper. She wanted
to give them the opportunity to see Tyrone
again, and tried not to dwell on needing
them as a buffer against the confusion she
felt every time she was within ten feet of
Tyrone Justice. To her surprise and Martha's delight, Tyrone had gifts for them, as
well.

"Why, it's a needle holder," Martha said,
holding up the item for all to admire.

For Henry there was a carved bone tooth-
pick.

"Fine work, Tyrone," he said. "Did you do
this yourself?"

"Yours and Mrs. Wofford's, but not Miss
Hudson's brooch," he replied with a nod
toward Caroline. "I learned scrimshaw from
one of the mates on a whaling ship when I
was just a cabin boy. It's been a while since
I had the time or materials to do the work,

but while I was in New Bedford one of the men I was working the docks with gave me a small piece of ivory he'd collected. Apparently he'd tried his hand at the craft and realized he hadn't the patience for it."

"Fine work," Henry repeated. "You might think about doing more pieces. There could be a market for your work here on Nantucket."

"A man can't make a living for his family etching and inking a piece of bone, Mr. Wofford."

"You can never tell. Times are changing. We're beginning to see more strangers on the island, especially in the summers. Folks from the mainland who come here to escape the heat of the city find our little piece of the world 'quaint' and they want something to take back with them."

"Why?" Jerome asked.

Henry grinned. "So they can look at it and remember how great it was to be here."

"You've got a gift, all right," Martha said as she helped Caroline clear the table and serve Eliza's pie.

Tyrone had his first bite of dessert halfway to his mouth before Eliza frowned at him.

"Yep," Henry said, "it's a changing world we live in. Whaling won't pay the bills for very much longer — at least for us on this island. As for trade — importing and exporting — even before the fire, that business had started to leave here for New Bedford. You should think on it."

"If you could sell your work, Papa, then could we stay here on Nantucket?" The hope that gleamed in Eliza's large eyes was heartbreaking.

"You children are staying with Miss Hudson," he said, glancing at Caroline. "She's offered to let you live here with her while I'm away."

"We're already staying here," Jerome pointed out.

"Away where?" Hannah's eyes narrowed.

"I have to work, little one. And the best way for me to earn enough money for us to afford a house of our own and pay Miss Hudson for your clothes and food is to join the crew of a ship."

"But you promised —"

"How long?" Jerome had never asked such a direct question in all the time Caroline had known him.

"The ship's sailing for South America and then on to India. I can show you on the map in the classroom after supper."

"I know where those places are," Jerome muttered. "They're a long way from here."

"Children, your father is here for tonight

166

only. Let's not waste precious time going over things we cannot change," Caroline said. "Eliza, perhaps you and Jerome could show your father what you've learned to play on the harpsichord and harmonica. And Hannah, you can dance for him."

"I don't want to," Hannah mumbled.

"Come on, Hannah," Ty coaxed. "I'll dance with you."

"What do you say, Hannah?" Martha asked, taking the child's hand. "It's a very special evening when we can offer our guests supper and entertainment."

"I used to play harmonica myself," Uncle Henry said as he and Martha followed the children to the parlor. "Where is that harmonica, Martha?"

"I hid it."

Relieved that her suggestion had worked, Caroline had begun to clear the dessert dishes and failed to notice that Tyrone had not gone to the parlor with the others.

"Thank you," he said.

"I'm just so glad you enjoyed the meal and —"

"Not just for supper. You know what I mean. Thank you for turning their attention away from my leaving. It'll come soon enough."

"How soon?"

"I can stay tomorrow, but I have to be in New Bedford first thing Monday morning."

Caroline felt the stack of dishes teeter slightly. She set them back on the table and took his arm. "Then we must make the most of the time you have with the children." And she led him across the hall to the parlor.

Ty spent the night at the Woffords, but he didn't sleep. He'd accomplished what he'd come to do. Against anything he'd thought possible, his children were safely settled in Caroline's care, with the added bonus that Henry and Martha had taken to them almost like grandparents. Jerome would have someone to look up to in Henry, and perhaps could learn barbering, as well. That, at least, was a trade a man could count on. There would always be a call for barbers — unlike whalers.

Both girls clearly admired Caroline and, as far as Ty could see, the feeling was returned. Caroline had praised all three children that evening and it was evident that Hannah had the teacher wrapped around her little finger, as she did most adults.

Ty folded his hands behind his head and stared up at the ceiling. He was going to miss them so. Life at sea might sound exciting to some, but he knew it for what it was — days and weeks of exhausting work interspersed with boredom, living in confined quarters with little opportunity for privacy.

The months he would be gone stretched out in front of him like a jail sentence. And maybe it was no less than he deserved. Maybe everything they'd been through since the fire was punishment for the fact that he should have been able to save Sarah.

"At least You don't take it out on the little ones," he muttered, still staring heavenward. "I guess I can be thankful for that. Thankful You brought Caroline into our lives."

He stretched the length of the bed and listened to the night sounds — the soft, methodical breath of a foghorn, the wind rattling the shutters and warning of harder weather to come, Henry snoring in the room next door.

"And if I take this job, make this voyage, will we be square then? Can I come home to Nantucket and my children and start fresh?"

And will Caroline Hudson be part of that fresh start?

Ever since Tyrone had appeared unexpectedly at her door, the weekend had taken on hooves on the cobbled street. Expecting to see Uncle Henry, she was surprised when it was Ty who climbed down from the wagon and headed for the kitchen door. He was carrying a basket draped with a checkered towel. And Caroline realized how very glad she was to see him.

"Come in." She swung the door open and stood aside as he entered the warm kitchen on a rush of frigid air. His cheeks were ruddy with the cold and she couldn't help noticing that the high color softened his scar.

"Your aunt sent you these. They're still warm." He handed her the basket, then held his hands out to the stove to warm them.

"Oh, the children will love them. Aunt Martha makes the best cranberry muffins. Thank you, Tyrone, but you certainly didn't need to —"

"I was hoping to spend as much of the day as possible with the children," he explained. "I could be gone for some time, Caroline, and —"

"Is this truly the only possible way?" she asked and knew by the sudden shallowness of her breathing that his answer was important, not just for the children, but for her. She was going to miss him terribly.

Ridiculous, she thought. *You hardly know*

the warmth of his breath on her fingertips, she jerked her hand away.

He smiled. "Why, Caroline Hudson, I would never have taken you for being superstitious."

"I'm not," she protested. "Not at all. It's just that we both know the risks, so why dwell on them?" She busied herself with setting a place for him at the table.

"I just need to know you'd take the children — permanently."

She didn't hesitate for even a second. "Of course."

Ty pulled a paper from his pocket and handed it to her. "This signs over to you all my wages and any part of the profits I might earn from the voyage. Your uncle helped me put the wording together and he and Martha witnessed it."

Caroline's hand shook as she unfolded the document and tried to focus on the words.

"It's all legal," he said.

"I'm not questioning you, Tyrone. I'm just so moved by the trust you are placing in me. Thank you."

"And the money is to be used however best serves the children. You can put it into the school or —"

"I would never use any of your funds for my needs, Ty."

"Caroline, if I die and you end up raising my children, you're going to need an income you can count on. Investing in the school is for the children." He smiled. "Of course, I might not wash overboard, so don't go counting on anything."

"Don't talk that way." Caroline was horrified at the very thought that Tyrone might not live through the voyage. But she also saw that he was trying to lighten the somber mood that had fallen around them like a fog. "Besides, I might decide to marry again, and then the children would have security and an inheritance."

To her surprise, he frowned. "I hadn't thought about you marrying — about some other man raising my —"

"Oh, Ty, I was joking. Look at me. I am well past the point where I am likely to marry again. Besides, my reputation as strict and plain and bossy precedes me. Most men on Nantucket are a little afraid of me."

"I'm not," he murmured as the children came clattering down the stairs.

Ty surprised himself and certainly Caroline by succumbing to Hannah's assumption that he would join them for church.

"You don't have to go," Caroline said after breakfast, while the children were busy getting their outer garments.

"It's no problem — might even do me some good." He grinned, hoping she would drop the subject.

"You know, Ty, God forgives. All we need do is ask."

"I know that, Caroline. It's not God's forgiveness I need. It's my own." He turned away. "Liza? Hannah? Jerome? We're going to be late."

The last time he'd sat in this church was the day of Sarah's funeral. It had not changed in the four years that had passed since then and neither had the minister. Reverend Groves's only sign of surprise at seeing Ty cross the threshold of the church was a slight lift of his bushy gray eyebrows before he turned to greet the next arrivals.

Hannah led the way down the center aisle, greeting people as she went and drawing smiles and waves in return. Jerome and Eliza were more reserved and shy, but Ty saw Liza cast a quick look at a lanky boy about her age seated in the pew across from the one they took. He waited for the children to file in, and then Caroline, before he took his place on the aisle. He glanced at the boy, who looked away, and then he turned his attention to Hannah, wiggling her way to a new position between Caroline and him.

It crossed his mind that, with Hannah between them and the older children seated Caroline's right, any stranger might assume they were a family. But until he was able to financially secure a future for his children, he had no business thinking about such foolishness. Besides, what woman would want him, scarred on the outside as well as inside? Certainly not a woman as beautiful and accomplished as Caroline.

Now, where did that come from? It's just because she's so close and you've come to depend on her for the children. It's the children that you're thinking of.

He reached for a hymnal at the same time Caroline did. Their hands brushed — his mottled with the scars of the fire and hers clothed in soft fawn kid leather. She pulled away as if stung, as she had jerked her fingers from his lips earlier. He had his answer.

The ritual of the service came back to him as easily as he knew the rhythms of working on a ship. He stood for the hymns, bowed his head for the prayers and tried without success to find a comfortable position on the hard, narrow pew once the minister started his sermon.

He was more aware of Caroline than he

had any right to be. She was wearing the brooch pinned to the lapel of her coat. She kept her hands folded in her lap and sat as still as a windless day, listening intently to the minister's words. Halfway through the sermon Hannah laid her head on Caroline's lap and fell asleep to the soothing rhythm of Caroline's fingers smoothing her curls.

A family. A home of his own. It was all he'd ever wanted, but as the now familiar bile of grief rose to his throat, he reminded himself that such dreams had gone up in flames the day Sarah died.

After church they stepped outside to find that the October day had warmed up enough to burn off the fog. Martha suggested they all go home and change, then meet again for the ride out to the flats of Eel Point at low tide to dig for clams.

"I'll make chowder for our supper," Martha said. "We'll need plenty of quahogs," she instructed the children. "Barring that, I'll accept steamers."

"What's quahogs?" Hannah whispered to Eliza.

"Great big hard-shelled clams," Jerome told her. "Steamers have soft shells. I'll help you, Hannah."

It was October and Caroline was weighing

the wisdom of having the children get their feet wet and dig in the sand, even if the sun had come out and turned the day into one of the warmest in weeks. "But, Aunt Martha, low tide isn't until three and . . ."

"So we'll be there at two. Plenty of time to find what we need and get back to make that chowder. Henry, are you going to bring that wagon around or do we have to walk?"

After taking Caroline and the children home, her aunt and uncle headed for their house, taking Ty with them.

"You're going to need old clothes," Caroline said as she followed the children inside.

"We've got our old things from before," Eliza reminded her. "You know, the clothes we wore when we first came here."

Seeing the excitement on the faces of all three children, Caroline put aside her concerns and smiled. "So you do. Go and change while I make you some lunch."

"What will you wear?" Hannah asked. "Your clothes are all so pretty."

It was a fair question. Since founding the school Caroline had always felt the need to maintain a certain image in the community. So whenever she went out she was careful to select her clothing and accessories with an eye to representing her livelihood. It was important to her that people assume that she was running the school to occupy her time, rather than because she needed the money. "I'll surprise you," she said, thinking, *and myself,* as she mentally catalogued her wardrobe. "Now, go and change."

Ty rolled the wagon to a stop just before two. Her aunt and uncle were nowhere in sight. Caroline climbed onto the front seat while Ty helped the children into the back of the wagon.

"I thought we were all to go," she said.

"Martha set Henry to chopping wood and she's busy making bread. She said she'd meant all along for this outing to be just for the youngsters. According to her, we must have misunderstood."

Caroline suspected that her aunt was up to her old tricks of matchmaking. Martha had made no secret of her belief that Caroline had married Percy more out of desperation to spare herself the label of "spinster" than out of love. And when Percy had left for California without taking Caroline, that had been the last straw for Martha. "You deserve better," she had argued when Caroline offered excuses designed to soothe the sting of Percy's desertion. It was clear that Martha liked Tyrone, and she'd been hinting that Caroline should find herself "a good man" long before the traditional year of mourning had passed.

"I'm sorry, Ty."

"I'm not." He grinned. "That's quite a hat, Miss Caroline."

She had pulled out an old, faded poke bonnet with a brim that hid most of her face. She was also wearing one of her late husband's old shirts over a plain navy-blue skirt. "This is what I wear for chores," she said. "Well, not the hat, of course, unless I'm gardening."

"Of course."

She could see that he was fighting to keep from laughing, and the truth was that she probably did look ridiculous. She certainly would not want the parents of her students seeing her out and about in this garb. "Stop laughing," she muttered, but she felt a bubble of giggles percolating in her breast, as well.

A moment later they were both laughing as Caroline loosened the ties of the bonnet to let it fall free on her back. All three children turned their attention to the front of the wagon.

"What's so funny?" Hannah demanded.

"You are," Ty answered and snapped the reins to urge the team of horses to move at a faster pace.

At the beach, Caroline watched while Ty

took the children out onto the flats, which would be covered over again in a matter of hours. She thought of protesting when he bent down and removed his shoes and socks and then did the same for Hannah, but reminded herself that they were his children.

He took Hannah's hand and guided her onto the soft sand, their heads bent low as they took slow steps and examined the sand for the telltale spurt of water that would signal the presence of shellfish.

"Found some," Jerome crowed and fell to his knees as he started to scoop up the wet sand with both hands.

"Don't cut yourself," Caroline warned in spite of her determination to let Ty handle the children.

"I know how to dig," Jerome assured her, and true to his word as soon as he had made a deep hole, he began exploring the side walls of it, digging in with his fingers until he produced a large clamshell. He held it up for all to see, then dropped it in the bucket next to him. "That's one for me," he shouted.

Next Eliza found a spot and about the same time so did Hannah and Ty. Caroline watched them on their knees, oblivious to their clothes getting wet and muddy as they laughed and kept count.

"We've got five already," Hannah shouted to her brother as she ran to Eliza to show her the clam she'd just found.

"Come and help us," Ty called to Caroline. "Your Aunt Martha says we need at least thirty for chowder."

Caroline hesitated. What if someone she knew was out for a Sunday ride and saw her digging in the sand? Well, what of it? She pulled off her shoes and walked across the sand in her stocking feet.

"Right there," Ty directed, pointing to a spot next to the hole where he was harvesting. "Stick your finger in that hole."

Caroline did as he instructed, expecting the dot on the sand to be no more than a small indentation, and squealed with surprise when her finger sank to the knuckle.

"Looks like you found one," Ty said as he crawled over to face her and started opening up a wider, deeper hole.

They worked in tandem for several minutes, surrounded by the soothing lap of waves against the beach and the laughter of the children as they raced each other to find the most clams.

After an hour the children lost interest and amused themselves making sand forts from the piles of wet sand they'd dug up in the search for clams. Caroline and Ty kept digging as if they'd been doing this together for years.

Caroline saw the edge of a shell and reached for it at the same time Ty spotted the prize. Their fingers were slimy with wet sand, but instead of pulling away or freeing the clam, they slowly laced their fingers together, neither looking up at the other.

"Caroline?" His voice was husky with emotion.

"I know, Ty. Don't worry about the children." Her voice choked.

He tightened his grip. "I'm not." At last he looked at her. "That's what I wanted to tell you. I want you to know how grateful I am for the peace of mind you've given me." He leaned closer and with his free hand brushed a glob of wet sand from her cheek. "If anyone had told me it would be a schoolteacher who saved me, I would have thought them mad."

"Oh, Tyrone, I can't save you. Only God can do that."

"Perhaps you are His emissary, then, for surely it is you who has made the difference."

For the first time since meeting him, she followed her instinct to trace the trail of the burn on his cheek. She heard his breath catch but he did not reject her touch. "Does

183

it hurt?" she asked.

"It did but no more. It's more like it brands me."

"As a man of rare courage."

"Hardly that, Caroline. Just a man trying to make a place for himself and his children."

"I wish you didn't have to go so far or for so long. The children will miss you very much." She smiled. "I'll have them write to you every night — a few lines at least."

"Even Hannah?"

"Yes. She can draw you pictures. We'll bundle their work and send it and hopefully it will find you. But even if the letters miss you, Ty, you will know they are out there and you must write the children as well, no matter how weary you are — a few lines. Promise me that."

"Yes."

"And we'll put up a map and follow your voyage. I'll have all the children learn about the countries you visit and if your letters come to us, we'll read about all the things you're seeing and the people who live in these far-off places and —"

He uncurled his fingers from hers and returned to the task of digging. "Don't raise their hopes, Caroline. It would be cruel."

She sat back on her heels and watched

him retrieve another clam and drop it in the bucket. "Why can't you believe in hope, Tyrone? You must have faith."

"In God?" His handsome face twisted into a smirk.

"In yourself. God can't help you if you won't even acknowledge your need for that help."

"I'm fine on my own, Caroline, so just let it go, all right?"

Caroline pushed herself to her feet and started across the beach. The man was impossible. Caroline felt sorry for any woman who would allow herself to be swayed by that smile, that devotion to his children, that proud, stubborn streak that ran the length of his six-foot frame. "Come along, children. It's time to go."

CHAPTER TEN

The children were so filled with excitement about the day they had spent at the beach that Caroline was sure no one noticed the distance between Tyrone and her. But she should have known that her aunt would be eagerly watching for signs that her match-making had produced some results.

"Well?" Martha demanded when the two women were washing the dishes.

"What?"

"You know very well what, Caroline. Tyrone is a good man. You could do a lot worse, and given your age and . . ."

"I am not exactly ancient," Caroline protested with a laugh she hoped might get Martha off the subject.

"You're past thirty. Are you determined to ignore the one opportunity that may come your way and keep you from spending the rest of your life alone?"

"I am hardly alone and, besides, Mr.

Justice is shipping out to sea tomorrow. He could be gone for over a year. Would I not be alone if we were married?"

"So you have thought on it. He's a handsome one in spite of those burns. In fact, because of them, I think. They give him a certain air of mystery, don't you agree?"

"I hadn't really thought about it one way or another."

"Ha!"

"Aunt Martha, I know you have my best interests at heart, but many women — especially women here on Nantucket — have chosen not to remarry following the loss of their husbands."

"Most of those women are my age. They've had their families, and in many cases a long, full life of marriage before their husbands died. Your situation is entirely different."

"I can't see how."

Martha sighed. "Oh, Caroline, I don't think you know what marriage is. What you had with Percy was a sham from the beginning. He was a charmer and a con man who set his sights on the prettiest girl in town — you — and romanced you until you agreed to marry him. Then once the conquest was made, he —"

"I know what Percy was," Caroline interrupted. "And I also know that what we shared was not the kind of love that you and Uncle Henry have been so blessed to know. But, Tyrone Justice is still mourning."

"It's been four years, Caroline. He isn't mourning. He's censuring himself. He has dedicated his entire life to making certain that his children are all right. He's even willing to take a job that will remove him from their lives for many long months — perhaps forever — if that job can provide them with the security he wants for them."

"I know all of that and I wish there were another way."

"He has entrusted you with his most precious possessions, Caroline. What other indication do you need that the man —"

"Children are not possessions. He has asked me to care for them and I have agreed."

"Why?"

Caroline stumbled for words. "Because it is the Christian thing to do," she finally managed.

Martha rolled her eyes.

"And speaking of those children," Caroline said, "tomorrow is a school day and it is past time that Hannah should be in bed. Thank you for a lovely day, Aunt Martha." She kissed her aunt's wrinkled cheek. "And thank you for caring so deeply. It means so much more than you know."

Martha's eyes welled up and she hugged Caroline hard. "I only want you to know some happiness, child."

"I'm happy," Caroline said. *Aren't I?*

Ty insisted on walking Caroline and the children home. He carried a sleeping Hannah up to the room she shared with Eliza. He laid her on the bed, then gathered his two older children close.

"I have to leave at dawn," he said, "so this is goodbye for now. I need to know I can count on the two of you to be strong and care for your little sister and help Caro— Miss Hudson as much as possible."

Eliza and Jerome nodded.

"I'll be back as soon as I can, but you know that means a long, long time."

"Yes, sir."

"I'll write to you every night and even if you never receive a single letter know that I am thinking of you and writing to you."

At this Jerome swallowed hard, his face reddening with the strain of keeping tears at bay. Eliza wrapped her arms around Ty. "I love you so much, Papa," she whispered and Ty almost lost all composure as he tightened his hold on her.

Over her shoulder he saw Caroline standing in the doorway. Tears were streaming down her cheeks and when she saw him watching her, she turned away and he heard her footsteps descending the stairs.

"Get some sleep, now," he said, gently prying Eliza's arms from his neck. "Everything is going to be all right. It's just going to take some time."

He walked Jerome down the hall to his bedroom. "If I got a job, you wouldn't have to leave," Jerome said just as Ty turned to leave. "I mean, if we were both working . . ."

"No. Your job is school. Learn all you can, son, so you never need worry about finding a good-paying job to support yourself and the family you'll have one day. Right now this is my responsibility. The lesson for you is to understand that sometimes a man must make hard choices for his family's sake."

Jerome made no pretense of hiding his tears then, and Ty wrapped him in a bear hug and held on until the boy's sobs had calmed. "It's all going to work out, son," he said, and wished he could be sure.

Downstairs Caroline sat in the parlor, staring into the dying embers of the fire.

"I'll say goodbye, then," Ty said. "I know I can never repay the kindness you and your aunt and uncle have shown me, but know this, Caroline — whatever this voyage has in store for me, I'll go easier knowing my children are here with you."

She had not stirred, had not turned to look at him, had sat so stone still that he thought she might be asleep. And then he saw her shoulders start to quiver and he realized that she was crying. No one other than his children had cried for Ty in a very long time. For a moment he felt his knees go weak with the longing to stay here with her, with his children.

Then he pulled himself together and crossed the room, where he knelt beside her chair and placed his hand on her back. "Ah, don't cry, Caroline. There have been enough tears for one day, don't you think?"

"There must be another way," she blubbered. "Children should not have to endure such heartache."

He felt a twinge of disappointment that she wasn't crying because she would miss him, but rather for the children. Then he understood that her tears were a kind of assurance that he had made the right choice. With the children in her care he could put all of his energy into building a future for his family.

"Come here," he said as he stood and pulled her to her feet to face him. "I want to ask one more thing of you, Caroline." She looked up at him with those huge emerald eyes filled with tears and her undeniable trust, and he was lost. "Will you kiss me goodbye?"

It was the last thing Caroline had ever expected to hear him ask of her. And as if her heart had taken charge of her brain she nodded.

Slowly he lowered his face to hers and she realized that he was giving her time to reconsider. Instead she touched his cheek, laying her fingers along the curve of his jaw, and took half a step closer.

When his lips touched hers his gentleness surprised her. His mouth was soft and warm in the moment before he pulled away just enough to look down at her.

"Come back to us," she whispered. "The children will miss you."

"And you, Caroline?"

She wrestled with the wisdom of admitting that her feelings for him had blossomed so quickly over these last two days that she hardly understood them herself. And in her hesitation he read rejection and stepped away. "I'll go now. I'll write the children."

And me, she wanted to plead. Instead she trailed after him to the front door, then onto the front stoop and finally on down the steps and path, until they were standing on either side of her front gate as they had the day they first met.

Only this time the gate is open. My heart is open. Oh, please see that, Ty.

And just when she thought he might not pause or look back, he turned, pulled her into his arms and kissed her without any of the hesitancy or shyness he'd displayed just moments earlier. "Goodbye, Caroline."

Reliving the feel of Caroline in his arms, of her lips pressed to his, made the early-morning voyage from Nantucket to New Bedford seem like a journey of no more than a block. After leaving her, he'd gone down to the docks to clear his head and found his friend Roscoe Anderson preparing to set off for New Bedford.

Roscoe had offered to take him along and Ty had been glad for the opportunity to save a bit of money and say goodbye to his old friend. At first the two men had talked about Ty's eviction, the arrangements he'd made with the teacher to care for his children and his intent to go to sea for one more voyage.

"I can earn enough to come back and start a small fishing business," he told his friend.

"The children will have a roof over their heads and, most important of all, we'll be together."

Roscoe had nodded as he bit down hard on his pipe. "*The Libertine,* you say."

"That's the one. Do you know it?"

"Aye. There's been some talk that the company that owns her has fallen on hard times."

"The captain mentioned that when he had us all on deck once he'd selected his crew. He said this voyage was especially important for that very reason. It was clear that he was feeling some pressure to make the voyage in record time and come back with the hold refilled with goods the owners could sell here in America."

"Makes sense, then. You want a voyage that will bring you home sooner rather than later, and the captain needs an experienced crew to make sure he delivers on his promise to the owners."

Gratified that he had Roscoe's approval of his decision to return to sea, Ty had settled back against the wall of the pilot's house to catch some sleep and think about Caroline.

At first he had thought that he'd only imagined asking her, but then she had stepped closer, touched his face as earlier she had traced the scar left from his burns.

He sat bolt upright. That was it, of course. The way she had traced the scar was all the evidence he needed to decide that she had agreed to the kiss more out of pity than anything else. He felt the tissue beneath his scar tingle as it always did when he was upset, embarrassed or both. He'd been a fool to imagine there had been anything more to her kiss than simple pity for a man who had suffered the loss of his wife and gotten maimed in the bargain. And he'd been a double fool to think that her following him to the gate meant anything at all, and yet he had kissed her again. Only this time he had not asked. He had simply taken.

He would write her and apologize for his behavior. As soon as *The Libertine* was out to sea and he had a few minutes to himself, he would write the promised letter to his children and add a separate note to her.

Dawn was just breaking when Roscoe steered his craft into the harbor. He navigated his way past a double row of ships, each floating low in the water, testament to the fact they were loaded and ready to set sail. With winter coming on, Ty knew the captains were anxious to be on their way so they might cross over the equator and enter the warmer waters of the southern hemisphere as soon as possible.

He leaned against the railing, ready to help Roscoe dock and tie up his small fishing craft. But a feeling of dread seemed to envelop him like the morning fog. Something was amiss. He scanned the horizon for signs of bad weather, but the day promised to be fair.

They slipped past *The Libertine* and Ty looked back to see a group of men gathered at the foot of her gangplank. They seemed agitated, and shouts he couldn't quite make out went up whenever a new man joined the group.

"Something's not right," he muttered to himself and then shouted back to Roscoe as he pointed to the gathering of men that seemed close to exploding, "I've got a bad feeling about *The Libertine.*"

As soon as they tied up Roscoe's boat the two men ran toward the ship. The crowd had grown now, and a thin, prissy man in business attire stood on the top deck looking down on the gathering mob.

Ty and Roscoe decided to split up and move among the crowd to see what they could find out. Those dock workers they could get to talk to them seemed more interested in getting their hands on the dandy on board than explaining to Ty what had happened. One man reported that the ship had been sold and would set sail later that day.

"Then they'll still be needing a crew," Ty said, feeling slightly relieved. He worked his way toward the front of the mob, where he could see the expressions on the faces of men reading an official-looking document posted on a piling next to the gangplank.

He heard the words *receivership, insolvency* and *auction* and knew from the utter defeat on the faces of the men who now turned away from the ship and worked their way back through the crowd that *The Libertine* would not be back on the high seas this season — if ever.

"I spoke with the harbormaster himself," Roscoe reported. "*The Libertine* won't be sailing anytime soon, Ty. I'm sorry." Roscoe squeezed Ty's shoulder. "Count your blessings. The harbormaster also told me that the load she was carrying was confiscated as illegal goods — profitable but illegal. You're well out of it."

"I don't have a job," Ty said, gritting his teeth to keep himself from slamming his fist into the nearest wall. It was small comfort that he was in good company. Dozens of men now wandered the docks, wondering where their next job, their next meal was coming from. "All the other ships have their crews in place and, even if they're short a man, there are plenty younger they would take ahead of me. Short of stowing away and hoping to prove my worth en route —"

"I'll see if anyone I know needs an extra hand and put in a word for you," Roscoe offered.

"Fishing season's nearly over," Ty reminded him.

Roscoe shrugged. "There's always work, Justice. Nets that need mending, barrels that need building, ice that needs cutting. You just have to be willing to do what nobody else wants to do no matter how desperate they are for money."

Ty thought about how Jerome had smiled when Caroline complimented him on his skills with numbers, and how beautifully Eliza had described a Nantucket autumn in a poem she'd written for one assignment. He thought about Hannah dancing joyfully around the parlor while Caroline played the harpsichord and Jerome did his best to conquer the harmonica.

And he thought about Caroline. She had taken in his children at a time when he knew she could barely afford to keep the school running. And she had done so without a moment's hesitation. If she was willing to do that, then the least he could do was find a way to hold up his end.

"All right," he told his friend. "Let's go see who's hiring."

The first letter for the children arrived just two days after Tyrone had sailed for New Bedford. A sailor hand-delivered it to Caroline's kitchen door just as she and the children were about to have their supper. Then he disappeared before she could get her coin box and pay him for his trouble.

"Read it out loud," Jerome instructed Eliza when Caroline handed her the letter.

Eliza smiled as she slit the flap and pulled out a single sheet. "He wrote it the first day," she said and began reading from the letter.

29 October 1850

Dear Liza, Hannah and Jerome,
After leaving you last night I took a walk to the docks and Roscoe was getting ready to set sail for New Bedford to deliver a load of clams. He invited me to sail with him so we left well before dawn so he could be here at first light. New Bedford's harbor is very busy — ships of all sizes and people from foreign places all talking at the same time.

I look forward to hearing how you are doing with your studies. Remember me to Miss Hudson.

Love,
Papa

All three children chattered on about the letter through supper, recalling tales of their father's friend Roscoe and wondering aloud how far their father's ship had gotten on its voyage.

"We know he started from New Bedford," Eliza announced.

"That's right."

"Let's go mark the map with the first pin and maybe tomorrow or surely by next week we'll have the next letter."

They hurried off to the classroom, leaving the letter lying on the table. Caroline picked it up and read through it again.

Remember me to Miss Hudson.

His handwriting was bold, the letters well formed and the words all correctly spelled. For a man with little formal education, Ty had taught himself well. The fact that he had found a way to include her was touching, and she could not help but reread the words several times.

But she also could not shake the feeling that there was something about the rest of the message that was not quite as it should be. She studied each word for what was not being said. He talked of other ships but not the one he was to serve. He talked of other crews but not his own.

On the other hand, Ty was a quiet man, a man who took the time he needed to get his bearings, find his way. Surely the next letter would be more forthcoming. And maybe — just maybe — he would enclose a note just for her.

She closed her eyes, reliving the kiss they had shared in the parlor and then the far more disturbing one he had given her before walking away. She had replayed both in her mind a hundred times in the days since he'd left. She'd lain awake at night wondering if she was only fooling herself in thinking that just maybe there had been more than simple gratitude in those kisses.

She touched her lips as she recalled how it had felt to be in the arms of Tyrone Justice — how different from the embraces she had shared with Percy. His demonstrations of affection had been perfunctory, an afterthought more often than not. And she had convinced herself that he showed his love in other ways — the house, the furnishings ordered from Boston or New York, the fine clothes he insisted on choosing for her. She had been so grateful that a man of his standing would notice her, much less marry her, that she had turned a blind eye to the mounting debt until he'd left for California.

"But it's practically the other side of the world," she had protested. "Let me come with you. We can —"

"No," he'd replied firmly, almost angrily. Then he had cupped her cheek and looked at her as if truly seeing her for the first time. "You'll be fine, Caroline."

Not "I'll be back soon" or "I'll send for you."

Then he had patted her cheek as he might a favorite pet and walked away. He'd climbed into the carriage he'd hired to take him to the docks and looked back once. But she realized now that he had not looked back at her. He had looked up at the house and there had been a sadness and regret in his expression that she had not understood at the time. It was only later that she realized he had never meant to come back or send for her.

With nothing other than that experience for comparison, Caroline reexamined her parting with Tyrone. True, he had kissed her with more passion than she had ever known before, but Caroline was nothing if not a realist. Tyrone Justice's passion was

202

for his children and their security. Whatever he had expressed in that kiss, it had nothing to do with desire.

And it's high time you put aside such foolish thoughts, Caroline Hudson. You are well past that time of life when romance and courtship come into play.

Tyrone Justice had written to his children as he'd promised. What he'd chosen to include in that message was really none of her business. She folded the letter and put it back in the envelope, then went to join the children in the classroom.

CHAPTER ELEVEN

The following day Caroline could not help noticing that Jerome had garnered some respect from the other boys in the class when he'd showed them his father's letter and the map and explained the plan to plot Ty's voyage.

"My parents are in Paris," Thomas Woodstock said, pointing to France on the map, "but your father is going all the way around the tip of South America." He traced the itinerary with his finger. "All the way over here." He pointed to India.

"Miss Hudson, I have an idea," Noah Johnstone announced with a rare show of enthusiasm. "Could we take some string and mark the path Mr. Justice will travel and then use pins to mark each stop he makes along the way as the letters come?"

"That's a fine idea, Noah. Eliza, please bring the ball of string and the scissors from the drawer in the kitchen."

For over an hour the students worked together, studying the map and carefully placing the string along the most likely path. "We could make a scrapbook of the letters," Helen suggested suddenly. "We could mount each letter on a page and decorate the page with pictures and drawings of the place it came from."

"We can save the stamps, as well," her sister Laura added.

Caroline felt the pride she always did when her class started to work together. It was the most rewarding part of teaching, that single moment when ideas seemed to fly from the children like the fluff of dandelions gone to seed and float on a late summer's breeze. She just hoped that Ty's letters would continue to arrive often enough that the children would not be disappointed.

"And we could all write to Papa," Eliza suggested shyly. "I mean from time to time. He'd love to hear from you."

"An excellent plan," Caroline said. "But we all need to remember that the delivery of letters in both directions will be uncertain. At best we may not hear from Mr. Justice again for many weeks."

"But we have to write anyway, Miss Hudson," Eliza said. "We promised and we have to believe that Papa will get our letters and write back."

Touched by such faith, Caroline smiled. "Of course. Why don't each of you take out pen and paper now and introduce yourself to Mr. Justice?"

The classroom grew still except for the scratching of pen tips on paper as every child concentrated on writing a letter. Caroline had no idea how she was going to get all of them to Ty, but she was definitely not going to thwart such exuberance. She only hoped that Ty would see the importance of holding up his end of things. Perhaps she should include a letter explaining the project to him.

Ty worked the docks every day from dawn to dark. Every job was backbreaking work, but Ty pushed himself to the limit. The more odd jobs he could pick up in a day, the more he could add to the cash he was saving to send to Caroline.

At night he stayed on Roscoe's boat, giving his friend a quarter of his earnings in exchange for a bunk to catch a few hours' sleep and enough food to keep him going. Roscoe was a good ten years older than Ty. He was small and wiry with thin white hair and a shaggy beard. He spent his days fishing in the bay or netting shellfish to sell to his customers in New Bedford. Every night he docked his boat and headed for a run-down tavern where he knew the owner and his wife.

The two men had been on this schedule for several days when one night Ty heard Roscoe returning earlier than usual from the tavern.

"Mail for you."

Roscoe tossed Ty a thick brown parcel addressed to Mr. Tyrone Justice, c/o *The Libertine,* then stood by to watch him open it.

"How'd you come by this?"

The older man shrugged. "A mate was sorting through the outgoing mail, getting it ready to send out with ships leaving tomorrow. Lucky I was there to intercept it."

Ty examined the handwriting and return address. "It's from Car . . . the woman who is caring for my children." He unfolded the top sheet and quickly scanned her message and frowned. Then he spread out the half-dozen other sheets of papers on his bunk.

"Must be quite a talker," Roscoe said, making no secret of his curiosity about so many pieces of paper in one letter.

"She's a teacher. She runs a school for the children of rich families out of her home and . . ."

"I know the one." Roscoe sucked on the

stem of his pipe as he lit it, without taking his eyes off Ty. "None of my business, but how can you afford —"

Ty gathered up the letters, tied them back together and stuffed the bundle under his mattress. "Like you said, none of your business," he growled, then turned away. "I'm beat."

But Roscoe didn't take the hint. Besides, there was really nowhere for him to go in the tiny cabin. He sat on his cot smoking his pipe and saying nothing while the small craft rocked gently. Then Ty heard him rummaging around. A moment later the cabin was filled with the warble of a harmonica sounding the mournful tune of a sailor's lost love. He gave up any pretense of sleeping and rolled over until he was knee-to-knee with his friend.

"Want to tell me about her?"

"It's not her that's the problem," Ty admitted.

Roscoe slapped his harmonica against his hand a couple of times and set it aside. "If you say so, but you've been moping around for a week or more now and I don't think it's because you've been working so hard that you can barely move without crying out in pain. Shouldn't you let her know things have changed?"

Ty had to admit that Roscoe had one thing right. He was definitely in pain, except in his case the pain was all inside. "I need some air," he said. "Want to take a walk?"

"Nope. You go along. Think things through a bit."

Ty reached under his mattress and pulled out the packet of letters. Roscoe pretended he didn't see, but Ty could tell he was hurt by the action.

"You can see them," he said. "I just want to read them first, okay?"

For an answer Roscoe handed him a lantern. "Then you'll need some light."

Instead of walking along the wharf, listening to the sounds of the ships creaking and groaning as their weight shifted to balance in the water, Ty found a spot on deck out of the wind. He lit the lantern and pulled out Caroline's letter. It was dated two days earlier.

Dear Mr. Justice,
Your children were so happy to receive their first letter from you. Jerome came up with a wonderful idea and now all of my pupils are eagerly awaiting your next correspondence.

She briefly explained the plan to chart his

voyage and to make a scrapbook of his letters. Did the woman not understand that a man at sea had only a few opportunities to send or receive mail? Months could pass before his next letter reached them — if he were away at sea. He felt a twinge of irritation with Caroline that perhaps she had raised false hopes for all the children — especially his.

He leaned closer to the lantern and kept reading.

Of course I do understand that the number of letters that will actually reach the children before your return is limited to two or possibly three. But they are so caught up in the idea of following your journey that I must admit I have postponed explaining that to them for the time being.

I would ask that when you receive this you might find the time to outline the ports you are most likely to reach on your way to India and back again. That way the class could create a kind of log of your travels and perhaps once you return, you might agree to meet with them and let them ask questions and show you their work.

Twice she had mentioned his return. He tried not to read too much into that, but could not deny that the idea that she might be anxious for him to return warmed him despite the damp night. Eagerly he read on.

Enclosed you will find letters from each of the students and a drawing that Hannah made for you. I have surmised the course your ship might take. Tomorrow I will work with the class to chart that course on our classroom map. We can make corrections as needed once we hear from you by return letter.

The children are all well — missing you, of course. They are a joy to me and I thank you for the opportunity you have given me to spend time with them. May God bless you on your journey and bring you safely home again as soon as possible.

Yours truly,
Caroline Hudson

He searched through the other papers until he found the letters from Jerome and Eliza. Jerome's was brief and more a list of the activities of his day. He showed no emotion. *He's learned that from me.*

Eliza's small script filled both sides of her

sheet of paper and was full of details about what they were learning, visits with Henry and Martha, meals they had all shared. And Hannah's drawing looked like a cross between a ship and a whale. Only a small stick figure standing on top of the object made Ty decide that it was supposed to be him on the ship.

The letters from Caroline's other students were brief and formal. They inquired after his health then launched into a few brief sentences about themselves. Each covered less than half a page.

Ty set them aside and reread Caroline's letter. He realized that he was searching it for some sign that their parting kiss had meant something to her. But no matter how many times he read the words, he had to admit that there was nothing. She was apparently as skilled at hiding her feelings as he was.

You're assuming she has feelings, Justice.

Three weeks had passed with no word from Ty. Caroline had done her best to keep the project going, but with no information to feed their curiosity, the pupils had begun to lose interest. Eliza still wrote to her father faithfully every night before going to bed, but Jerome's letters had dwindled from four a week to barely one.

"Jerome, I believe you once mentioned a sailing friend of your father's. A Mr. Roscoe?"

"He's just Roscoe," Jerome mumbled, but she saw the first flicker of interest she'd had from him in days.

"And you say he lived down on the docks as you did before you came to live with me here?"

"He lives most of the time on his boat," Eliza said.

"I see. I thought I might pay him a visit and invite him to come to class one day. While we wait to hear from your father, surely his friend could answer some of our questions and give us more insight into the voyage your father is on."

"He's kind of shy — like Papa is," Jerome said.

"I understand. And certainly if he prefers not to speak with the class, then perhaps he can recommend someone else. Would you accompany me to the docks on Saturday, Jerome, and introduce me to your friend?"

"Yes, ma'am. If he's there. He works pretty much every day. But I can show you where he ties up."

"Lovely. Why don't we make a morning of it? We'll go into town and do some shopping, then stop to see Mr. Roscoe and perhaps have lunch with Uncle Henry and Aunt Martha."

The promise of an outing always seemed to lift the children's spirits. And Caroline was not at all surprised to find them dressed and ready to go at first light.

"I'll hitch up the wagon," Jerome announced as he gobbled down his breakfast.

"There's no great rush, Jerome. The shops will hardly be open at this hour."

"But Mr. and Mrs. Wofford are sure to be up and maybe she's made some of her muffins," he replied with a grin so like his father's that Caroline thought her heart had momentarily stopped.

"Excellent point," she replied and noticed that her voice came out as if she'd just run a race.

"Are you all right, Miss Caroline?" Eliza had come around the table to place her hand expertly on Caroline's forehead. "You don't seem to have a fever, but . . ."

"Fine," she assured the children. "Now you girls finish eating and help me wash up while Jerome gets the wagon ready. We'll need lap robes, Jerome. They're stored on the shelf below the harness."

"I'll get them," Hannah exclaimed as she grabbed her coat and ran after her brother.

In town Jerome expertly pulled the wagon to a stop across the street from the Wofford's house. Aunt Martha was opening the door before they had climbed down.

"Get in here out of that damp," she fussed. "Henry, set four places. Caroline and the children are here." She pulled off Jerome's knit hat. "You could use a haircut, young man."

In minutes the children were having a second breakfast of Martha's hot biscuits and fruit compote. Aunt Martha was regaling them with the story of the time she had failed to properly tie up her father's wagon and the horse had bolted and run away. Caroline used the opportunity to take her uncle aside.

"Uncle Henry, do you know a sailor by the given name of Roscoe?"

"Roscoe Anderson — old as Methuselah — and twice as spry," Henry replied. "Why?"

She told him her idea of contacting the elderly sailor to invite him to speak to the class. "There have been no letters since that first one and I think the children are beginning to lose heart."

Henry nodded. "I expect even Eliza is too young to remember how long it was between letters when Tyrone was away before. Of course, she had her mother back then. I expect that made a difference."

"Do you think this Mr. Anderson would come to the school?"

"Why don't we go ask him? We'll leave the children here with Martha. I can make the introductions and maybe soften the way for you."

The way he flicked his gaze over Caroline's costume, complete with gloves and small bonnet, told her that she might have over-dressed for this particular meeting. "I'd appreciate that."

Caroline was relieved to have her uncle's company. A woman alone on the docks even in broad daylight might attract the stares and unwelcome comments of those who lived and worked there. Her uncle was well known and respected by islanders of all classes and she felt perfectly comfortable walking with him the few short blocks to the waterfront.

"That's Roscoe's boat there. Looks like you're in luck."

Henry led the way down the narrow pier. "Ahoy there, Anderson," he shouted.

Caroline could smell fish frying and cof-fee as she waited with her uncle. She heard the clank of utensils on tinware and the mumble of men's voices inside the small cabin of the boat.

"Perhaps we're too early," she said just as a small, wiry man dressed in canvas trousers anchored by suspenders over a heavy sweater emerged from below. His face was weathered to the color of a coconut shell, no doubt due to his many years at sea, and he had the bluest eyes Caroline had ever seen. Those eyes twinkled now as he greeted Henry but focused all his attention on her.

"My niece, Caroline Hudson," Henry was saying.

"I'm so pleased to meet you, Mr. Anderson," she hurried to say.

"My niece is a teacher and she has something to ask you, Roscoe, if you've got a few minutes."

"Of course. Must be providence that brought you here today. I've been tying up over in New Bedford these last several weeks."

Instead of inviting them aboard, he hopped onto the pier. "How can I be of service, ma'am?"

Even as Caroline explained her idea, she had the uneasy feeling that something was amiss. She told Roscoe of the student project to follow Ty's journey and could not help noticing that when she fumbled for words to explain how the entire thing had begun, he was quick to fill in the blanks. If she didn't know better she would think he had heard all about the project. Of course, perhaps he had. After all, the pupils had been excited and had undoubtedly told others.

You're just nervous, she thought, but could not for the life of her understand why she should be.

"I'm afraid I can't pay you, sir." *I can barely meet my bills now,* she thought.

"I'd enjoy talking to the young ones, miss. You just tell me what you want me to talk about. Life at sea? The types of work and specialties the crew members need to have?"

"I had hoped that you might be more successful than I've been at explaining to the children why there have been no further letters from Mr. Justice, even though he promised he would write."

"That's easily handled. Ships come and go and they have their main business to consider. The mail gets to where it's meant to be eventually." He chuckled. "Sometimes though, eventually comes a long time after the sender has returned home. I expect you might find that's the case with Ty . . . Mr. Justice."

"Oh, thank you, Mr. Anderson. We shall all look forward to your visit to the classroom — at your convenience, of course. I know you have your work and . . ."

"Season's almost at an end, miss. How's Monday?"

Caroline could hardly believe it. "Monday would be fine. In fact, it would be perfect." She was so surprised that the man had agreed so readily that she felt suddenly shy with him. "I do hope you will plan to join us for lunch, Mr. Anderson," she said. "Perhaps you and your crew would enjoy sharing one of my apple pies?"

She glanced toward the cabin, smelled the cooking within and caught a glimpse of a man's hand. The sun highlighted deep purple marks on the palm. Was she seeing things? Of course, there were many men who had suffered burns fighting the fire of '46.

"An apple pie would be more than generous payment, Miss Hudson," Roscoe said, drawing her attention away from the porthole and back to the business at hand.

"Monday, then," her uncle said as he took her arm to guide her back up the pier. "You know the house?"

"Aye," Roscoe said. "I know it well."

Caroline stumbled slightly as she turned to look back at the boat, trying to catch a glimpse of the man inside. Tyrone could not possibly be in there, could he? And yet the glimpse she had caught of the burn — she knew that pattern. Hannah had once commented that her Papa carried a star with him everywhere he went. And when she had asked Eliza about that, she had explained that the burn on Ty's left hand resembled a star and that was the story he had told Hannah.

"Ten o'clock all right with you, Miss Hudson?"

Caroline steadied herself and met Roscoe Anderson's cheery smile. "Ten o'clock would be fine, Mr. Anderson." *And perhaps you could bring your friend with you, so his children can see him and he can explain why he has spent nearly a month pretending to be somewhere he obviously isn't.*

Chapter Twelve

"She's one to make a man look twice," Roscoe observed as he ducked below the narrow door and resumed eating his breakfast. "No wonder she has you all tied up in knots."

Ty gave his friend a look of warning that fairly shouted, "Back off."

Roscoe ignored it. "A bit straitlaced for my taste but nevertheless, a fine woman. Anyone can see that. You could do a lot worse, Justice."

"I didn't see my children with her."

"Me neither. Just her and her uncle." He sopped up the last of his egg with a piece of bread. "How do you want me to handle this business of going up to the school?"

"I don't know. Why'd you agree to do it?"

Roscoe grinned. " 'Cause nobody ever thought to ask me before. Nice to think I may know something those high-class youngsters would find interesting."

"Do you think we might be able to lay our hands on an old envelope postmarked from Portugal?"

"And then what?"

"I could write a letter and you could take it to them as if it just happened to come into your hands, the way their letters did when we were in New Bedford."

"Pretend you've been in Portugal?"

Ty nodded. "And I wrote that as we were setting out for Buenos Aires suddenly —"

"You're tying yourself up in lies. And in the end when it all starts to unravel — and it will — you'll come out the worse for it with your kids and Miss Hudson."

Roscoe was right, of course. He should never have started the lie to begin with. He should have gone to Caroline, told her about the ship's financial failure and the men left without work. Those men like him had had to scramble for the few jobs there were. Some, like him, had taken anything that would pay them. Others had taken other paths — petty thievery to collect enough to get them away from New Bedford and on to Boston or New York, where their chances for earning a living might improve.

"I just wanted to make good on my promise to come back with enough money to pay

222

her and set my children up in a proper house."

Roscoe clutched Ty's shoulder. "You've gathered quite a tidy sum these last weeks — not what you could have made on a ship's crew, but a decent amount. It might make the difference."

Not in Caroline's eyes. Not if I lied to her and my children while earning it.

Her uncle seemed oblivious to Caroline's sudden foul mood on their walk home, but Martha saw immediately that something had changed.

"Roscoe Anderson turned you down," she stated the moment she saw Caroline's pinched expression.

"Not at all," Caroline hurried to assure her and the children, who took this announcement to heart. "He's coming to class on Monday morning. He's quite a charming and well-spoken man and I assume he will have the children enthralled with his tales of life on the high seas."

"It went well, then?" Clearly Martha was not convinced.

"Very well," Caroline assured her. And it had, insofar as it had been her purpose to find some way to reenergize the class. Half a dozen times on the walk back from the pier she had gone over the details of what she thought she had seen in that small porthole. The sun had been very bright and the movement so quick. Surely she had imagined the purplish color of the hand pressed against the glass.

And even as she shepherded the children out to the wagon and into town to attend to the rest of their shopping, Caroline continued to chastise herself for what she had convinced herself was wishful thinking. The truth was she missed Tyrone intensely, and more than once she had been in town and caught a glimpse of a man walking away from her, or the top of a seaman's cap, and her heart had beat faster with the rhythm of hope.

No, there had to be some other explanation. When Mr. Anderson came to speak to the class on Monday she would find a few moments to talk with him privately. He had taken Ty to New Bedford that morning. He would confirm that the ship had indeed sailed. He would be able to set her conflicted thoughts to rest.

Ty had forgotten how truly beautiful she was. The way the sun highlighted her golden curls, the way her eyes came alive whenever she was engaged in a conversation that interested her, the way her small mouth pursed as she worked through the logistics of a potential problem.

He closed his eyes, reliving as he had a thousand times the touch of those lips on his, the feel of her in his arms. After Sarah died, the only thing that mattered to him was making sure his children were safe and cared for. After a year or so mates he had worked with or known when Sarah was alive began to suggest that it was time he sought a new wife.

Ty had rejected any such notion as disloyalty to Sarah's memory. But when Roscoe had suggested he owed it to his children to find them a new mother, he'd seen some sense in that. It was for the children, not him. The problem was that the few women he'd found suitable had rejected him. They wanted children of their own. They wanted love and romance. They did not want a man whose grief for his late wife was forever burned into his face.

"You gonna sit out here all night?" Roscoe growled as he struck a match and lit his pipe.

"Maybe."

Roscoe squatted next to him and stared out into the blackness. "Winter's coming on. The steady work will dry up soon, Ty."

"I know."

"I was thinking of maybe heading south. I'm getting too old for these winters. Besides, there's work to be had further south. A guy with a boat — two guys with a boat — even better." He drew on his pipe. "We could take your boy with us."

Ty was deeply moved that the old man had obviously been doing some thinking of his own. "You're a good man, Roscoe."

The old man shrugged. "Seems to me the plan was for you to go to sea. I'm just making that happen and getting a first mate in the bargain." He groaned as he stood up and stretched. "You think on it some. I'm going to bed."

When Ty opened his eyes and saw the sun trying to fight its way through the mountain of clouds that had appeared on the horizon, he realized he'd fallen asleep on deck. He heard church bells and remembered with relief that it was Sunday morning. No work today. He was stiff and cold and hungry, but there was no sign of movement from inside the cabin so he decided to let Roscoe sleep.

Instead of going into town, where he ran the risk of someone seeing him, Ty wandered out into the countryside. Hour after hour he walked, barely aware that he had reached the newly constructed Sankaty Head lighthouse before turning back. Mile after mile he let his feet take him where they chose while his brain seemed to run in all different directions.

He went over the events of the last several weeks again and again. The bargain he and Caroline had struck to have Eliza and Jerome attend classes while he repaired her home and school. The eviction from the fishing shack. The search for work and the decision to go to sea once more. And Caroline agreeing to not only school the children but house them, as well.

He had begun to believe that he might be on a path to redemption. They would be a family again. All he needed was enough money to maybe buy a small boat. He'd even thought about asking Roscoe if they could be partners. When he was feeling particularly confident he imagined the two of them building a fishing business to rival those that had been destroyed in the fire or had moved to New Bedford.

He'd had it all planned out and then it had all disappeared — all his plans and dreams for his children. Even the fantasy that someday Caroline might come to care for him.

There was nothing I could do once the job

with The Libertine *fell through,* he told himself. *Yeah, I could have come back, but what would that have solved? I still couldn't take care of my children and work for the money we need to start over. I still have nothing to offer her.*

Ty had always been one to face hard facts. The facts were that he had lied to his children, lied to Caroline and lied to himself. He could either let the lie stand and go south with Roscoe or he could stay and face the consequences of his actions. The first was the easier path by far and it had the added advantage that he would return with the money needed to start fresh. The children need never know. He'd traveled the world before. He could certainly convince his children and even a smart woman like Caroline that he had done it again.

But a lie of omission is still a lie.

Shaken by that realization, he stopped and looked around. Without being aware of it he had nearly walked back into town. He hesitated. Up the hill stood the church. The other way led back to the docks. He walked up to the closed double doors of the church. Judging by the sun it was well past noon and everyone would be home now, enjoying their Sunday dinners and a day with family and friends. Ty tried the handle and stepped inside the shadowed vestibule.

Rays of filtered sunlight cast the colors of stained glass onto the pews and altar. Ty snatched off his cap and started up the center aisle. The sanctuary seemed larger than it had that Sunday he'd come here with Caroline. And the silence was far more powerful than any choir's anthem or minister's sermon.

And yet he felt surrounded by calm, as if he had been at sea in a raging storm and all at once everything had gone quiet. He was tempted to surrender to the overpowering weariness of mind and spirit that had been his constant companion. But for the sake of his children, he had to keep on trying to find his way through this.

If he went with Roscoe, the children could stay with Caroline and he could return with at least a portion of the money he might have made on *The Libertine.* But he would still have to face the lie — the fact that he had been close by all this time. Would his children understand and forgive him? And how would he explain his actions to Caroline?

He stood before the altar, hat in hand, and understood that the silence he'd taken at first for solace was no more than the eye of his personal storm. The worst was yet to come. He must go to Caroline, tell her the truth and hope that she would agree to continue to be the only safe harbor his children had known since their mother had died in the fire.

He started to shiver violently. His hands shook and he felt blood rush to his head and then plummet just as suddenly until he felt light-headed and weak. He grasped at a pew and missed. He needed some fresh air. The church was suddenly too close, too warm. He stumbled up the aisle toward the door, where a figure in black robes had just entered the church. Ty fell into the man's arms.

Next thing he knew he was lying on a hard pew and Roscoe was leaning over the back of it. "That's him, reverend. Thanks be to God, he came here. When he wasn't on the boat this morning, I was afraid he'd done something drastic. He's been through some hard times."

You might say that, Ty thought just before he lost consciousness.

Caroline was truly grateful when Martha insisted that the children come home with her and Henry following church.

"We're going to make apple butter," she announced, "and then we're going to eat some on the bread I made this morning."

All three children grinned, then turned immediately to Caroline. "May we go?" Eliza asked.

"Of course. Let's all go. I could help," Caroline offered.

"Do you really have time to add making apple butter into your routine?" Martha asked.

Caroline smiled weakly. "No, but . . ."

"Then go home. Perhaps you'll find the time to work through whatever problems have been keeping you up nights. Henry will have the children back after they've had their supper."

It had been weeks since Caroline had been in the house alone, and she could not deny that the brief respite from the constant presence of the children was a welcome change. She had the whole afternoon in front of her and she could use it to catch up with work she often put off until after the children were in bed.

She changed out of her Sunday best and into a more serviceable plain skirt and shirtwaist, then went immediately to her desk in the parlor. She pulled out the ledger where she kept careful records of money coming in and money going out and stared at the two columns. John Woodstock had not paid her for Thomas's tuition.

Of course she was well aware that he assumed his son was attending the public school with the other Woodstock children. He and Matilda were due back any day now from their trip to Europe. Caroline decided the best course would be to write them a letter that they would receive upon their return requesting the opportunity to sit down and discuss Thomas's much improved classroom performance over previous years.

Just as she started the letter, there was a knock at the kitchen door. It was odd for anyone to call at the rear of the dwelling on a Sunday. Perhaps one of the neighborhood children was playing a prank. A little irritated at the interruption, Caroline went to the door and saw Roscoe Anderson waiting patiently on her back stoop.

"Why, Mr. Anderson," she exclaimed as she opened the door wide. "Please, come in."

"No, miss, thank you all the same. I just came to deliver this." He handed her a folded piece of paper and waited. "I've been asked to wait for your reply," he explained, and turned up the collar on his coat against the sharp wind coming off the bay.

Caroline unfolded the paper.

Dear Miss Hudson,

I apologize for the suddenness of this request, but please come to the church at once with Mr. Anderson. There is someone who needs your help.

Regards,
Reverend Jeremiah Groves

The church was just up the hill, less than two blocks away. Caroline could see it from her front gate. "Is someone ill? Mrs. Groves is away visiting her sister, is she not? Has Reverend Groves had an injury or a fall?"

"Just come, won't you? He needs you."

Caroline looked up from the brief note she'd been trying to understand and saw that Roscoe was near tears.

"Is it Mr. Justice?" It was a ridiculous question. Surely Ty was halfway around the world by now. But when Roscoe nodded, Caroline grabbed for the wool shawl she kept on a peg by the kitchen door and wrapped it around her shoulders. "Let's go," she said, her voice thin and hesitant even as her stride was sure and steady. Without another word she led the way up the hill to the church.

Caroline almost didn't recognize the man stretched out on the last pew of the church. He was gaunt and hollow eyed as he stared vacantly at the rafters above him. Doctor Hopkins had just finished examining him.

"I suspect he's suffering from exposure and exhaustion. He's undernourished, for one thing. You say he was out all night?"

Roscoe nodded. "Not unusual for him. Most nights he's working until the wee hours. Last night he was just sitting on the deck. We had a few words before I turned in. Then I got up this morning and his bunk hadn't been used and he was nowhere to be seen. I didn't think much of it until he didn't turn up by noon. I started checking places I thought he might be like the cemetery here. He used to come here."

Caroline reached over the back of the pew and laid her hand against his cheek. Tyrone blinked up at her, then turned away.

The doctor folded his stethoscope into his medical bag and snapped the bag shut. "He needs rest, plenty of fluids and a place to spend several days out of the damp and cold."

"Thank you for coming, doc," Roscoe said as the two men walked out to the doctor's buggy. "We'll see that he gets the care he needs."

"I'm fine," Ty muttered as he tried to stand, then immediately had to sit down again.

"I was just warming some soup that Mrs. Groves left for me when I saw Mr. Justice enter the church," Reverend Groves said. "Do you think you could make it to the parsonage by leaning on me, Mr. Justice? A bowl of soup might help."

Ty nodded. "Thanks."

As soon as Reverend Groves had helped him to his feet, Ty looked at Caroline. "Where are my children?"

"Making apple butter with Martha and Henry."

He nodded and started the short trek from the church to the house, leaning heavily on Roscoe and the minister.

For a moment Caroline stood frozen in the doorway of the church. When she'd first realized that it was Ty who needed her help, she had acted instinctively. It had been all she could do not to run the few blocks to the church. And when she had first seen him lying there, she'd had to restrain herself again from wanting to cradle him in her arms.

But now that he was at least semi-ambulatory, she was beset with questions. Where had he been all this time? Why had he stayed away? What would she tell the children? Why hadn't he come to her and let her help? Why — after all that she had done — did he not trust her?

The fear that had driven her to run to his aid was now replaced by fury. Fury at the stubborn pride that drove men to choose self-destruction when, through trust and faith — and yes, love — all problems could be faced and resolved.

She clenched her fists and followed the trio of men across the churchyard and into the parsonage. By the time she got there, Tyrone was sitting on the sofa while the minister went to the kitchen to get soup. Roscoe was standing uncertainly near the door.

"Well, Justice, looks to me like you're in good hands here. I'll come by later to see how you're faring — see if you . . . what you've decided about that other thing. See you and the children tomorrow, Miss Hudson."

Ty just sat hunched forward, staring at his hands.

Caroline saw Roscoe to the door, then went to the kitchen. "Reverend Groves, I don't understand. Why did you send for me?"

"He asked for you. Just before he passed out he distinctly spoke your name. I asked Mr. Anderson to go for the doctor at once, and when he arrived and Mr. Justice regained consciousness, he again asked for you."

"I see." *No, I don't understand any of this.*

"Perhaps you could take him this soup — I put only a little broth in the cup until we're sure he can stomach more." He held out the mug to Caroline as if offering her Communion. When she hesitated, he smiled. "From what I could gather from Mr. Anderson, Tyrone has come to us with a heart that is weighed down by doubt and guilt and broken promises. He seems to have chosen you as the one he most needs to hear what he has to say. I'll be nearby in my study should you need me."

Caroline took the soup and returned to the parlor, where Ty was still sitting in that pose she had come to associate with him — the one where he seemed always about to take flight.

"Drink this slowly," she said, handing him the mug.

He cupped it in both hands and sipped the broth. "Thank you." He looked up and glanced around, obviously a little taken aback to be alone with her.

"Reverend Groves is in his study right across the hall." She sat down in a straight chair next to the settee. She rolled into one all the questions longing to spew forth from her. "Tyrone, what happened?"

CHAPTER THIRTEEN

He looked at her and realized that over the last weeks she had struggled, as well. The circles under her eyes told a story of sleepless nights. She looked drawn and yet every muscle in her slim body seemed ready for a fight. Her fingers were so tightly interlocked that her knuckles had turned white. Her spine was as straight at the chair she sat upon. Her mouth was pursed as if to contain her abject disapproval. He realized that she was furious and only the fact that he was no match for her at the moment kept her from attacking him with the full frenzy of her ire.

"Will you hear me out before passing judgment, Caroline?"

"I have no cause to judge you, Mr. Justice. Whatever your reasons for . . . for . . ."

"Deceiving you?"

"Deceiving your children." She spat out the words. "Do you have any idea what this news will do to them?"

Ty held up his hands in surrender. It was a mark of how infuriated she was that she was refusing to call him by his given name. "Please let me try and explain."

She crossed her arms and glared at him.

"I'll start at the beginning — the morning Roscoe and I sailed for New Bedford. The morning after . . . after that night at your house with the music and the laughter and . . ."

The kiss.

He took some comfort from the fact that her eyes seemed to soften just a bit, and pressed on. He told her about their arrival in New Bedford, the mob gathered next to the ship, the posted sign, the complete lack of recourse. "Not only for me, Caroline, but for all the men. We had all counted on that work and suddenly it was gone and we could do nothing about it. You can't possibly understand how completely invalid a man feels knowing he has no control over how he might earn a decent wage to support his family."

"I understand more than you give me credit for, Mr. Justice. Perhaps in some ways I am on the other side of things. It is my business that suffers when I cannot collect the tuition due me."

"So your sympathies lie with the ship owner."

"My sympathies lie with three wonderful children whose love for and trust in their father is absolute. Were there not other ships in need of a crew?"

"No. By the end of that first week most had already put out to sea, and the likelihood of more ships sailing before spring was small."

"Yet the idea of coming back here seems to have never crossed your mind."

"I thought that if I could work the docks — odd jobs that no one else would take — then perhaps someone would hire me. In the meantime I was able to save a good part of my wages. Roscoe let me sleep on his fishing boat and shared his food with me. I gave him a small part of my wages and saved the rest."

"And what is your plan now?"

"Roscoe has offered to take me with him when he leaves day after tomorrow to fish waters along the southern coast from now until spring. By then I should have enough to buy a small craft of my own. I'm hoping that Roscoe and I will form a partnership."

"And what about the children?"

Ty stretched out one hand as if to touch her, but withdrew it immediately. "Everything I do is for the children, Caroline. Don't you know that?"

"I know you believe that with all your heart."

"You doubt that it's true?" He was incredulous. His red-rimmed and feverish eyes demanded, *What more could I have done?*

Caroline released a long, slow breath. It was as if she'd been holding it in for some time now. "In so many ways your story is like the biblical story of Job. You are a good and decent man who loves his family and wants only the best for them. Do you know the Scripture?"

"Of course, I know it, Caroline. Job was tested. Are you saying God is testing me?"

"I am saying that while you are trying very hard to do the right thing for your children, in spite of one setback after another you stubbornly refuse to accept the help that is right there in front of you."

"I've accepted help. From you. From Roscoe. From your aunt and uncle."

"But perhaps not from God." Reverend Groves came into the room and stood behind Caroline's chair. "Forgive me for interrupting, Mr. Justice, but perhaps instead of trying so hard to make things right for your children and yourself, it's time for you to be still and listen for God's voice."

"With no disrespect, sir, God does not speak to people like me."

"Because you are poor?"

"Because I am unworthy." He collapsed against the settee cushions. "My head is pounding and I am also very tired and not thinking clearly. Caroline, I am pleading with you to keep my presence here secret from my children until tomorrow evening. By then I will have made a decision about whether to go with Roscoe or stay here. Either way, I would be grateful if you would continue to —"

"How can you even suggest that I would do otherwise?" Caroline said, coming to her feet as if to advance on him. Her voice wavered with emotion as she told him, "I love those children. Perhaps not in the same way you do, but no less."

Once again Reverend Groves interceded. "Caroline, why don't you return home? Mr. Justice indeed needs his rest. He can stay the night here with me if he is willing. I promise not to preach but I cannot promise not to pray for you, young man."

"I'd be grateful for the hospitality — and the prayers. Thank you." He watched as Caroline wrapped her shawl around her. He saw that the fabric was frayed and worn and noticed for the first time that she had sewn a twill tape around the hem of her skirt. Was that to disguise the fact that it too was showing wear? "Caroline? Could we have a word before you go?"

The minister patted Caroline's shoulder and returned to his study, leaving the door open. As soon as they were alone Ty pulled out a tattered envelope and handed it to her. "I did work, Caroline, and while this is not the amount I had hoped to bring you, the money is yours. If I go with Roscoe, then there will be more."

Caroline took a half step away, as if he were offering her something foul. "I don't want your money."

"And I don't want your charity," he growled. "Take it. Use it for Eliza and Jerome and Hannah. Food, clothes, medicine." He shoved the envelope into her hands and closed his eyes. "Please do not deny me this small opportunity to provide for my children."

"Very well," she said stiffly. She folded the envelope into the pocket of her skirt and turned to leave.

"Caroline?"

There was something about the sound of her name coming from him that she knew would always make her pause, no matter how impossible she found his behavior.

"We both have a lot to think about to-night," Ty said. "And I dare to ask that, as you go over the details of the choices I made, you remember that the only thought behind my actions was that I must care for my children."

She wheeled around and advanced on him, but he looked so completely spent and miserable that she softened her intended reprimand from a lecture to a suggestion. "And in return, Tyrone, I hope you will think on the fact that there is an answer in all of this — one that will assure us both that the children are safe and well cared for. You're in good hands here with the rever-end, and your children will always have a place with me." She reached out to him but stopped short of actually touching him. "Get some rest, Tyrone. We'll talk tomorrow."

It was pure fear that had added fuel to her anger at the man. When she had seen Ty ly-ing in the church pew — so thin and pale and haggard — the fury that had gripped her as she'd followed Roscoe up the hill to the church had turned to terror. Her image of him had always been the agile, vigorous man scaling a ladder to the heights of her house as if it were no more than climbing over a low fence. When she thought of him as she so often had these last weeks, she saw him walking alongside her in the rain or lifting Hannah high in the air and laughing at her squeals of delight. The man lying on the pew was a stranger.

Her one thought had been that losing him would break the children's hearts — and hers. He was a good man, completely dedicated to the welfare of his children, often to his own detriment. Surely such a man deserved some happiness, some peace. And in that moment she had realized that she had come to care deeply for Tyrone Justice.

"Please, God," she prayed as she walked the short distance back to her house, "help us find a way. Show us Your path. For I am as much a part of this now as Tyrone and the children are. You brought those children to my door and their father followed. Help me to understand Your purpose here."

Back inside the house, she walked from room to room — upstairs and down — as if the very walls might speak to her and provide answers. But all she saw was the deterioration of the mansion — the cracks in walls and ceilings, the drapes that had begun to fray over the years, the loose floorboards. How ironic that Ty struggled to find work and in this house the work waited around every corner.

She wandered into the classroom. A large part of running the school, aside from serving as teacher and administrator, was to provide a steady flow of new students to keep the school going. New enrollees rarely showed up at her door as the Justice children had.

But Ty's children living with her challenged her to stretch limited funds further for the term. And although John Woodstock had decided to send his children to public school, she realized she had yet to recruit a single new student. Even if Thomas Woodstock stayed the year, in the spring he and Noah Johnstone would graduate, leaving two more empty desks to be filled.

The truth was that she could barely afford to keep the doors open, much less care for Ty's children. And yet she had grown so used to having them with her. They had become a family in so many ways. In fact, the children's conversation often seemed to assume that indeed they were a family.

"When Papa comes home . . ." or "Papa says . . ." or "You and Papa . . ." as if they were a couple. As if they were parents. As if they were married.

■ ■ ■ ■

The following day Caroline arrived at the parsonage late in the afternoon and handed the minister a basket of food. When Reverend Groves ushered her into the parlor where Ty was sitting by the fire, she refused to sit, preferring to pace back and forth as if organizing a lesson she needed to teach him.

"What did you tell the children?" Ty asked after the minister had gone to his study.

"I told them the truth. I told them I was going to visit a sick friend. You are ill and in spite of your recent actions I do consider you a friend, Tyrone."

He wondered if she had any idea how enchanting she was when she assumed what he had come to think of as her schoolmarm demeanor. She had this way of saying things that sounded like a reproach but could also be taken as a compliment. He remembered how Jerome had blushed when she had commented on his ability with numbers, and imagined that her young male students must all fall madly in love with her at some point.

"Are you feeling better?" she asked.

"Yes, thank you. Solid food, a hot bath and a warm bed can be the best medicine."

"I'm glad." She continued to pace and he realized that she was not so much agitated as nervous.

"Reverend Groves and I talked for some time last night," he told her. "He was taken by your comparison of my circumstances to those of Job. We sat in his study until quite late with him showing me comparisons of Scripture between Job's story and that of the Good Samaritan."

"With Mr. Anderson cast in that role?"

Ty shrugged. "I suppose he's another example."

"What example did Reverend Groves use?"

"You."

She dismissed the comparison with a wave of her hand. "I didn't come here to discuss theology, Tyrone. We have to think of the children. Of what's best for them."

"What's best for them right now is to remain in your care — if you'll have them — while I go with Roscoe. How was he as a guest in your classroom today?"

For the first time since she'd arrived she smiled. "He was quite wonderful. The class was engrossed in his stories of life on the high seas and his knowledge of places they could only read about in books."

Ty laughed. "He should have been on the

249

stage, I think. He loves an audience."

"He did something quite remarkable, Tyrone. Something I'm sure he did only for you."

"What?"

"He made a point of telling the children that sometimes voyages do not work out and must be terminated before the purpose of the voyage can be achieved. He added that sometimes a ship never leaves the dock, and he made a point of impressing upon them that members of the crew have no control over such decisions — only the officers on board or the owners can decide such things."

Ty was touched by his friend's attempt to prepare his children for the disappointment he would possibly have to bring to them. But Roscoe's explanation would not answer their questions of why he had not returned immediately, or at least let them know he was still close by.

He pushed aside the blanket that Reverend Groves had insisted on, and stood up. Caroline had stopped her pacing and was looking out the window as she told him about Roscoe's visit. He took a step closer.

"Caroline, when I talk to the children, will you be there? They are going to be so hurt and perhaps even angry and —"

The sigh she released was one of weariness and defeat. It shuddered through her narrow shoulders and softened her spine. "Let's sit down, Tyrone. I have an idea I'd like to discuss with you. One that you may find shocking or perhaps simply amusing, but it's the only plan I could think of that will best serve the needs of Eliza, Jerome and Hannah."

Without looking at him she took the chair opposite his next to the fire. He returned to the other chair and waited.

"I have prayed long and hard for most of the night on this, Tyrone. More importantly I have been still and listened for God's answer, and it seems to me that for the children's sake, you and I should marry."

Ty could not have been more shocked if she had suddenly announced that she had decided to join forces with Sarah's parents and have the children permanently removed from his care.

"Marry?" He could barely frame the word. Surely he had misunderstood. "You? And me? Why?"

"Just hear me out," she snapped, then focused on her hands primly folded in her lap as she delivered a speech he was sure she must have rehearsed numerous times. "I have looked at this from every possible

251

position but always with consideration for the best interests of the children in mind. Beginning with the very idea of a union between you and me, it occurs to me that neither of us is likely to remarry for reasons of . . . for personal reasons."

For love, he translated. "Unlikely but —" *not impossible.*

"And people at our stage of life," she rushed to add, "have been known to form unions of convenience for far less noble causes than the welfare of three innocent children."

"Man and wife — you and me?" He was still wrestling with the full ramifications of that idea. "Exactly how would that — I mean how would we —"

Her cheeks grew rosy with embarrassment. "The marriage would be in name only, of course. In practical terms, there is a room next to mine with a dressing room between that you could use, or share the room with Jerome if you prefer. Or there are small rooms on the third floor you could convert to an apartment. The house is spacious enough to accommodate both of us."

"I see." *A business arrangement.*

"Oh, please don't dismiss this out of hand, Tyrone. Your children miss you so much, even though I believe that over these last several weeks they have become fond of me. And while I would never presume to take the place of their dear mother, if you could be here and we were together as a family, they would have a certain stability that has been sorely lacking in their lives."

Ty braced himself against the litany of failures she would present as evidence. But to his surprise she looked up at him and her expression did not accuse. It pleaded. "Marriages have been based on far less, don't you think?"

"I suppose that's true." He was not yet past the fact that the very prim and proper Caroline Hudson had just proposed marriage to him, whatever her reasons.

She pressed her case. "Working together I believe that we can both find our way through the financial challenges we are currently facing. For example, if you agreed, then we could use the funds you gave me yesterday to purchase supplies so that we could make necessary improvements to the school and then —"

"Use my money to refurbish your school?" *Ah, now we're coming to the crux of it.*

"I can see how that might sound as if I want to take advantage, rather than thinking of your children. But we would consider it a loan. Enrollment is down and unless I

253

can recruit new students, the school will fail. I can't recruit new students if I am teaching, trying to keep up with the most minimal repairs and renovations, handling the administrative tasks and —"

"And caring for my children."

"If the school fails, Tyrone, I would have no choice but to sell the house. On the other hand, if the school's roster is filled I could repay your investment and maintain the school. You could then purchase that boat and join Mr. Anderson in business as you proposed. And most important of all, the children would have a stable home environment that included your presence and they would be receiving a good education."

Ty took his time considering the idea from all angles. She'd had all night to work through the details. And clearly she had looked at things from the point of view of keeping her livelihood afloat. In that way they were more alike than perhaps either of them had realized.

"I don't see where I fit into this. You clearly need my money, so if I go with Roscoe I can send more money. I don't see how this is different from the arrangement we previously had — I work and send money for the children's room, board and tuition."

"They need you, Tyrone, not your money. These are such formative years for the children. Jerome is on the brink and could go either way — he could become a closed-minded, angry young man or a productive member of society. Eliza is already doing a woman's work in worrying about you and her siblings. She deserves a childhood. And Hannah? Well, Hannah adores you and misses you so."

"All right, I can see your point. But if I stay here, how will I make a financial difference?"

Her shoulders slumped. "I haven't yet worked out all the details, but for the time being you could help me run the school, and as opportunities for employment — locally — arise, you could certainly consider them. The money you gave me earlier is substantial enough to see us through to the end of the year and cover some of the most needed repairs if we do them ourselves."

Ty studied her for a long moment and she met his gaze without looking away. "If we are to marry, Caroline, there are no loans to be repaid. Even a marriage of convenience must include the elements of trust. We would be equal partners, equally invested in the other's welfare." Ty could not believe that he was actually considering this. "How do you think the children will react?"

"Oh, Ty, this will not be simple. The children — especially Eliza and Jerome — will struggle with many of the ramifications of such a decision. They will feel a certain disloyalty to their mother's memory. They will be disappointed in you — that you stayed away even when you could have been with them."

"I did what I thought best," he replied through gritted teeth.

"Whatever your motives were, they will not matter. They are children, Tyrone." She waited for him to respond and, when he didn't, she added yet another problem to the growing pile. "We shall all have to face the curiosity and gossip that will come with the news. My pupils are bound to hear their parents discussing such an unusual and sudden arrangement, and they are likely to mirror their parent's attitudes in their dealings with your children."

"I won't have my children suffer because of my actions or some local gossip, Caroline."

"Your children are far more resilient than you may realize. Eliza especially has a unique gift for earning the respect of others."

Ty searched her eyes for some clue to her

true motivation in suggesting such an outrageous idea. She met his gaze directly without guile or any hint of cunning. She looked as tired as he felt, and he realized that these last few weeks had been no easier for her than they had been for him.

"Do you have a better solution, Tyrone? If so, I am more than willing to hear it."

"No."

Was he actually about to agree to marry her?

He swallowed once and then again, then stood up and took the step necessary to stand before her. He noticed for the first time that she was wearing the brooch he had given her. "Caroline Hudson, will you be my wife?"

To his surprise her eyes filled with tears and she did not smile but pressed her lips tightly together and nodded.

So, it's as the minister said, Ty thought. *Caroline is a Good Samaritan, willing to do whatever she can to help a Job who has run out of options.*

CHAPTER FOURTEEN

Caroline saw his lips move, heard the words, but still could not believe that Tyrone had agreed to marry her. She had not missed his hesitancy when he had stood and come to her. And she would not deceive herself into imagining that perhaps one day he might come to love her. Theirs was a partnership for the sake of his children — nothing more.

"Then we have an agreement," she managed, then cleared her throat and stood, as well. "I suggest that we tell the children tonight. On Friday after classes if Reverend Groves is available, he can conduct the ceremony."

"You don't want more time?"

"For what?"

"To send invitations and . . ."

"Tyrone, this is not a first marriage for either of us. No, the simpler the better. If it's all right with you I'll ask my aunt and uncle to serve as witnesses." Her mind raced with the practical details that would need to be in place now that they had actually agreed to proceed. "You can stay here for the time being and after the ceremony move your things down to my . . . the house."

"How do we tell the children?"

That was, of course, the most pressing issue. "I could bring them here this evening."

"Yes. That's a good idea," he said.

She looked around as if trying to come up with something more they needed to decide. "Well, then, until this evening."

"And Caroline, I'll need some of that money I gave you." He smiled for the first time since proposing. "I'd like to be married in my own clothes, not those borrowed from your uncle."

"I'll bring the envelope when I come with the children." They were standing close enough to embrace, but the space between them seemed solid and impenetrable. Suddenly Caroline felt that, if she did not get out of this room, she would shatter into a thousand pieces. "Will you ask Reverend Groves if he is willing to perform the ceremony while I go and give the children their supper?"

Ty nodded and Caroline started to step around him but he stopped her by taking her hand. "We can make this work," he said.

"Yes. For the sake of the children we must make it work." He was stroking her fingers with his thumb. She could not bear his tenderness or his gratitude, so she pulled her hand free of his and walked away as quickly as possible without actually breaking into a run.

Instead of going directly home, she made a detour to see Martha and Henry. She had quite possibly just made a mistake of monumental proportions. If anyone would set her straight, it would be her Aunt Martha.

"I think it's the best possible solution," Martha said. "Not that there's any good solution to this mess, but it seems to me that you've come up with a plan that will at least keep a roof over the heads of those darlings and food in their stomachs."

But Henry did not seem as enthusiastic as Martha. As Caroline had outlined her reasons for a marriage of convenience with Tyrone, Henry had folded his arms across his broad chest and leaned his chair back on two legs. "Uncle Henry, what do you think?"

"I'm wondering why you wouldn't come to us if you were having trouble meeting your bills. We're your family, Caroline. Why

260

would you tie yourself down to a man you hardly know? Don't mistake my meaning. Tyrone Justice is a fine man. I don't know many who would have gone through what he has and still be trying to provide for those children. But what's this business about borrowing the little money he's been able to save and repairing the school, all with the idea you're going to be able to attract a new crop of pupils in the spring?"

"It's true that the future of the school is in doubt, Uncle, but that is only part of this, and a secondary part at that. My primary consideration is the welfare of those children. They have been through quite enough. They lost one parent and have barely seen the other this autumn. I have always believed that God sent those children to me for a reason. I thought I was supposed to save them. It never occurred to me that perhaps God's purpose was to have me save their father in the bargain."

"But you'll still be married to the man." Henry looked over at his wife of nearly forty years. "I had always hoped that one day you might meet a man who loved you the way I love my Martha."

"Sometimes, Uncle, the best a woman can hope for is a man who respects her, and I do believe that I have Tyrone's respect."

"And does he have yours?"

"I . . . he . . . As you have said, he is a good man who cares deeply for his children."

Martha came up behind Henry and wrapped her arms around him. "Besides, Henry, sometimes it's necessary to set a pot to boil to rid it of a certain bitterness, then let it simmer a bit before it becomes palatable. Romance is like that, as well."

Caroline blushed. "Martha, I am not some girl. I am past thirty."

"Well, so is Tyrone."

Henry laughed as he patted his wife's hands and rocked forward on his chair. "Whatever the cause or outcome, it seems we're destined to have a wedding."

"Something very simple," Caroline insisted. "Just you and Aunt Martha to witness, while Reverend Groves performs the ceremony."

"Surely . . ." It was Martha's turn to be taken aback.

"No. Let's all remember that the union is for the sake of the children. I don't want Tyrone thinking that I am trying to manipulate him into marrying me."

"Oh, Caroline, he cares for you. He's so very grateful for all you've . . ."

"Nevertheless, it's best if we keep things

as simple and private as possible. This is for the children. The sooner Tyrone and I are officially married, the sooner we can begin the work of assuring the children that they have a home to call their own and two people who will care for them." She gathered her things. "And now I must hurry. The children need their supper and then we must go to the parsonage."

She could not hide her concern. Her hand shook as she reached for her shawl. Martha took it from her and held it for her to put on.

"Why don't you take Jerome and Eliza to the parsonage and I'll come and stay with little Hannah? She's too young to understand what this all means and if the older children become upset —"

"I hadn't thought of that. Yes, do come." She hugged her aunt. "This is not going to be easy," she murmured.

"No, but if you believe that God has led you to this moment, then you will have faith that He will continue to walk this path with you until you find your way."

Ty wished he could turn the clock back to the night before he had left for New Bedford. When they heard Caroline's knock, Groves suggested that Ty wait in the study and let him break the news of their father's return to the children.

"I can explain to them that you've been ill. Soften the shock, so to speak."

Against his better judgment Ty had agreed. He heard Caroline telling Groves that Martha had stayed behind with Hannah. "It's close to her bedtime," she said.

"A wise decision," the minister agreed. "Jerome, Eliza, please come sit by the fire. It's gotten quite cold this evening."

Ty strained for a glimpse of his two older children through a crack in the door. For the first time he realized the adult burden he had allowed his elder daughter to take on her narrow shoulders, and he saw Jerome's scowl — so like his own. His son's eyes were lowered to the ground, but watching and questioning. They were both well dressed and groomed. Caroline had kept her word.

Once they were all settled in the parlor it became more difficult to hear what the minister was saying, so Ty stepped into the hall and stood just outside the entrance to the stuffy and excessively furnished parlor.

"Miss Hudson has brought you here this evening to receive some news." Then Groves explained to the children that, even when people start down one path, God may intercede to take them down a different one.

"That is the case with your father," he said.

Suddenly Eliza burst into tears, heaving sobs that she could not disguise. "Papa is dead?"

Ty couldn't stand it. It had been a mistake to let the minister prepare the children. How could anyone prepare them for this?

"I'm right here, Liza," Ty said firmly as he entered the parlor. His eldest child ran to him and, as he embraced her, he met the eyes of his son. "I'm here, children, and I am not going away again." That he had made his decision came as much as a surprise to him as it did to his children.

"You're back so soon?" Eliza asked.

"I never left. I've been in New Bedford all the time."

Jerome's head came up with a jerk. "But we told everyone in class and they told their friends and families that you were sailing to India," he protested, his fists clenching and unclenching as he realized the lie his father had been living and fought for control. "All the guys think —" He paused and glanced at Caroline.

"What do they think, son?"

Jerome ran from the room and out the front door.

"Let him go," Ty advised when Caroline started for the door. "He needs some time."

Still upset, Eliza looked from her father to Caroline. "What news? What else has happened?" Her eyes were wide with panic.

"Let's all sit down while your father explains what happened in New Bedford and where he has been these last weeks," Caroline said, taking Jerome's vacated chair and indicating that Tyrone should bring Eliza to sit on the settee. "Go ahead, Mr. Justice."

Ty faltered his way through the story of how *The Libertine* had been taken over by others and never sailed.

"Like pirates?" Eliza asked, her hysteria finally abating.

"No. The owners of the ship had not paid their bills and the bank seized the ship. Many men besides me were left without work, Liza. I didn't know what to do."

"You should have come home." The child's logic was almost his undoing and he looked to Caroline for help.

"Your father wanted very much to come home, Eliza, but grown-ups sometimes have responsibilities that must come before what we want. Your father needed to earn the money necessary to care for you children. He worked very hard for many weeks — so hard that when he finally had enough money to come back to Nantucket, he became quite ill."

"Oh, Papa, you should have sent word. I would have come. I would have taken care of you."

So, this was what he had done to his oldest daughter. He had allowed her to assume the role of mother to her siblings and caregiver to him. "No," he said more harshly than he intended, and Eliza pulled back.

"What your father is saying, Eliza, is that he has come back to take care of you and Jerome and Hannah."

"But I realize that I cannot do that alone," Ty added, taking his cue from Caroline. "And so Miss Hudson and I have agreed to work together."

"I don't understand any of this," Eliza said.

Ty was at a loss. He could find neither the words nor the logic to make it clear to her how the arrangement would work. To his relief Caroline leaned forward so that she could take Eliza's hands in hers.

"Eliza, you know that I have come to care for you and Jerome and Hannah very much. You have all been more than just a great help to me. Having your children living with me has given me such joy, and your father and I have become friends, as well."

"I don't understand," Eliza said.

"What Miss Hudson is trying to say, Liza, is that —"

"Your father and I are to be married. We will be a family and we will all live together in my — our — house."

"Married?" Eliza whispered the word as if trying to decipher its meaning.

"Yes, on Friday evening," Caroline told her. "I — we — hope you and the other children will come to understand that —"

Eliza flung herself into Caroline's arms. "Oh, Miss Hudson, it's the best possible news."

Caroline looked at Ty over Eliza's shoulder and he smiled at her with relief. He just hoped Jerome would be as pleased with the news as Eliza was.

"We should go," Caroline said. "Tomorrow we can talk some more. The news has been a shock and the children need their rest."

"Jerome?" Ty asked.

"He just needs a little time," she said.

Ty frowned. "But he'll come around."

"Give him time," Caroline repeated as she touched his face, drawing his attention away from the son who had rejected him and back to her. "Be very sure about this business of our marrying, Tyrone. It's not too late to change your mind. Sleep on it, and if tomorrow you decide —"

He held her hand. "I won't change my mind, Caroline. Will you?"

She suddenly wasn't sure. She had been so certain that he would reject her idea of marrying that she had never truly thought beyond laying out the plan. "I don't know," she whispered and fled the room.

When Eliza and Caroline reached her house, Jerome was there. He was sitting on the back stoop and did not look up as they approached. Caroline realized that he had no idea of how to deal with his rage and disappointment.

Without a word she gently touched his shoulder. "What are you going to tell the class tomorrow?" Jerome asked.

"I will tell them the truth, Jerome. I will tell them that through no fault of his own your father was denied the position on the ship's crew. I will remind them that he could have given up. Many men in his position would have turned to drink or some other vice to bury their disappointment, but your father found work."

"Not on a ship. He didn't go anywhere. Not to South America or around the horn

or into the Pacific. He was right over there."
He lashed one arm out in the general direction of New Bedford, then shoved his hands into his pockets. "He lied to us and everybody is going to know it."

He ran into the house and when Eliza and Caroline went inside, Martha was waiting for them, her expression one of questioning and concern.

"Where's Jerome?" Caroline asked.

Martha nodded toward the classroom. "Hannah is sleeping," she added, then hugged Eliza. "Are you all right, child?"

Caroline left Eliza with her aunt and followed the sounds of Jerome's fury to the classroom. He had ripped the pins and string away from the map, tearing it in the process.

"What do you think you are doing, young man?" she demanded and it had exactly the desired effect.

Jerome froze, his clenched fists still clutching the length of string they had used to plot the course of *The Libertine.* Then his thin shoulders began to shake and he collapsed into her chair. He put his head on her desk and started rhythmically pounding the surface with his fist.

"It's not fair," he chanted again and again.

Caroline went to him and placed her hand

lightly on the back of his head. "No, life rarely is fair, Jerome." She felt him go still as if waiting for reassurance, but she had none to give. Over the next several days, if not weeks, there would be gossip and speculation about the marriage. She wished she could shield the children from such things, but the reality was that she could not.

"Jerome, are you concerned about the other boys in the class?"

His head was still buried in his folded arms but he nodded. "I bragged about how my father was going to return with all this money and presents for me and Eliza and Hannah and how we were going to buy a big house — bigger than this one. I could see they didn't believe me but then when that first letter came and then yesterday when Roscoe was here I could see that they were starting to believe those things might happen."

Caroline hesitated. She was an excellent teacher, but surely this moment called for the love and reassurance of a parent. "There's nothing wrong with showing your pride in your father, Jerome. Granted, you may have gone a bit far, but you have every right to be as pleased with your father's accomplishments as Thomas or Noah are of their fathers."

"Their fathers are rich."

"Monetary wealth is no comparison to the wealth of having a loving father who puts the needs of you and your sisters above his own. And that is exactly what happened here."

Jerome rolled his head to one side and looked up at her. "But if he'd come back right away and told everyone about the ship not going, everybody would have understood."

"Who is everybody, Jerome? Whose opinion do you value so highly?"

"Everybody," he repeated.

"Well, everyone who knows now — my aunt and uncle, Mr. Anderson, Reverend Groves, your sister Eliza — every one of them understands and is simply glad to have your father home again."

"Roscoe knows? He knew today when he spoke to the class?"

"Mr. Anderson has been with your father the entire time. He was concerned enough to house your father on his boat so that the money your father was earning working on the docks could be put aside for your welfare."

"Then he lied, as well. And you taught us that lying was always wrong."

"It is wrong, Jerome, but as human beings

we are not perfect. Your father made a mistake in not revealing to you and your sisters how things had changed for him, but in blaming him for that you must also be willing to accept that he withheld that information so as not to worry you. He erred out of love." Caroline considered whether or not to tell him the rest, but he deserved the full story. "Your father and I are to be married at the end of the week."

Jerome took a moment to digest that, then sat up. "He's going to be living here with us?"

"Yes, he will be living here as your father and as my husband."

"What does Liza say?"

"Why don't you go upstairs and ask her? Take her to your room so you don't wake Hannah." Caroline was sure that Eliza would reassure her brother that the plan to become a family was a good one.

Jerome pushed away from the desk and crossed the room. "Miss Hudson? Do you think Roscoe might come back here tomorrow when you tell the class about my father?"

"Why?"

"The others really liked him, and maybe if he told them what happened it wouldn't be so bad."

She hated to disappoint the child again. "Mr. Anderson is leaving tomorrow to sail south for the winter season, Jerome."

"Oh." The boy looked beaten down with disappointment.

Instinctively Caroline went to him and wrapped her arms around him. "It's all going to work out, Jerome. I promise you that."

She blinked back tears when she felt his thin arms circle her waist and hang on. She loved this child as she had come to love each of Ty's children. Not as she loved her students, but as if they were her own.

CHAPTER FIFTEEN

Ty had lain awake most of the night trying to imagine how they would carry off this marriage. Where would he sleep? Her first suggestion had been a room next to hers. Why? Surely she didn't think anyone would know or care whether they slept together as man and wife, or in separate but connecting rooms. Of course, then she'd been quick to add that he could share with Jerome, or have a room of his own on the third floor.And that didn't even begin to address the issue of exactly what his role in running the school was to be.

By the time he arose the following morning Ty had made up his mind. If he and Caroline Hudson were to marry — for whatever reason — then he was going to make it clear from the outset that he intended to assume his rightful role as head of the household.

In spite of a slight fever and occasional

chills, Ty insisted on coming down to the school the following day. "I'll handle this, Caroline," he said firmly when she stopped by the parsonage early the next morning to let him know that Jerome was working through the news in his own way and that she was going to tell her class the truth.

"Mr. Anderson has agreed to be there and there's really no need —"

"There is every need," Ty replied. "I have embarrassed my son and I am well aware of how cruel boys his age can be. If his class-mates intend to ridicule him, then they will have to do so in my presence."

"You intend to stay the entire day?"

"If necessary and come back tomorrow and the day after." He saw her eyes widen in surprise. Clearly she had not considered this specific piece of their union — how he would spend his days. "I will attend to the repairs and maintenance of the school and dwelling, Caroline, while you give the students their lessons. I remind you that you presented this union between us as one of business partners, and I will not allow these youngsters or their parents to see me as a schoolmarm's version of the hired hand."

That brought the reaction he had been expecting. She pressed her lips so tightly together that they almost disappeared.

"You may as well state your thoughts, Caroline, so we can settle the matter once and for all."

"I thought we had an understanding, Mr. Justice."

"Ah, so, it's back to Mr. Justice, is it? And what shall I call you when we argue, Caroline? Mrs. Justice?"

Her mouth worked but no sound came out, and he couldn't help himself. He grinned down at her. She obviously had no idea how fetching she was when she got her back up this way. Those green eyes flashing, that chin jutted stubbornly forward, and every inch of her stretched to her full height, irritated that she was still forced to look up at him.

But Ty found he could not hold the teasing grin, for the truth was that she was so beautiful it took his breath away. To fight against his feelings for her he tightened his own jaw and met her defiant glare. "Well?"

"If you insist on mocking me, we will get nowhere."

"I wasn't mocking you. I was teasing you. There's a difference. Now, can we get back to the subject at hand?"

"Your role in running the school?"

"Or to put it another way, how we will

work together to maintain the business in such a way that it will provide a good living for our family." This time the slight lift of her eyebrows indicating her surprise at his question annoyed him. "Surely you've considered this, Caroline. You proposed marriage — a lifetime commitment between us. I would assume you of all people had thought through every aspect of how this would work."

"Well, I haven't," she snapped.

Her uncertainty was as reassuring as her honesty. It put them on an even keel, and Ty felt for the first time in weeks as if he might actually have the opportunity to prove his worth — to his children, to Caroline and, most of all, to himself.

"All right, for example, then, in addition to the maintenance tasks, I can help with the bookkeeping and collection of that overdue tuition you mentioned once. I've done accounts on a couple of voyages. Of course, I would understand if you didn't trust me to —"

"If I didn't trust you, Tyrone, I certainly would not marry you."

"So during the day you'll teach and I'll see to the maintenance of the building. After school while you prepare lessons and grade papers, I'll attend to the ledgers and bills."

"Yes, that would be a great help."

Ty was beginning to feel as if this whole idea might just work when she added, "But in the matter of telling the class of your return and our . . . this new arrangement —"

"I said I would handle that, Caroline."

She hesitated and then to his surprise gave in. "Very well. The class begins promptly at eight. Shall we expect you at half after the hour?"

"I need to go into town first. Why don't we plan for me to come to the classroom just after lunch?"

"At one o'clock, then. Was there anything else?"

"Yes, ma'am. After I speak with the class I'd like to take a look at that bedroom."

"On the third floor? Of course."

"No, Caroline, the one on the second floor. I want to be close to the children."

He watched a rosy glow spread across her fair skin. "I had thought you might want more privacy than that."

"A family man doesn't need his privacy, Caroline. He needs to know that if his wife and children need him, he will be close at hand."

"I'll ask Eliza to show you the room and prepare it for you to move in your things," she said, her voice almost a whisper.

"Papa!" Hannah ran into the room and catapulted herself into Ty's arms. "Oh, Papa, you've come home ever so much sooner than everyone expected."

"Are you glad, little one?"

"Yes, yes, yes," she cried, punctuating each affirmative with a kiss. "And now Miss Caroline is to be our mother. Isn't that wonderful?"

"It is," Ty said, his eyes meeting Caroline's. "It's quite wonderful."

Later that morning Ty moved his meager possessions from the parsonage into the large bedroom, connected by twin dressing rooms to hers. If he had tried the door to her dressing room and found it locked, or seen the dresser she had pushed against the door after returning from her morning visit with him, he made no mention of it.

"I'll be back at one o'clock," was his only comment.

As scheduled he appeared at the door of the classroom, freshly shaven and wearing business attire. "Good afternoon, students," he greeted the class after Caroline had stumbled through her introduction.

"Good afternoon," they mumbled back. He took a position in the back of the room and waited. Caroline saw Eliza look over her shoulder at him and smile. Jerome ignored his father by taking a sudden interest in the book of poetry that Caroline had asked him to read.

The other boys in the class eyed one another and snickered. The girls, clearly impressed by Ty's dress and demeanor, cast sidelong looks back at him and then at each other, communicating through gesture and expression rather than actual words. Helen Johnstone sat up a little straighter in her chair and tossed her curls as she glanced back at Ty and smiled. Her sister, Laura, was as always far less obvious, but could not resist a peek and, when Ty smiled at her, her cheeks instantly changed from their usual fair peach to a flaming red.

"Mr. Justice, as you all know, is the father of Eliza and Jerome."

"I thought their father had gone to sea," Noah Johnstone said, casting his eyes at Thomas Woodstock and grinning.

"Please stand when you wish to address the class, Noah, and phrase your comment in the form of a question that is intended to add to our enlightenment and learning."

Noah got slowly to his feet. "Wasn't Mr. Justice supposed to be in South America or on his way to India at this time, Miss

Hudson?" With an insolent smile, he remained standing, waiting for her response.

"May I?" Ty asked, and when Caroline nodded he moved to the front of the room. "Mr. Johnstone raises an excellent question. I was supposed to have sailed with *The Libertine* three weeks ago, but the ship's owners had fallen behind in their payments to the bank and the ship was repossessed, thus canceling the voyage. I believe your father is a banker, Mr. Johnstone?"

Noah did not like being singled out. He glared at Ty, sat down at his desk and gave a curt nod.

"Well, then, I'm sure that he could explain far better than I can how these things work. Perhaps Miss Hudson will invite your father to speak to the class, Mr. Johnstone."

Helen Johnstone shot to her feet. "I'm Mr. Johnstone's eldest daughter and I'm sure he would be more than happy to come and speak to the class. Shall I ask him, Miss Hudson?"

"Why don't I prepare a letter that you and Laura and Noah can take to him?" Caroline replied.

Helen smiled at Ty and actually curtsied before taking her seat again.

"Then we'll let Mr. Johnstone explain that part of the story. Now, let me ask you a question. What would you have done if you had thought that you had a position that would pay a fair wage and give you the means to provide for the needs of your children, and suddenly that position was no longer available? Mr. Johnstone?"

Noah slunk farther down in his seat.

"Mr. Woodstock?"

Thomas leapt to his feet. "I would have found work on another ship, sir."

"And what if the ships remaining in the harbor had already hired their crews and were loaded for sail within the next week? What if there were no positions available?"

"I would have . . ." Thomas hesitated. "I would have sought other employment, sir."

"And that is exactly what Mr. Justice did, children," Caroline said. "Now, then —"

"On the other hand," Ty interrupted, "I have sailed on many ships and to all the places Miss Hudson told me you had planned to study." He turned to the map, now stripped of the pins and string that had once marked his journey. "Mr. Justice, would you give me a hand here?" He held out a length of string to Jerome and waited.

Reluctantly Jerome stepped forward.

"Please pin one end of the string to Nantucket," Ty said. "And now, Miss Johnstone — Miss Helen Johnstone, please

283

draw the string out into the Atlantic toward Portugal. Not all the way there — just into the Atlantic a bit. Excellent."

One by one he called the students to the map and had them connect the string until the route that Jerome had destroyed the night before had been restored. "With Miss Hudson's approval, class, I would like to take you on a voyage over the coming weeks — a voyage much like the one I would have been on had *The Libertine* set sail."

"Oh, that's ever so much better than waiting for a letter that could never come," Laura whispered to her sister.

Caroline was astonished by his perception of exactly what would appeal to the class and rob Noah Johnstone of any opportunity to ridicule or mock Jerome. She was well aware that the other boys in the class looked up to Noah and followed his lead. "I think that Mr. Justice has offered an excellent suggestion, class. Perhaps each of you can prepare a list of questions for Mr. Justice to address at his first lecture."

"So I'll bid you good day, class," Ty said. "Miss Hudson, may I speak to you a moment, please?"

"Take out your slates and list three questions each by the time I return," she instructed as she followed Ty into the hallway and shut the double doors to the classroom. "That was inspired, Tyrone. Thank you," she said. "I was frankly concerned that Noah would cause a stir and then Thomas would follow suit, but you disarmed them both."

Ty dismissed her compliments with a curt nod. "Do you think Jerome is all right?"

"Give him some time, Ty. I certainly think your lecturing to the class about your adventures on the high seas will be a positive influence."

"I wanted to talk to you about that. Lecturing is not exactly something I'm good at. Maybe you've noticed that I'm not much of a talker, Caroline. I was thinking that maybe I could come up with activities the youngsters could do along with me — like knot tying or mending a sail or fishing net. Something a little less formal."

Caroline frowned. "That's quite unorthodox, Tyrone. I do have to consider how such activities might be perceived by the parents. Mr. Woodstock, for example, is quite vigilant about Thomas learning the basics, especially his arithmetic."

"Is the boy good with numbers?"

"Not as good as Jerome is," she admitted. "And that's been a bone of contention for both Thomas and his father — the fact that

Jerome is —"

"Smarter, in spite of his background?"

Caroline nodded. "It rankles the elder Mr. Woodstock."

"Then let's make Thomas the ship's purser for the journey. We'll give him a starting amount and a list of the fixed expenses, and then let him decide how best to deal with that money and the profit he can earn by delivering his goods."

"I see your point. We could choose roles for each student according to his or her most difficult subject. But what about the girls?"

Ty grinned. "Crews have to be fed, Caroline. And nursed if they become ill. Beyond that, I'm sure at least one of the girls in the class would happily assume the role of ship's captain."

"Are you thinking of Helen?"

"You wanted to choose a role that would address a weakness. It appears to me that working with others is sometimes a challenge for Miss Johnstone."

Caroline had never considered that Ty might be such a good judge of people, and she couldn't help smiling. "If we appoint Helen as ship's captain, we'd best prepare for a mutiny."

They both laughed at that and Caroline

could not help thinking that they made a good team. She was talking in terms of *we* and she was starting to feel an excitement about the future that she had not felt in some time now.

"Will one o'clock be all right for my sessions with the class?"

"Yes. And Tyrone? Your new clothes make you look quite distinguished."

"It's good that you like them — this is my wedding suit, my work suit and my . . ."

"Sunday suit?" She could not disguise the fact that she hoped he'd had a change of heart after staying at the parsonage these last few days.

But Tyrone avoided the question. "I'll stop by to see the children this evening, all right?"

"You're welcome to come for supper if you like."

"Thank you, but I want to gather some things I'll need for the session with the class tomorrow. I'll be by in time to put Hannah to bed and say good night to Eliza and Jerome." He walked to the door, then retraced his steps and kissed her lightly on the forehead just as Helen Johnstone slid open the classroom door.

Once Helen had witnessed Tyrone kissing

her, Caroline knew she had no choice but to tell the class about the impending marriage. It was either that or let Helen's considerable imagination run wild. Either way the news would be all over town by supper, so better the truth than rampant gossip and speculation.

"Class, I have an announcement to make," she said, cutting short the hum of Helen's excited whisperings to the girls around her. "On Friday we will end the day at noon."

This got their attention. "It's not a holiday, Miss Hudson," Thomas noted.

"No, but for Mr. Justice and his children and me, it is indeed a day of celebration."

All eyes fastened on her as if she had just announced that the world might indeed be flat and they were all in danger of stepping off the edge. Eliza gazed at her with unabashed joy. Jerome's scowl told a very different story. He was still smarting from the embarrassment of having bragged to the others and then learning that Ty had lied. Now to become the schoolmarm's son?

"As you know, the mother of Eliza and Jerome and little Hannah died tragically a few years ago in the great fire. It was only a little over two years ago that my own husband died unexpectedly. Mr. Justice's children have been residing with me for the last few months and, now that he has returned to Nantucket, we have decided to marry."

"Miss Hudson is going to be your mother?" Thomas whispered to Jerome.

Jerome shrugged.

"Can we all come to the wedding, Miss Hudson?" Helen wanted to know.

"What will you wear?" Laura asked.

"I will wear my Sunday best, as will Mr. Justice and the children. Because this is a second wedding for both of us, it will be a quiet ceremony in the parsonage with only family in attendance — Mr. Justice's children and my aunt and uncle. The ceremony will take place this Friday evening."

There, she had told them the facts, and she was determined to keep things simple so that when they relayed the details to their parents there was some hope that it would not get distorted.

"So on Monday we need to call you Mrs. Justice," Laura said, and she actually sighed aloud. "It's so very romantic."

No, Laura, Caroline wanted to say, *it's not romantic at all. I only wish it were.*

For the rest of the afternoon it was difficult to get the students to concentrate on their spelling and reading lessons. The girls all wanted to talk about the wedding and what role Eliza might have in it. Noah continued to rib Jerome about the fact that Ty had never left the area, while Thomas struggled between his loyalty to his longtime friend Noah and his sympathy for Jerome.

By supper Caroline was mentally and emotionally exhausted and in no condition to deal with her conflicted feelings for Tyrone Justice. Of course, that was the very moment that he showed up at her — their — back door.

"Papa!" Hannah exclaimed. "Liza made a cake. Come, sit here so you can have a piece."

"Have you eaten?" Caroline asked as Eliza sliced a large piece of cake for her father.

"Reverend Groves invited Roscoe up to the parsonage for a kind of farewell meal. He's leaving tomorrow."

Caroline studied Ty for any sign that he had regrets about not going with his friend. "You should take the children down to the docks in the morning to see him off."

Ty smiled. "That's a fine idea."

"We have school," Jerome mumbled.

"I'm sure Mr. Anderson will be anxious to be on his way at first light, Jerome." Caroline softened her tone and added, "You'll just have to get up earlier than usual, but he's a good friend of yours and your father."

"Yes, ma'am."

"We should take him a present," Eliza said.

"Why don't you wrap up the rest of the cake and take that to him?"

"And we could draw pictures for him to have on his boat to remember us by," Eliza added. "May we be excused, Miss Hudson?"

"Not just yet, children," Ty said. "I need to talk to you."

The children settled back onto their chairs and glanced quickly at each other before giving their father their attention. Ty cleared his throat.

"You know Miss Hudson and I are to be married on Friday and after that she will have my name — our name. She will be Caroline Justice and we'll all be living here together as a family."

Caroline glanced around the table and saw that Jerome was looking at his father with his usual suspicion, Hannah with impatience to be excused so she could start on her drawing and Eliza with the dawn of full understanding.

"You'll be our mother," she said.

"Not exactly," Caroline hastened to assure them. "I will take on the responsibility of raising you with your father — we will be your parents." She looked down the length of the table to where Ty sat, her eyes pleading with him not to upset the children any more than they already were. "This can wait."

"I was thinking that we need to consider how you will address Miss Hudson once we are married. In school, of course, you must call her what the others call her — and beginning on Monday that will be Mrs. Justice, just as they will call me Mr. Justice whenever I have dealings with the class. But when we are together as a family — when you are calling me Papa, what shall you call Miss Hudson?"

"Mama," Hannah shouted as if she had gotten the answer to a very difficult question right. She looked to her sister and brother for their approval and her face fell. "Mother?"

"She is not our mother," Jerome said.

Caroline placed her hand on Hannah's. "You see, dear, Eliza and Jerome are old enough to remember your mother. They have very special feelings for her and it would be hard for them to think of anyone else as mama."

Hannah twisted her mouth as she concentrated on the problem at hand. She looked across the table to Eliza for help.

"What if we were to call you Mother Caroline? Would that be all right?" Eliza suggested.

"What do you think, son?" Ty asked.

Jerome shrugged. "I suppose."

"Jerome, I would hope to prove myself worthy of that title. It may take me a while to learn the difference between being your teacher and a parent, but with the help of your father as well as you and your sisters I'm sure I could learn."

"We would be your teacher," Hannah said.

"Precisely," Caroline agreed.

"Jerome?"

Jerome looked up at his father. "I suppose it might work out," he said.

"It will, son. We'll all work together as a family." Ty waited a beat to see if they had any further comments, then added, "Now, off with the three of you to draw those pictures for Roscoe."

As the children clamored from the dining room and up the stairs, Caroline could not help noticing that Ty wiped a corner of one eye with his napkin.

"You miss her terribly, don't you? Your Sarah?"

He busied himself with clearing the table. "Sarah will always be with me, Caroline, but we are about to begin a new phase of life for all of us. I think it best that we keep our sights on what lies ahead, rather than those places and people who dwelled in our past."

Caroline watched as he carried the dishes into the kitchen and wondered if some day, years from now, they might look back on this time with regret for what might have been, if only they had opened their hearts to each other as well as to the children.

CHAPTER SIXTEEN

Although she had told herself a hundred times that the wedding was nothing more than a formality, Caroline could not help being nervous as she stood before her mirror on Friday afternoon. In less than an hour her life would change forever.

Martha had suggested the timing — five o'clock at the parsonage, followed by a wedding supper at her house. She had even offered to have the children stay the night with her and Henry.

"To give you and Tyrone a bit of privacy your first night."

But Caroline had squelched that idea, threatening to call off the whole thing if Martha did not stop trying to make more of it than it was. She was going into this marriage a very different person from the naive girl who had married Percy. Back then she had imagined their life together filled with children and adventures.

Marriage to Tyrone would indeed bring her children, but the children of another woman — a woman whom Caroline's husband-to-be had loved deeply. As for adventure, the marriage itself was a leap into the unknown.

She selected a day dress of soft fawn-colored wool with deep chocolate embroidery around the hem, cuffs of the full sleeves and outlining a row of self-covered buttons down the front of the gown. The neckline was high with a little stand-up collar and a bow of pale peach satin. The same peach satin ballooned out from the bell-shaped sleeves at her wrists. Accenting her small waist was a thick braided-silk cord.

A bonnet seemed wrong for the evening, but Aunt Martha came up with just the right accessory — a lace cap with a dark brown moiré bow at its center. In the single side pocket of the gown, Martha tucked a handkerchief that she had edged with lace and embroidered with the date.

"You look lovely," Martha said as she placed the headpiece on Caroline's blond curls.

"Thank you, Auntie. Thank you for everything," Caroline whispered as she hugged her aunt. "Are the children ready?"

"I sent them on ahead with Henry. He'll

be back for us in a few minutes. Shall we?" Martha opened the bedroom door and waited for Caroline to precede her down the stairs. "Oh, Caroline, child, don't look so forlorn. It's all going to be fine. It was God's will that brought those darlings to your door, and God's will that has brought you to this day. Now trust in that and smile."

Ty had been in a foul mood most of the day. The weather was as turbulent as his emotions — one minute clear and the next blustery and dark. Roscoe had been gone only a few days and he missed the old man already. He was surrounded by strangers. Although admittedly he had begun to feel more comfortable with Martha and Henry than he could say he felt alone with his bride-to-be. He was more certain by the minute that Caroline had realized her mistake in proposing this whole idea. Surely any moment he would receive word that she had changed her mind.

But things kept moving forward. Henry brought the children to the parsonage and Ty hardly recognized them, so serious and somber were their faces. Jerome kept running one finger under his starched collar and Eliza looked as if she might cry any minute. Only Hannah was her usual sunny self.

Then Reverend Groves's wife took her place at the small pump organ in the corner of the parlor and began to play music that sounded to Ty more like a dirge than a wedding tune.

"Mr. Justice? Shall we wait by the fire?"

Ty nodded and followed the minister to the front of the room. He smiled at his children and then fixed his gaze on the foyer beyond the open parlor door. He heard the front door open and close and the low murmur of voices, then Henry escorted Martha to a chair next to the children, lined up on the settee.

"For better or for worse," Ty muttered as he accepted the reality of what was about to occur.

"I'll cue you with the vows, Tyrone. No need to memorize them," Reverend Groves assured him. Then he turned his attention to the foyer, where Caroline had taken Henry's arm, and entered the room.

For one terrible moment Ty thought he might have forgotten how to breathe. She was radiant, a vision in a one-piece dress of finely woven wool. With the grace of a princess she moved toward him, each step perfectly synchronized to the music Mrs.

Groves was playing.

And now the music he had heard as ominous seemed lighter, more hopeful and full of promise. Caroline's gaze was focused on the floor at first, but as soon as he stepped forward she looked up at him. And when she smiled, he knew in his heart that with Caroline at his side, he could conquer any calamity. He placed her hand in the curve of his arm as he led her the rest of the way.

"Dearly beloved . . ."

Martha had outdone herself on the wedding supper. The meal began with mussels steamed with garlic and stuffed cherrystone clams, followed by a seafood bouillabaisse. The main course was a dish of lobster chunks seasoned with fresh herbs and baked in a cream sauce, with side dishes of rice, baked beans, squash, onions and peas. For dessert she had made egg custard pie, for which she was renowned, and a small plum pudding that she set on the table between Ty and Caroline.

"A plum pudding to share," she announced as she presented each of them with a spoon. "Just as you will share your lives from this day forward."

"I want a taste," Hannah said.

And to everyone's surprise, instead of correcting her sister as she often did, Eliza grinned. "Me, too," she said and nudged her brother.

"Yeah, me, too."

"Mrs. Wofford made this for the bride and groom," Ty explained. "But in a way we all married Caroline today, so gather round, children."

They all took turns feeding each other from the pudding. Caroline offered a spoonful first to Hannah and then another to Jerome, while Ty gave a spoonful to Eliza, then refilled his spoon. Caroline was laughing when she turned to him, and he popped the silver spoon into her mouth before she could stop him.

"Now you give some to Papa," Hannah instructed.

Shyly Caroline dipped her spoon into the pudding and offered it to Ty. When only seconds earlier they had all been laughing and shouting encouragement to one another, now the room went still. Ty covered her hand with his and guided the spoon to his lips, his eyes locked on hers. It was as if everyone in the room had disappeared except the two of them.

"Thank you, Mrs. Justice," he murmured as he swallowed the pudding.

"You're welcome, Mr. Justice," she replied.

Hannah clapped her hands. "Are we married now?"

Everyone laughed and Ty lifted Hannah onto his lap as the older children stood on either side of him. "Yes, little one, we are married — a family."

"And now if you children will come with me," Henry announced, "I feel like a game of duck, duck, goose."

Caroline knew the game was a favorite of all three children, and she was grateful to her uncle for suggesting it. "What a good idea. Aunt Martha and I can . . ."

"You and your new husband should take a walk, Caroline," Martha said. "Tyrone, the wraps are on the rack in the hallway there."

"But —"

"Go," Martha whispered as she shooed Caroline toward the door. "The children will be fine and the two of you have to be alone sometime."

Caroline swallowed. It was the very moment she had dreaded. She had thought that, by the time the festivities at her aunt's house ended and they got the children settled for the night, Ty would be so exhausted that he would excuse himself and go immediately to his room. Then the following morning they would start the day with chores and breakfast and gradually fall into a routine that would serve them over the weeks and months to come.

Ty had already put on his coat and wrapped a wool scarf around his neck. He held out her cloak and she stepped into it, far too aware of his hands resting lightly on her shoulders as he waited for her to close the fastenings.

"We won't be long," Caroline called out in the general direction of the parlor, where the children were fully engaged in the game. Ty was holding the door open and she stepped out onto the front stoop.

It was a cold, clear night.

"Good sailing weather," Ty murmured as he closed the door and then took her arm to guide her down the front path to the street.

"Yes."

They walked along in silence for a block.

"I'm sorry the ring was too large," he said.

"Only a bit," she assured him, as beneath her glove she felt the presence of the narrow silver band he had presented during the ceremony. "It's a lovely ring."

"We'll get it properly fit to your finger tomorrow."

"There's no rush."

A one-horse carriage clopped by and the driver tipped his hat in their direction. Otherwise the street was deserted.

"Are you warm enough?" Ty asked.

"Yes. Thank you."

This is ridiculous, she thought. *I wasn't this nervous before the ceremony.*

"Caroline?"

"Tyrone?"

The fact that they had been completely silent and then spoken at the same time broke the pall that had hung over them like a gathering fog.

"You first," he said.

"I was just going to ask what you were thinking."

He paused and turned her so that they were facing each other, his face in shadow, hers reflecting the light of a full moon.

"I was thinking, Mrs. Justice, that I had not yet had the opportunity to kiss my bride."

And before she could even gather her thoughts to form a proper response, he was kissing her.

Was it possible that he had developed feelings for her beyond simple gratitude for what she had done for his children? Surely a kiss like this — a kiss that lingered — carried more than token appreciation for kindness given.

Caroline's heart beat so rapidly that it felt like a butterfly longing to break free of the prison of her chest. She tried to take in every facet of the moment. His arms around her. The way she fit so perfectly against the length of him. His mouth on hers, soft, gentle. The awareness that they were pledged to each other for all time. The comprehension that she could indeed come to love this man — might love him already.

He held her close and murmured, "How can I ever repay you for all you have done, Caroline? You have quite literally saved me."

Her heartbeat steadied to a predictable thud as she pulled free of him. "It's the children we've rescued, Tyrone. Both of us. And my life stands to be greatly enriched by their presence, so there's little need to keep thanking me."

He started to say more but she pulled the collar of her cloak higher around her face and turned back toward the house. She'd been fooling herself as she had fooled herself into believing Percy would one day love her. Ty was not Percy. He would care for her, respect her and surely that was enough. "It's quite chilly and it won't do for one or both of us to take ill. We have a great deal of work to do over the coming weeks."

She was already several steps ahead of him by the time he realized what had just happened. She had allowed the kiss. He hadn't imagined that. Furthermore, she had enjoyed it as much as he had. He hadn't imagined that either. And yet she was marching back to the house as if he had offended her. Sometimes the woman could be so hard to read, and he had just signed on for a lifetime of trying to understand her.

"Wait," he called, but she kept right on walking, her bell-shaped skirt swaying from side to side. He lengthened his stride until he could reach out and take her arm again. "Just hold on a minute."

She jerked her arm away and then had the audacity to smile at him as if he were one of her students. "Really, Tyrone, it's well past Hannah's bedtime and . . ."

"Hannah can sleep later tomorrow. It's Saturday and she doesn't have school."

"She has her chores, as do the other children and . . ."

"Why are you acting this way? Was it because I kissed you?"

Her laugh was brittle and without a trace of humor. "Of course not. You took me by surprise is all."

"I am your husband, Caroline, and while I fully understand that ours will never be a marriage of — well, a marriage like —"

"Like you had with Sarah." She sighed heavily as if it had all suddenly become too much for her. "Let's just get the children and go home, Ty." She touched the back of her gloved fingers to his face. "Please."

He fell into step with her but this time she did not take his arm, and it seemed to him that the chasm between them had just widened.

When Caroline walked into her uncle's house, she was greeted by all the sounds of merriment of a celebration. But she felt as if the entire day had been a sham. Furthermore, what irritated her the most was that she was the perpetrator of all that had transpired. It had been her idea to marry, her idea to have Tyrone and the children live with her, her idea that she would be able to set her growing feelings for the man aside and accept the situation for what it was.

"Back so soon, dear?" Martha studied Caroline closely for some clue to what might have happened on her walk.

"The air is quite damp. We need to get the children home and in bed. They've had quite a full day."

At that moment Ty entered the house. He was scowling at no one in particular, but Martha immediately guessed the situation. "Ah, your first spat as husband and wife." She sighed and took Ty's arm. "Well, best to get it over with early on. Come, I think there's a surprise waiting for you in the parlor that just might lighten your mood."

"Roscoe!"

Caroline watched as the two men grasped each other by the shoulders. "Good evening, Mr. Anderson. This is indeed a most delightful surprise."

Roscoe grinned at her and bowed. "And a good evening to you, Mrs. Justice. I'm sorry I missed the ceremony."

"What are you doing here?" Ty asked.

"I got as far as the coast of New Jersey and turned back. Decided there was plenty to keep me busy until spring. And the truth is I've gotten used to these three ragamuffins hanging around." He wrapped his arm around Eliza and Jerome and grinned down at Hannah.

Caroline could not help noticing that Ty looked as if he'd just been thrown a lifeline. And she couldn't help feeling a bit of her own pressure lifting at the sight of the wizened fisherman.

"Well, that's just fine," Ty said and then repeated himself. "Fine. Isn't it, Caroline?"

"Yes. I do hope, Mr. Anderson, that you will consider our home your home and come for visits often."

Roscoe frowned. "Well, now, ma'am, I'd like that, but there's going to be a real problem unless I can convince you to call me by my given name."

For the first time since returning from her walk with Ty, Caroline felt the beginnings of a genuine smile. "Agreed, Roscoe. And you must call me Caroline."

"Will you come back and talk to the class?" Jerome asked.

"Just waiting for the invite."

"Consider yourself invited," Ty said before Caroline could form words. "In fact, you can help with a project Caroline and I have started with the class. Come on, I'll walk with you back to the docks and tell you all about it."

Martha puffed up with indignation. "Don't you think —"

"You and Roscoe go ahead," Caroline interrupted. "I'll take the children home and get them settled for the night." As an afterthought she stood on tiptoe and kissed Ty's cheek. "Don't stay out in the damp too long. You haven't been well," she reminded him.

The fact that the children needed little prompting to go to bed was a mark of just how full the day had been. Hannah yawned and curled onto her side. "Mother Caroline?"

"Yes, Hannah."

"Do you think tomorrow will be as happy a day as today was?"

"It's possible. Let's wait and see what it brings." Caroline kissed her and Hannah closed her eyes and sighed.

Eliza was just getting into bed. She pulled up the covers but remained sitting up, hugging her knees. "It was a lovely wedding. Papa looked so happy. It's been a long time since I saw him smile so much."

"Eliza, you and Jerome do understand that everything he does is done with you children in mind. He loves you so very much."

"I know. And now that we're a family, I hope he will be happy again."

"So do I, Liza. Now, go to sleep."

She covered Eliza and took the lamp with her as she moved down the hall to Jerome's room. He was already in bed, turned away from her, but she knew his breathing was far too even for him to be sleeping.

"Sleep well, Jerome," she said softly as she

adjusted the covers and brushed his hair back from his tightly shut eyes.

Downstairs she set the lamp on a hall table so that the light would show through the side windows of the front door. Would he stay late with Roscoe? Would the two men go to a tavern to commiserate over Ty's fate? Would he come back drunk and stumbling about and making a ruckus that might rouse the neighbors, as Percy so often had?

What did she know of the man, really? His manners whenever they had been discussing the children or working together on repairs for the house had been impeccable, but now she was to know him as he truly was. She thought about how he had come to the school dressed in his new clothes and setting rules as if he already resided in this house.

She twisted the thin silver band he'd placed on her finger earlier that evening. Ty had presented the ring to Reverend Groves for a blessing and then taken Caroline's hand in his as he slipped it onto her finger. It was so loose that she had to hold it in place with her thumb once he'd released her hand.

She had not expected a ring. The truth was she had not even thought of it until they'd come to that part of the ceremony.

She had been prepared to explain that a ring was unnecessary, but suddenly she felt the cool metal slipping over her knuckle, saw the candlelight reflect its shine and she had thought, *I am this man's wife.* It had been the first time she had thought of their union as anything other than a convenience for providing care for the children.

She held up her hand and let the moonlight illuminate the band of silver. It was so delicate — almost fragile. A fitting symbol perhaps for the fragility of her union with Ty.

With each click of the hands on the clock Caroline became more anxious. She stiffened her spine and clenched her fists tightly, as if by doing so she might contain all of the questions and doubts that assailed her. Then she heard the clank of the gate and panicked. Should she rush upstairs and into her room so that he would think she was asleep? Should she meet him at the door, take his coat, hang it on the hall tree and ask how his time with Roscoe had gone? Surely that would be more wifely.

She waited until she heard him in the front hall removing his coat and boots, then walked into the hallway and picked up the lamp. "Do you want something more to eat?" she asked, surprised that this had been her first thought.

"No, thank you. The children are sleeping?"

"Yes. They were quite worn out by all the excitement of the day."

On stocking feet he walked to her and relieved her of the lamp. "Shall we go up, then?"

"I —" The words froze in her throat.

"I haven't forgotten our arrangement, Caroline," he said. "I only thought to share the light."

"Of course." She was close enough that if he had been drinking with Roscoe she would have smelled spirits on him, but all she could smell was the salty scent of the night and smoke from the lamp. "And tomorrow —"

"No more talk of tomorrow, Caroline. Let's get through this one day at a time." He stepped aside and waited for her to climb the stairs. At her bedroom door he handed her the lamp. "Good night, Mrs. Justice."

Her thumb worried the ill-fitting ring as she watched him move down the hall. "Good night, my husband," she murmured, but Ty either didn't hear her or chose not to respond as he entered his own room and closed the door.

CHAPTER SEVENTEEN

Caroline had prepared herself for the whispers of neighbors and speculations of shopkeepers and others, but she could not have been more mistaken. Certainly there was curiosity — ladies of the church came calling with a basket filled with baked goods and bread still warm from the oven or a jar of jam or pickles they had put up during the harvest.

The men who frequented Uncle Henry's barber shop came home singing the praises of Tyrone Justice — a man who had risked his life to save others in the great fire; a man who had been down on his luck until he'd met the schoolmarm. And finally there were those who had — like Ty — lost loved ones and their livelihood in the fire. Many of them had managed to rebuild their lives financially speaking, but they understood how close they had come to being in the same position Tyrone Justice was in when he'd met Caroline.

The women listened and added their own romantic fantasies to the connections, and after a week Martha told Caroline that most everyone in town thought that she and Ty were a perfect match. Through Roscoe, Ty was able to pick up work on the docks, and at least twice the elders of the church had sought his help in managing some repair.

But after a week any gossip about Ty and Caroline had been replaced with curiosity about Caroline's new teaching methods. The rumor that she was permitting Ty and Roscoe to instruct the children, in spite of their lack of any formal education, spread through town like wildfire.

Colleagues of Caroline's who taught in the public school and the one run by Quakers questioned the wisdom of straying from the fundamentals, as they put it. Meanwhile the students in their classes waited eagerly for Caroline's pupils after class to hear what they had learned that day. And Martha reported that conversations around the dinner tables in homes up and down India Street often revolved around how Caroline's students were assuming adult roles as ship's captain and doctor.

But as excited as the youth of Nantucket were about the unorthodox classroom that

Caroline was running, the parents remained skeptical. Helen Johnstone had tearfully reported one morning that her father had announced that once the term ended, she and her siblings would not be returning to Caroline's school.

Finances continued to be a source of concern for Caroline. With the threat of losing the Johnstone children, she could see no way that they would be able to keep the school open after Christmas. Finding the money necessary to run the school had become all-consuming. On the one hand she hated giving in to the will of others, especially when she could see that the entire class was thriving under the new system.

On the other hand, there were no signs of new enrollments, in spite of the fact that she had personally called on several families on the island with children who had recently reached the age of thirteen. The money Ty had earned in New Bedford, along with whatever he was able to pick up doing odd jobs on the island, would certainly see them through Christmas if they watched every penny. But one evening as they were going over the accounts while the children did their homework, Ty pointed out that there wasn't nearly enough money to make repairs to the roof and refurbish the gardens this spring.

Ty ran his finger down each column. "What's this outstanding balance here under tuitions paid and owed?" he asked.

"The Woodstocks took all their children out of school at the beginning of the term and then left for an extended tour of Europe. Thomas wanted to continue coming to my school and I didn't have the heart —"

"Caroline, you can't run a business on heart," Ty said gently. "I'll take care of this. When are the Woodstocks due back?"

"I think they returned late last week. Matilda sent word that she would be calling on me tomorrow afternoon after school."

"I'll be here then."

"No, Tyrone, this is a social call."

He grinned. "Why, Mrs. Justice, haven't you noticed? I can be very sociable, given the right occasion."

"Still —"

His smile disappeared. "I won't embarrass you, Caroline. Trust me."

"I do. Oh, Tyrone, I'm sure that the Woodstocks removed their children from my class because I agreed to enroll your — our — children. They are quite class-conscious when it comes to such matters."

"Are you telling me that you gave up an entire term's tuition times five for Eliza and Jerome? Why?"

"It was the right thing to do. I do not allow others to dictate my decisions, Tyrone, and I make no attempt to dictate the actions of others. Clearly the Woodstocks had their reasons. Let's just leave it at that."

"Nevertheless, John Woodstock owes you for Thomas's tuition and I fully intend to collect."

"I had no idea that you and Mr. Justice had been seeing one another socially, Caroline," Matilda Woodstock said. "Of course we've been out of touch. The continent is so lovely this time of year. Have you traveled to Paris or London, dear?"

"No, but my husband has traveled widely."

"Yes, so I heard. On whaling voyages, isn't that right?"

"Yes." Caroline poured tea and passed a cup to Matilda. "He started as a cabin boy when he was younger than his own son is now and rose to the position of first mate. He had just received a commission as a ship's captain when the fire came."

"So I've been told. Our Thomas has been singing the praises of Mr. Justice and his friend Mr. Anderson." She took a sip of her tea and sighed heavily. "Unfortunately, that brings me to the rather serious matter I came to discuss with you today, Caroline. This idea of having the children taught by these common sailors — I mean, what is their qualification, Caroline?"

"They have traveled the route and spent time in the countries we are studying."

"Still, it's one thing for you to instruct them. You've had formal instruction in the geography and history of such places. But these men — forgive me, but do either of them have academic education?"

"They have firsthand knowledge of the lands we are discussing, Matilda. Think of it as if the children were reading a story about these men and their travels in a book. The only difference is that my husband and Mr. Anderson are right here telling their stories. And at the same time they are assisting me in teaching the children valuable skills. Why, Thomas is the purser for the voyage, and your husband would be most impressed with the manner in which he has managed the ship's accounts."

As usual, when anyone complimented one of her children, Matilda preened.

Caroline heard Ty's step in the hallway. "Mr. Justice, please come and join us. Mrs.

Woodstock and I are just enjoying a cup of tea."

Matilda gave Ty a coy smile and extended a limp hand in his direction. "I've seen you in church, of course, but I don't believe we've had the pleasure of meeting. Do you know my husband, John Woodstock? He's president of the Nantucket National Bank on Main Street, you know."

"I have met your husband. In fact, Mrs. Justice and I are hoping he will agree to come and address the class on the subject of business economics in the near future."

Matilda smiled. "Yes, he received Caroline's invitation. He's quite busy, you know."

"Perhaps one day when he has more time, then." Ty smiled down at the woman. "I've certainly been looking forward to meeting you, Mrs. Woodstock. Caroline was just telling me the other day how well Thomas is doing in class this year."

"He is an extremely sensitive boy, but gifted, don't you agree, Caroline?"

"As are all your children, Matilda."

Ty lifted his eyebrows in mock surprise. "Of course, those two handsome youths I've seen with you in church are Thomas's siblings. And the two lovely young ladies I see sitting in your pew are as well?"

"Oh, yes, there are the twins, Jasper and

Jeremiah, and my two daughters, Bettina and Mildred."

Ty frowned. "Forgive me, Mrs. Woodstock, but how is it that only Thomas is attending classes? Of course, it's none of my business but I do hope that the cause is not that the children are unwell."

Caroline smiled tightly at Ty, warning him off before he made things worse. Was he not aware the power a woman like Matilda could wield over the opinions of others? All their hard work could be undone with a single word from her.

But Ty sat on the edge of the settee and continued to gently hold the matron's hand as he stared into her eyes in a way that Caroline was sure no woman could resist. He unleashed the smile that had more than once set her heart beating to a faster rhythm and saw Matilda Woodstock's breathing quicken.

"Surely, Mrs. Woodstock," he said, his voice low and intimate, "a lady of your standing — the wife of a pillar of the community — wishes all her children to receive the very best education possible."

Matilda withdrew her hand and smiled uncertainly. "I . . . that is, Mr. Woodstock and I thought perhaps to give them the experience of the public school while we were abroad."

Ty nodded as if considering this. "Very wise. A term there would surely make them more fully appreciate the very special attention that Mrs. Justice gives each of her pupils. I do hope that when the new term begins after the Christmas holiday, we might welcome all your children back into the classroom?"

Matilda fluttered her lashes at Ty, then focused on his burn scar. "I understand that you were quite the unsung hero in the great fire, Mr. Justice. I am so very sorry for the loss of your wife — your first wife. I believe she was the daughter of the Copelands of Boston?"

Caroline saw Ty stiffen but his smile held. "Yes, ma'am. Mr. Copeland is also in the banking business. Perhaps your husband knows him."

"I'm sure they've met. Mr. Woodstock knows so many important people. Oh, my, look at the time. It's been lovely seeing you, Caroline. My best wishes to you both."

"Thank you, Matilda. Please call again."

Ty walked the lady to the door and held her cape for her. "Perhaps you and your husband would like to stop by one day and observe the class in comparison to the curriculum at the public school."

"My husband is a very busy man, Mr. Justice."

"Yes, I'm sure he has a great deal to manage after being abroad these last several weeks. Would it be convenient then for me to stop by your home one evening next week to clear up the matter of payment of Thomas's tuition?"

Matilda's mouth opened, then closed, then opened again. "I . . ." She took one step closer and lowered her voice to a hiss as she cast her eyes around to see if anyone was within earshot. "Mr. Justice, I do not discuss financial matters and I certainly do not discuss them in public. Good day, sir."

"So nice to make your acquaintance, ma'am. Mrs. Justice and I look forward to seeing you and Mr. Woodstock and the children in church."

Caroline's fury took the form of silence. At dinner she directed all of her conversation to the children. After the children were in bed she retired to her room without a word and, while Ty could hear her moving around, she did not reappear until the following morning.

"We need to talk," she said, her lips drawn into a tight, thin line as she prepared his breakfast.

"I'm listening."

"You simply cannot afford to upset Matilda Woodstock," she blurted.

"I wasn't trying to upset her, Caroline. I was making a point. Her husband is in arrears with the tuition for Thomas. I walked over there last night after you went upstairs, and we talked about it."

"You . . . why would you do that?"

"Because we are trying to run a business here, Caroline, and we need every dollar that's rightfully owed."

"John Woodstock owes nothing. It's my fault that Thomas got away with disobedience for so long." She set a plate in front of him. "I should have insisted Thomas attend the public school instead of staying on here."

"Or another way to look at it is that John Woodstock knew full well Thomas had continued to attend your school and he either needed to pay his debt or insist his son leave."

"He was in Europe."

"Come on. Do you honestly think the Woodstocks were not informed of Thomas's rebellion? He chose to deal with it once he returned and that's all fine, but the fact remains that in the meantime it was you — not the public school — teaching his son."

He buttered his bread. "Were you planning to just let this go, Caroline?"

"I had hoped that once the Woodstocks returned I might persuade them to reenroll all their children. The loss of one term's tuition in exchange for that would have been worth it. But now . . ."

"You're running a business here, Caroline."

"Stop saying that," she snapped, then slumped into the chair next to him and twisted a dishcloth around her fingers nervously. "I'm beginning to realize that while I am a very fine teacher, I am not good at business."

Ty smiled. "Fortunately I am — or I used to be." He fed her the last bite of his buttered biscuit and pushed back his chair. "Roscoe has lined up a job for the two of us this morning. We'll be back in time for this afternoon's lesson on the whaling voyage."

She nodded but it was evident that he had not relieved her anxiety over the meeting with Matilda the previous day.

"Hey," he said, lightly touching her hair, "do what you need to do — place the blame on my lack of manners if you feel you need to mend fences. She'll come around."

"I will not give her the satisfaction of appearing to be disloyal to you, Tyrone. You are my husband."

I wish that were really true, Caroline.

They heard the class beginning to gather in the front hall, their voices excited and muffled as they hung up their outerwear and raced to warm themselves by the fire in the classroom.

"Go on," Ty said. "There are children in need of teaching. I'll take care of mending fences with the Woodstocks."

"No," Caroline cried. "Please. Leave them to me."

Ty's spirits plummeted. She didn't trust him to conduct himself properly with people above his station. She was above his station. How could she ever come to love him if all she saw when she looked at him was someone lesser?

But when Caroline entered the classroom she was met by the smiling faces of all five Woodstock children. Thomas stepped forward and handed her an envelope that she recognized as stationery from John Woodstock's office.

Dear Mrs. Justice,
After speaking with Mr. Justice last evening, Mrs. Woodstock and I have reconsidered our decision to enroll the

children in public school. We do hope that this will not be too much of an inconvenience for you. I have enclosed my check in the amount I have calculated to cover the full tuition for the term for Thomas and half terms for each of the others. Naturally Mrs. Woodstock and I reserve the right to stop by your classroom unannounced to observe this unusual new curriculum you are currently teaching.

Sincerely,
John B. Woodstock III

The check had fluttered to the floor when Caroline had unfolded the letter. Thomas handed it to her and for the first time since he had enrolled in her class, he was meeting her eyes directly. He was also smiling. "Father and Mother were going to insist I leave and attend public school with the others, but I stood my ground, just like Mr. Justice and Mr. Anderson taught us. I laid out my case for staying here, showing Father my improved grades and the project I'm doing for the voyage as purser. He was very impressed. And then right after that Mr. Justice came calling, and he and Father talked for some time and — well, here we are."

"But I never thought that —"

Helen pushed her way into the circle. "Oh, Mrs. Justice, don't you know that everyone wants to attend your school? Once they heard about the way we're learning all those subjects that used to be boring, like arithmetic and geography and history, they were ever so envious. I mean, when I told them that I was the ship's captain — well, you should have seen their faces. I don't wonder that you'll have a waiting list for next term."

Caroline studied the check, trying to absorb the incredible amount of money this little piece of paper represented. They could do all the repairs, refurbish the classroom and still have enough to live comfortably.

Thank You, Father, she prayed silently. *It is not my place to question how You have brought this to pass, but I thank You for this incredible blessing.*

"Jerome, please go and find your father," Caroline said as she reinserted the precious check into the envelope and placed it in the drawer of her desk. Then she took out a sheet of paper. "Take him this note and be sure he reads it right away." Her pen flew across the page and she realized how very happy she was to have someone who would share her excitement and joy. "Go," she urged as she gave Jerome the note. "And

327

don't forget your cap and mittens."

She looked at her class, still clustered together where they had been when Thomas had given her his father's letter. "Well, please take your seats, ladies and gentlemen," she said, but she could not stop smiling, knowing that for the first time all term every desk was going to be occupied. This was Ty's doing. She did not know what he had said to John Woodstock, but clearly he had gained the banker's respect — as well as hers.

CHAPTER EIGHTEEN

The weather in early December was mild and calm. With their future looking considerably brighter, Caroline found that she had more time to spend with Ty and the children. In the evenings they often gathered around the harpsichord, where she and Eliza would play a duet while Jerome and Ty played their harmonicas. Hannah danced around the room, spinning until she was dizzy and Ty had to rescue her.

They fell into a tradition of going to Martha's for Sunday dinner after church. Caroline was well aware that Ty attended services only as a courtesy to her and to set an example for the children. Whenever she had tried to include him in her morning devotional or weekly Bible study with the children, he had made some excuse about needing to see Roscoe or promising a neighbor that he would help with a repair or chore.

He was gaining a reputation as a fine

carpenter, and a steady flow of jobs had translated into a consistent income. At the same time Matilda and John Woodstock's apparent endorsement of Caroline's teaching methods had resulted in a flurry of inquiries for admission in the new term.

Because things were going so smoothly for them, Caroline had not pressed the issue of his lapsed faith for she had never forgotten what he had told her. "How can I expect God's forgiveness when I cannot forgive myself?" It was the depth of his love for Sarah that had kept him from coming back into the fold of the church. All she could do was pray that in time he would come to understand that he had done everything he could, and in God's eyes that was all that could be asked of him.

On clear Sunday afternoons she and Ty and the children would ride out to one of the glacial ponds that dotted Nantucket, where she would teach them about the geology of the island. Afterward the children would coax the adults to join them in a game of hide-and-seek. If the weather was dismal they might spend the afternoon playing cards or board games such as Our Birds or Errand Boy.

"Does everything have to teach a lesson?" Hannah sighed on one such afternoon.

Several times she had landed her playing piece on a square that described laziness or, worse, dishonesty and she'd had to move back a space or go to jail.

"Your mother is a schoolteacher," Ty said with a laugh and then, realizing what he had just said, immediately corrected himself as he passed the spinner to Caroline. "Mother Caroline, it's your turn."

"I think we ought to just call her Mama, since we call you Papa," Hannah groused. "It's hard to say Mother Caroline when you're in a hurry."

Caroline focused on spinning to see how many spaces she would move, but she was aware of glances passing between Jerome and Eliza.

"I wouldn't mind," Jerome said so softly that Caroline was not sure he had actually spoken or if she had only wished it.

"Eliza?" Ty asked.

"It's not the same."

Caroline's heart fell. She had thought that perhaps things were changing, that the children were coming to love her as much as she loved them.

"I mean," Eliza continued, "Mother is what we called our real mother, so in a way Mama is just a kind of nickname."

"Would that be all right with you, Caroline?" Ty asked.

"It would be an honor," Caroline replied, her voice on the verge of breaking. Then she pushed back her chair and held out her arms. "Oh, children, you have just given me the most precious gift of all."

"And it's not yet Christmas," Hannah said, as she and Eliza readily came to her embrace while Jerome stood off to one side, grinning shyly. Caroline glanced up at Ty. He was watching her, and in his eyes she saw that the decision had his blessing. "Thank you," she mouthed.

Later that night Caroline knelt by her bed to say her evening prayers. "Heavenly Father, thank You for the blessings You have bestowed on this house. I pray that I may always be worthy of the love and trust of these dear children."

Next door she could hear Ty moving around his bedroom. The scrape of a chair, the creak of a window being raised because he could not bear to sleep without fresh air, no matter what the temperature outside. Lately she had become aware that he stayed up late most nights, judging by the level of oil in the lamp the following morning.

"I pray for Tyrone that You will continue to keep him in Your care. In time I know he will find his way back to You. He is a good and gentle man, dear God, and I have come to care for him more than I had ever imagined would be possible."

I love him.

Caroline sat back on her heels, her eyes wide-open while her hands remained folded in prayer. *Impossible.* But when she thought of life without him, she could not help but wonder if, once the children were grown and away on their own, he would become more distant. She did not think she could endure the depths of loneliness she had known throughout her marriage to Percy and in the years before Ty's children had come to her door.

The house was quiet and yet it was so alive these days. The children had instilled it with a presence that filled every corner. She had thought that things would be little different once Ty moved in. After all, the days would be filled with school and the evenings would be filled with the children, and then they would each retire to their own pursuits — their separate rooms.

But she had been so wrong. She was aware of Ty every minute of every day. When he was away she found herself waiting for his return, and when he was there she felt as if by his very presence he had usurped her home, her school — her heart.

Even now the scent of his pipe tobacco wound its way under the door and into her room and she knew that he was not sleeping. And knowing that, she felt a kind of serenity that she had rarely known before Ty. The house no longer echoed its emptiness in the dark of night. She was no longer alone — or lonely.

After everything she'd done for him and his children, Ty had decided that the one thing he could do for Caroline was to absent himself from her presence unless the children were around. When it was just the two of them, it seemed to him that she was either nervous or annoyed, or a little of both. Weekdays were not a problem. She had her work and he had his. Saturdays were usually taken up with chores and on Sunday they attended church together, then took their main meal with Martha and Henry.

But the evenings after the children were in bed were the worst. He had tried sitting with her in the parlor while she read or embroidered a set of pillowcases for Martha for Christmas. They exchanged comments and observations about the children, the school, the need for this or that repair, but they never really talked.

One night she surprised him. "Will you tell me about Sarah? Not how she died. I'd like to know about you and Sarah. Your backgrounds were . . . well, it was unlikely the two of you would meet, much less marry."

"She came to the wharf one day with her father. His bank had financed the voyage we had just made. I had kept the ledgers on that voyage and so when I gave the accounting she was there."

"What was she like?"

"She was a good deal like Hannah — vibrant, mischievous." He smiled.

"No wonder you loved her."

"She was also stubborn like Hannah can be. I came home from a voyage once and found that she had opened her own business — a hat shop on the corner of Main and Pleasant Streets. Jerome had just started school and she decided to go into business." He shook his head as the memory came flooding back. "We fought over that for months."

"I remember that shop. I shopped there with Aunt Martha. She made the most beautiful hats. Why would you argue over that?"

"Pride. She had gotten the money from her father to set up shop. Her parents already thought of me as beneath her. I knew she had married me to rebel against her parents as much as because we were in love. I mean, we were so young. How could we even know what true love meant?"

Embarrassed that he had revealed so much, Ty stood up and stretched. "I think I'll go up, if you don't mind."

"Of course not. Sleep well, Tyrone."

But unable to sleep, Ty would go over the lesson he intended to teach the class the following week. He worked on his lessons for hours, determined not to let Caroline down, especially now that they never knew when John Woodstock or one of the other parents might show up unannounced to observe the class.

So far he and Roscoe had taught the class the intricacies of knot tying, how to properly mend a sail or fishing net and the steps involved in building a leakproof barrel. Caroline had suggested that he teach them the art of scrimshaw, but he had refused.

"I'm out of practice and if we're going to teach them something like that then I want to be good at it."

"Then practice," Caroline had replied. "The girls are losing interest in the project because the skills you and Mr. Anderson teach are so male oriented."

She had a point.

Roscoe had told him about a store of whalebone and walrus teeth that had been abandoned in a warehouse untouched by the fire. To Ty's delight the manager of the warehouse had been more than happy to give him the goods at no cost. Now all he needed to do was revive the skill he had once been renowned for — the skill to create intricate and detailed designs on the smallest piece of ivory.

Night after night he carved and polished the collected pieces as he considered what practical use each bone or tooth might have. And as he worked, he came up with the idea of making Christmas gifts for the children. It was a good way to practice his craft, and he knew the children would be pleased to receive something so personal. A bookmark for Eliza would be a good start. It was the simplest to carve and illustrate. If that was successful, his plan was to make a belt buckle for Jerome and a ditty box for Hannah. *And for Caroline?*

Among the collection he'd found a sperm whale's tooth that had been broken at the hollow end. At first he'd thought the piece ruined, but found he could not discard it. Again and again as night followed night and the work progressed on the gifts for the

337

children, he would return to that whale tooth. And night after night he would put it aside in favor of a piece of ivory that seemed more perfectly formed.

If Caroline had noticed that on recent evenings Ty had made no attempt to endure the hour he usually sat with her in the parlor or take his walk before going up to his room, she had said nothing. Likely she was as relieved as he was not to have to try to make conversation. Ever since the night she had asked about Sarah, she had seemed even more reticent around him when they were alone.

When he heard her come upstairs, he sat perfectly still and waited, his heart hammering. He could not help hoping that she would come to his door. He was aware that they had come to a point of mutual respect — even friendship.

Once John Woodstock had decided to re-enroll all his children in her school, Caroline had given Ty all the credit for this miraculous turn of events. And with the school's future seemingly secure, at least for the time being, she had begun to laugh more easily. He often saw her glancing his way, sharing a parent's amusement at something one of the children had done or said.

Every night he heard her stop to look in

on the children, but she always passed his room without hesitation on her way to her own. And every night he would ask himself what might happen if he went to her and told her that he was falling in love with her. How would she react if he admitted that he longed for a marriage in fact, not just in name?

He studied his hands, blotched and discolored beneath the lamplight, then pushed back his chair and lit his pipe. He stood at the window he always left open, smoking and chastising himself for fantasizing that a woman as beautiful and learned as Caroline could ever love someone like him.

Sarah did.

But Sarah had been young and rebellious when they'd met. Their love had grown out of defiance and a determination to prove her parents wrong about him. Over time the children had come — Eliza just nine months after they had run away to be married and Jerome the following year. They had settled into a routine that suited them both. He sailed away and she raised the children and ran a successful hat shop.

How odd that once again he had married an independent woman who ran her own business and loved his children. The difference was that Caroline had come into his life at a time when they both were well aware of how cruel and unfair life could be. He picked up the broken whale's tooth and balanced it on the end of his finger. He was fool to think that carving her a ring that offered her his heart — his love — would win him hers. How could a woman like Caroline ever love a man like him? He spun the hollow tooth on his finger and then dropped it back onto the pile of discards.

Caroline could not recall when she'd had a more complicated day. It had begun before sunrise when Eliza had come to her room to say that Hannah was complaining of a stomachache. Caroline had shoved her arms into the sleeves of her robe, heedless of how she might look, and hurried barefoot across the hall to the girls' room.

"I'm sick," Hannah moaned and proceeded to prove as much by throwing up all over the covers and herself.

"Get your father," Caroline told Eliza.

"He and Uncle Henry left early this morning," Eliza reminded her.

Caroline had forgotten. Her uncle was looking at the possibility of buying a piece of property in the village of 'Sconset at the east end of the island and had asked Ty to come with him to look it over. "I forgot."

340

"Will Hannah be all right?"

The little girl was wailing miserably and Caroline was sure she had a fever. "She'll be fine. Go wake Jerome and tell him to get dressed and go to Aunt Martha's. He's to ask her to bring the doctor and come as soon as possible, then come right back here. Meanwhile, please fill the washbasin here and then refill the pitcher and bring me clean linens. Come on, Hannah, let's get you out of those stinky nightclothes," she crooned as Eliza ran to do her bidding. "How would you like to sleep in my bed this morning?"

"Papa's," Hannah sniffled.

"Papa's, then." Caroline got the child changed and carried her across the hall to Ty's room.

It was the first time she had been in there since he'd moved in. He had insisted that he would take care of the cleaning and changing the linens, and she had respected his need for privacy. She was far too aware of the scent of him, the presence of him in the empty room. The hand towel neatly hung next to the washbasin. The precisely made bed, where she pulled back the covers and laid Hannah on his pillow.

"What's that?" Hannah asked, rolling onto her side and pointing to a collection of small tools and a covered box on the table next to the window.

Caroline took it as a good sign that the child was showing her usual curiosity. "I don't know. Your Papa will be back after lunch and you can ask him then."

"I can stay with Hannah," Eliza volunteered.

"No. You have your report to give today."

She knew how hard Eliza had been working on her project to illustrate how people might dress in the countries they had studied in the voyage. She and Hannah had spent hours in the attic going through fabric and clothing to find pieces she could convert into costumes to illustrate her report.

"If you could please change the linens on Hannah's bed while I get dressed. Then bring everything down to the kitchen, and I'll start boiling some water to soak them."

By the time the doctor arrived and declared Hannah out of any real danger, the class was gathering for the day. Martha insisted that she had nothing she'd rather do than sit with the child, so Caroline went downstairs to the classroom. But her thoughts were on Hannah. What if she were seriously ill? What if the fever came back suddenly?

"All right, class," she said clapping her

hands for attention, "take your seats and open your readers."

Christmas was only two days away, and the boys and girls were far more focused on the gifts they might receive than they were on their studies. Repeatedly through the morning she had to reprimand Helen for whispering, Thomas for daydreaming and even the usually docile Laura for passing notes and giggling.

She was just about out of patience when she heard Ty's voice coming from the kitchen. She instructed the children to read the next story in their readers and rushed out to tell him about Hannah.

Martha was stirring a pot of chicken soup and had already filled Ty in on Hannah's condition. "Bless her heart, she fell asleep as soon as the doctor left and has hardly stirred since. Her fever is down and she's going to need to eat something. I thought she might be able to stomach a little of this broth, and there's plenty here for you and Caroline and the class, as well."

The soup definitely smelled enticing. Caroline had not taken time for breakfast and she was ravenous. "Aunt Martha, you are a blessing," she said.

"I'll go look in on Hannah," Ty said as he started up the back stairs.

But just then they heard raised voices and then a crash coming from the classroom. "I'll go," Ty said. "You check on Hannah."

Caroline looped her shawl over her forearms to shorten its length so she wouldn't trip or spill, then filled a crockery mug with some broth and started up the stairs. "Hannah?" she said softly as she reached the doorway of Ty's bedroom and eased the door open. The bed was empty. She set the mug on the table.

"Hannah?"

Caroline went to the girls' room, then her own and Jerome's, but there was no sign of the child. Through her bedroom window she saw Ty standing on the front lawn, delivering what looked like a serious lecture to Noah Johnstone. At the same time she smelled something burning.

"Aunt Martha? The soup is burning," she called down the back stairs as she started up to the third floor, where Hannah sometimes liked to play when her older siblings were studying.

She moved along the narrow hallway, opening doors to the three bedrooms meant for servants that she and Percy could never afford. But there was no sign of Hannah. Caroline smiled as she remembered how just the previous evening Hannah had begged to stay home so she could hear Eliza present her report. Surely the little imp had sneaked down the front stairs and hidden herself somewhere outside the classroom.

She was just about to start back downstairs when she saw smoke curling its way out from under the closed door to the attic.

"Fire!" she cried, leaning over the banister. "Aunt Martha, get the children outside now and send Tyrone to fetch the fire brigade!"

"Hannah?" Aunt Martha called back.

"I think she's downstairs, as well. Check the parlor. I'll take one more look to be sure."

She was about to descend the stairs when she heard a muffled cry. "Mama!" Her heart stopped, then beat so rapidly she thought she might faint before she could reach Hannah.

"Mama!"

Hannah's cry was unmistakable — terrified, pleading. Caroline forced herself to remain calm and follow the sound of the child's call for help. "Coming, Hannah. Just stay where you are. Mama's coming."

CHAPTER NINETEEN

Ty collared Noah Johnstone and hauled him outside to cool off after breaking up a fight between Noah and Jerome. Noah was a good three inches taller and twenty pounds heavier than Jerome, and Ty was sure his son would have gotten the worse end of that battle. "You stay here," he barked at Jerome and was relieved to see that the boy obeyed without an argument. No doubt the blood coming from his nose had been a factor, especially when the girls all gathered around him offering handkerchiefs and sympathy. "Noah started it," he heard Helen say.

Outside, Ty reprimanded Noah for his disregard for the property of others in knocking over a table filled with test tubes and a microscope that Caroline used when teaching science.

"Now, give me your side of how this all started, Noah."

"Ask your son."

"I will but right now I'm asking you."

Noah scowled. "He thinks he's so smart. I know how to rig a sail." Roscoe had brought the class a model ship so they could practice raising and lowering the sails. "I sure don't need somebody like him teaching me," Noah added bitterly.

Someone like him. Ty felt like punching the boy himself. Determined to control his temper, he looked beyond Noah and saw what looked like steam rising from the roof of the house. Only it wasn't steam — couldn't be. He felt a dread he thought he buried long ago and then heard shouts from inside the house.

He grabbed Noah's shoulder. "Noah, there's a fire in the attic. I need you to run as fast as you can and bring the fire brigade."

Noah's eyes widened in panic. "My sisters —"

"I'll get them out. Just go."

Noah took off in one direction while Ty ran back to the house, but the front door was barricaded by the panicked students trying to get out. He could hear Martha shouting orders to them, but her instructions were drowned out by the hysterical screams of the girls.

"Back away from the door," he shouted,

but knew it was useless. He ran around the side of the house into the kitchen. "This way," he shouted. "Martha, bring them this way." Once the logjam at the front door was broken, some of the children fled the house through the kitchen while others used the now-accessible front door.

"Caroline? Hannah?" Ty shouted as he dashed up the back stairs. He ran from room to room, saw the rumpled covers of his bed and realized Caroline must have grabbed Hannah and run out the front. And not a minute too soon, as smoke had already filled the stairway leading down from the third floor.

Ty grabbed the hand towel and soaked it in water from the washbasin, holding it over his mouth and nose as he hurried back down the front stairs and through all the downstairs rooms to be sure that no one had been left behind. In the distance he heard the clang of the fire wagons.

Relieved that everyone was out of the house, he rushed outside just as the fire chief jumped down from the wagon before it had come to a full stop. "How did it start?" he asked Ty.

"I'm not sure. I saw smoke rising from the roof and then we heard Mrs. Justice shouting to the children to get out."

"Is everyone accounted for?" the chief asked as neighbors began to gather, bringing blankets to wrap around the frightened children.

"I'll check for sure. Some are here and the rest went out the front." Ty heard glass breaking and looked up at the attic window just as flames erupted. At that moment he had a sudden memory of something amiss when he'd gone into his bedroom — something beyond the empty and unmade bed.

The lamp. There had been no lamp on the table where he worked at night. Surely Caroline had taken it to clean and refill. He brushed off the thought.

"Get these children away from here," the fire chief shouted at Ty, then he hurried off to instruct his men on how best to control the fire.

Ty mentally counted the children — Helen, Laura, Thomas, Jerome, Eliza . . .

"Papa, we can't find Hannah or Mama," Eliza cried when she saw him. "Aunt Martha thought they must have come out the front but they didn't and . . ." She burst into tears.

For an instant Ty couldn't breathe. *Not again,* he thought. *Please, God, not again.* And ignoring the shouts of the fire chief and Martha, he rushed into the house.

■ ■ ■ ■

Caroline could hear Hannah whimpering, but she could not find her. She was hampered partially by the presence of trunks, wooden storage boxes and extra furnishings left by previous owners, along with things she had stored in the attic over the years. But it was the smoke that made it impossible to see. Her eyes stung as she tried to move through the large space, ducking around the slanted beams as she checked every nook and cranny, retracing her steps when the whimpering grew fainter. She covered her head and face with her shawl and pressed on.

"Stay where you are, Hannah," she called out, but her voice was already hoarse and it was hard to form the words. "I'm coming, darling."

The sound of breaking glass behind her caught her by surprise, and she spun around in time to see orange flames leaping about on the sill in a macabre dance. Hannah screamed and Caroline rushed toward the sound, the laces of her corset binding her like a vise and making breathing even more impossible.

The child was lying in a pile of fabric near

an open trunk just a few feet from her. "I'm right here, Hannah." She fell to her knees and lifted the sobbing child in her arms, cradling her, pressing Hannah's face into her breast and wrapping her in the shawl to shield her from the smoke and fire. She glanced around, but by now the smoke was so thick that it blocked out the light from the window.

She had to get them out, but which way? The window was not an option. She had to find the stairs. "Wrap your arms around my neck and hang on," she said, fighting to catch her breath as the heat seared her face and hands and smoke filled her lungs.

She tried standing but realized there was more air closer to the ground. *Heat rises.* She had taught the children that in a science lesson. Inching along, she used her hands to feel her way. She touched a smooth curve of polished wood and recognized it as the rocker on a chair she had stored until she would have time to repair the seat cushion.

She closed her eyes against the sting of smoke and envisioned that rocking chair placed just inside the attic door. She blinked until she could make out a change in the panorama of gray and black that the attic had become. Lighter gray. An opening. The stairway down. She inched her way closer and felt Hannah's arms tighten around her as her foot miraculously found the top step that would lead them to safety.

Please, God, she prayed as she mentally counted each step down to the third floor, *lead us through this. If not both of us, then save the child. Ty cannot lose another loved one. He has suffered enough. Please. Please. Please.*

But as she reached the bottom step she saw that the long, narrow hallway leading to the stairway down to the second floor was almost as smoke-filled as the attic had been. At the same time she felt Hannah's hands loosen and her body go lifeless against her.

"No," she croaked as she pressed the child to her heart and stood upright, stumbling as fast as she could through the blackness toward the stairway. She misjudged the distance and when her feet went out from under her she clung to Hannah as the two of them fell and rolled down the stairs. And as the blackness finally won out, Caroline imagined she could hear Ty calling out to her.

I found her, she wanted to assure him. *I'm here.* And her last thought before she lost consciousness was a prayer. *Please, God, save his child.*

■ ■ ■ ■

Ty tore through the house, his heart pumping like a steam engine as he dashed blindly from room to room, calling out her name until the smoke and heat made it impossible to do more than whisper, "Caroline."

Memories of another fire assailed him as he checked the downstairs rooms and then ran up the front stairway.

This is not the same, he tried to convince himself. Then he'd had to run for blocks. This time he was right here. Then he had not been able to get to Sarah. This time he would not turn back until he had Caroline and Hannah safe in his arms. Then the fire had entered the house through the front door. This time it had started in the attic. Then time had run out.

Not this time. Please, God, not again.

He forced himself to take the time to search every bedroom carefully, moving quickly but methodically from room to room, taking time to once again soak the towel he held over his mouth and nose, then having the presence of mind to soak additional towels for Hannah and Caroline. When he heard the thud of the boots of the fire crew making their way over the same

353

territory he'd already covered on the main floor, he realized he had been inside the house only minutes, yet it seemed like hours. Then came a crash from the back of the hallway and through the gray smoky haze that filled the two lower floors of the house, he saw a body crumpled at the bottom of the stairs that led up to the third floor.

"Up here," he shouted as he ran past the main stairway. "Hurry."

Caroline was lying at the foot of the stairs, her body so still that Ty feared the worst. It was happening again. He rolled her into his arms and there was Hannah, equally still. Blindly he covered their mouths and noses with the wet cloths, and still neither of them stirred.

"We found them," he heard one of the firemen shout as strong arms pulled him to his feet, still holding Caroline in his arms.

He saw one of the men lift Hannah and, as he cradled her against his chest, Ty saw her body twitch and her arms instinctively circle the fireman's neck. She coughed and he felt the stirrings of hope that maybe this time things would turn out differently. But when he looked down at Caroline, there were no similar signs of life.

The fireman carrying Hannah brushed

past Ty as he ran with her to safety, while two more men tried to take Caroline from him. He tightened his hold on her. "I've got her," he said, almost daring them to defy him.

When Sarah died he had turned away from God. This time he knew from that experience that he would never survive the loss of Caroline on his own. For the sake of his children he had to call on God for the strength they were all going to need.

Please, save her. Please give us another chance. I promise You I won't waste this one. If it be Your will, let her live. I love her so much.

As he stepped out onto the lawn, he scanned the crowd that had gathered for his children. "Hannah! Liza! Jerome!" He was shouting, but his voice was weak and there was so much noise.

"Tyrone," Martha shook his shoulder. "The children are all safe and now Dr. Hopkins is here. Let us take Caroline."

He realized that he had fallen to his knees and that he was clasping Caroline to his chest, his face pressed against her soot-covered hair. Jerome had run to him and was staring at him, his eyes wide with fear.

"Where's Hannah?" Ty asked.

"She's over there with Liza and the neighbor lady." Jerome pointed toward a wagon where Hannah was sitting up. Eliza was holding her, stroking her hair and adjusting the blanket someone had placed around their shoulders. Ty noticed how Eliza kept Hannah turned away from the house so that she wouldn't see Caroline. But Eliza was watching.

"Doc says Hannah will be fine, Ty," Henry said. "A few bruises from the fall, but Caroline must have protected her from the worst of it."

They eased his arms away and laid Caroline out on a garden bench. Martha and some of the other women gathered around her to form a shield while the doctor loosened her clothing and examined her.

Henry helped Ty stumble to his feet and stayed with him while they waited for some sign, some sound.

Nothing.

When the circle of women parted to allow the doctor to emerge, Ty was sure he was going to see the doctor shake his head — that terrible tradition of saying "nothing can be done" without actually speaking a word.

He bowed his head and felt Henry's comforting hand on his back.

Just one more chance, he pleaded silently.

"Well, Mr. Justice, your wife has swallowed a lot of smoke and she has some swelling in her ankle and bruises from the fall. I suspect the ankle is a sprain rather than a break, but we'll get her settled somewhere that I can make a more thorough examination. The thing we need to be most concerned about is how much smoke she inhaled before she got out of that attic."

"Caroline is one of the most resilient women I've ever known," Martha assured Ty. "She'll fight this and come back to us good as new."

"And if the damage is too severe?"

The doctor looked uncomfortable and said nothing. Ty had his answer. Her recovery was in God's hands now.

"Come on, Tyrone," Martha urged. "We'll take Caroline and the children to our house, where I can help them clean up and get Caroline properly settled in bed for the rest she's going to need."

He realized that Caroline's aunt and uncle were every bit as frightened as he was, but were trying hard to hold out some hope.

"Is Reverend Groves around?" Ty asked.

"I saw him earlier. I'll go find him," Henry replied, clearly relieved to have something to do.

Martha grasped Ty's arm. "Caroline will be real glad you asked for the minister, Ty."

"I need him there as much as she does,"

357

Ty admitted. "I mean, in case . . . If Caroline doesn't make it, I don't think I can face the children, Martha."

"You just hush, now. She's going to be fine."

But Ty saw the woman's chin quiver uncontrollably as she turned away and started shouting out instructions for moving Caroline and the children to her house.

Caroline was having the strangest dreams. One minute she was at the circus, running from tent to tent in search of something. Then she was a performer in the center ring swallowing fire as everyone applauded. Then Ty was there but she could only hear him, not see him. And she always seemed to be running, searching, her breathing becoming more difficult with every step.

Hannah! In her dream she shouted the child's name and it echoed down hallways and up stairways that led to nowhere or ended in darkness. She tried to run but could not move. Tried to breathe but could only wheeze. Tried to open her eyes to find her way, but her lids were impossible to lift.

Hannah!

What would she tell Tyrone? How could he ever forgive her? She should have sent the class home for the day, or asked Martha to maintain order in the classroom while she tended the sick child — *her* sick child.

Through the haze of her unconsciousness, she fought to hear sounds that would bring her a measure of peace. Eliza at the harpsichord playing the carols of Christmas. Jerome's harmonica. Hannah's giggle. And most precious of all, Ty's whispered assurance that all were safe.

But the more she tried to come awake, to decipher the activity around her, the more exhausted she was. She felt the panic and the struggle to get out of the house as if it were happening all over again. And in the end she would always surrender to the dreams that made no sense.

In spite of the doctor's assurances that he was doing everything possible to speed Caroline's recovery, she continued to drift in and out of consciousness. On those occasions when her eyes would flutter open, a film covered the usually sparkling green irises and she looked about, unseeing. She would mumble unintelligibly and clutch at the covers as if holding something she feared she might drop. All the while she would writhe so much that Martha worried she might further injure the ankle they had bandaged and elevated according to the doctor's instructions.

Once Ty had assured himself that his older children were safe and Hannah was unharmed, he insisted on staying with Caroline. Through that night and all the following day, he sat with her. By day to keep himself from pacing the room he worked on the scrimshaw gifts that Henry had rescued from the house, and at night he slept in a chair he had pulled close to the bed. When he ate at all, it was from a tray Eliza or Martha brought to him. When the doctor came to check on Caroline, Ty stood near the head of the bed, watching the doctor carefully for any expression that might signal a change in Caroline's condition.

"Her restlessness is probably a good sign, Mr. Justice," Dr. Hopkins told him. "And the swelling has gone down overnight," he added as he wrapped the injured ankle again. "I think it's all going very well."

You think? I don't want you to think. I want you to know. And it's going well for whom? You?

It was all Ty could do to be civil to the man.

"I know it's difficult," the doctor said, as if reading his thoughts. "You have every reason to hope, Mr. Justice. The fact that she was not exposed to the smoke for an

360

extended period improves her chances considerably."

"Thank you, doctor," Martha said, as she hustled him from the room and closed the door before Ty could say something he might regret.

Ty collapsed back into the chair and rested his forehead on the edge of Caroline's bed. "Come back to me, love," he whispered. "Please come back and let me show you how much you've come to mean to me — how much I love you."

"Papa?"

Ty looked up and forced a reassuring smile as Hannah edged into the room, her eyes on Caroline. "Hello, little one," he said, holding out his arms to her.

She scrambled onto his lap and nestled against his chest. "Is Mama ever going to wake up?"

"She needs her rest, Hannah. Remember once when you were sick and all you wanted to do was sleep?"

"I guess," Hannah answered. Her mouth worked and Ty tightened his hold on her and rocked her back and forth.

"I was bad, Papa," she said.

"How so?"

"I remembered something Eliza asked me to bring down from the attic that she

361

needed for her project, but I forgot. Liza said it didn't matter but I thought if I could get it for her, she would be so happy."

"That's a kind thing, Hannah, not a bad thing at all."

"I was in your room and I saw the lamp and it's always so dark in the attic even in the daytime, and I'd seen you light the lamp before and so I took a match just in case. I never meant to strike it, Papa. Only if I couldn't find the piece that Liza needed."

Ty went still as he imagined what had happened next. "It's all right, Hannah. These things happen and now you know. As Mama would say, you learned a lesson today. You won't make the same mistake again."

The child sniffled and cuddled closer. "I was so scared, Papa."

"I know, little one. I know, but you're safe now." *Thanks to Caroline,* he thought. Once again, she had saved them all from certain disaster. Surely that was love that could not be questioned.

He rocked her until she fell asleep in his arms.

CHAPTER TWENTY

Caroline opened her eyes and looked around. It was just before dawn, judging by the thin light that filtered through the lace pattern of her Aunt Martha's bedroom curtains. The window was open and she could feel the cold air on her face, but the rest of her body felt as if it were encased in some kind of oven.

She shifted and cringed. Every muscle ached but at least she could breathe. She tried to push herself upright, but she was so tightly bound in blankets lined with warm bricks on either side that she could do little more than simply lie there.

She turned her head to the opposite wall and saw Tyrone sleeping in the chair next to the bed. His long legs were looped over one arm of the chair and his arms were folded tightly across his chest. He had at least two days' growth of whiskers and his hair was an unruly mass of copper waves. And then she saw that his arms were pressing her open Bible tightly against his chest — his heart.

She tried to speak his name, but nothing came out. She tried to calculate how long she might have been unconscious — at least the day of the fire and the night that had followed.

The fire.

Had everyone gotten out? Was Hannah all right? She had to know.

She stretched out her arm but could not reach Ty, and she could not help wondering if that might not be symbolic of the future they now faced. If Hannah had been injured — or worse — how would he ever forgive her? How would she ever forgive herself? For the first time she understood how Ty had turned away from God. It had never before occurred to her that she might do something that would make her unworthy of God's love. But if anything had happened to Hannah . . .

"Caroline?" Ty unwound himself from the chair, closed and set the Bible on the bedside table and leaned forward until he could grasp her hand between both of his. "Oh, Caroline, you've come back to us." His eyes were red-rimmed from loss of sleep, and when she cupped his cheek he turned his lips to her palm. "I thought —" His voice broke.

"Hannah?" she managed to croak.

Ty swiped at his eyes and hurried to pour her a glass of water. "She's fine. Everyone is fine." He held the glass to her lips. "Small sips," he instructed.

She felt the water soothe her throat and reached for more, then grimaced. "My foot?"

"Sprained, not broken. That's the least of it. The smoke —"

She nodded. "It was so thick and putrid and I couldn't find my way and Hannah . . ." Suddenly the memory of her fear and panic overwhelmed her. Tears ran down both cheeks and her chest hurt as she tried to control her sobs. She reached for him and he sat on the side of the bed and wrapped his arms around her.

"Hannah is fine. Truly. Everyone is fine. It's you we've all been so worried about. You've been so ill these last two days."

"The house?"

"Henry went over there late yesterday afternoon. There's a lot of smoke damage and a pretty big hole in the roof. Nothing we can't fix. I'll get started on it right after Christmas."

Christmas.

"Is today Christmas Eve, then?"

"Yes."

"But the children were so looking forward to decorating the tree and they've been working on gifts for everyone and —"

"Henry found the gifts you'd put aside and the ones the children were making and brought them all back here."

"They must be ruined."

"A little smoke damage. Martha and Eliza have been able to get most of them clean. We're going to have a wonderful Christmas right here with Martha and Henry. Martha is making cookies with the girls and Henry took Jerome to get the tree. And now you've given us all the best possible gift." He rested his cheek against her hair. "The children are going to be so glad to see you when they wake. It will be like Christmas morning a day early."

"I hope I don't frighten them. I must look a mess." *Now, where had that come from?* Caroline had never been vain about her looks. And why would the children care how she looked?

You aren't thinking of the children. *You're thinking of how you look to Ty,* she thought, reproaching herself for her streak of vanity.

Ty lifted her chin so that she was looking up at him. "You're beautiful, Caroline." He stroked her face with his knuckles. And then he kissed her.

It was unlike any kiss they had shared before. It was a reciprocal kiss that spoke of relief and thankfulness. It was a kiss that acknowledged the near disaster they had survived. It was the kiss of a man and a woman who could love each other deeply because of all they had endured.

"I love you, Tyrone," she said, as for the first time since waking up she found her voice. "I know we married for the children, but I never again want to risk anything happening that might rob me of the chance to tell you that."

"When did you know?" he asked, and she bristled at the unexpected reaction.

"I'm not saying that anything has changed," she said. "I know that we have a bargain and I'm not expecting —"

Ty kissed her, then kissed her again. "Everything is changed," he said. "And all for the better. I love you, Caroline Justice. Merry Christmas, my love."

"I'm feeling much better," Caroline said. "Truly." *My husband loves me — truly loves me. How could I not feel as if my heart has sprouted wings?*

She could not stop smiling at Ty and he

seemed equally besotted with her. How had neither of them realized the love that had blossomed between them over these last few months? They had talked for an hour after he had declared his love for her, and then Martha had heard their voices. Once she realized that Caroline was finally conscious and able to sit up and take some nourishment, she sent Ty off to get Dr. Hopkins.

"Henry will go," Ty protested, reluctant to leave Caroline's side.

"Go," Caroline said. "Give me a chance to wash and change into a clean gown."

"And as soon as the doctor tells us Caroline is truly all right, then you can bring her into the parlor, but only for a few minutes. She still needs her rest."

"I'm fine," Caroline croaked, her voice still hampered by the dryness in her throat and the fullness in her chest. "I'm a little weak, but I want to see the children."

"Tell you what," Ty said as he stroked her cheek with the backs of his fingers, "let me bring the doctor and then I'll carry you to the parlor so you can see the children. They have a surprise for you."

"I thought I was the one who always came up with the bargains between us," she teased.

"Now, listen to me, Mrs. Justice," Ty said

sternly, "it's high time that you let us take care of you for a change. You're always the one caring for everyone else. Well, it's time we turned things around."

"Aye, aye, my captain," Caroline whispered and then she laughed. "I'm beginning to understand why you were appointed to captain that ship. You do have a tendency to enjoy giving orders."

He grinned. "A lot has changed, Mrs. Justice. Might as well get used to it." He kissed her forehead then. "I'll be back as soon as I can," he murmured, but still seemed reluctant to leave her.

"Well, if you don't get going, we're likely to be here all night," Martha said as she gave him a gentle push toward the door.

"Aye, aye," Ty said with a salute.

Later, as Dr. Hopkins examined Caroline without comment or a change in his expression, Ty stood by the bedroom door scowling.

"Breathe," the doctor instructed as he placed his stethoscope against her back. "Remarkable," he muttered as he put the instrument away.

"She's all right?" Ty asked.

"She'll need to continue to rest for the next several days, but there's been a significant improvement." It was evident that the doctor had not expected such a turn of events and was somewhat mystified by it.

Martha walked him to the bedroom door and called for Henry to see him to his carriage. When he was gone, she turned to Caroline and Ty. "He knows he gave up on you so he can't figure it out. Well, God is the original and greatest healer and that and Ty's constant praying brought you back to us, Caroline." She tapped Caroline's Bible. "There's your answer."

Martha flitted about. "Let's add this extra quilt. There could be a draft. The children have been in and out a dozen times or more already, letting cold air into the house with every opening of the door," she groused.

"Are you feeling well enough to see the children?" Ty asked, deliberately changing the subject.

"That would be the best medicine," Caroline said.

Then to her surprise Ty scooped her up into his arms, covers and all.

"Tyrone Justice, you put her down," Martha ordered. "The doctor said she needed to rest."

"But he didn't say she had to stay in bed," Ty called over his shoulder, as he carried Caroline down the hall to Martha and Henry's parlor, where the doors were

370

closed. "Children," he shouted. "Are you ready?"

Caroline heard giggles and whispers and then the doors slid open to reveal an evergreen tree far too large for the small room. It was decorated in gingerbread men, fruits made of marzipan, paper fans and cornucopias filled with nuts and candies. Popcorn strung together with cranberries formed a garland that swirled its way around the tree from top to bottom, and sprigs of holly and mistletoe peeked out from among the branches. Caroline saw that they had left off the usual candles for lighting the tree. The danger of fire was far too real for everyone, but the tree was so colorful and filled with other trim that the candles were unnecessary.

"Merry Christmas, Mama!" all three children shouted.

"Oh, children, it's the most beautiful tree I've ever seen," Caroline exclaimed.

"Sit her here, Papa," Jerome said, pointing to the settee beside of the tree.

"Are you really all better, Mama?" Eliza asked.

"I'm better," Caroline said. "Much better." She held out her arms and Hannah climbed into her lap.

"There are presents for you under the

tree," she whispered.

"Is there one for you?"

Hannah nodded. "Lots. And there's one for me and Jerome and Eliza all together," she confided.

"Oh, my, what could that be?"

"You'll just have to wait until morning to find out," Henry teased.

"Now stop that, Henry Wofford. These dear children won't sleep a wink. They're so excited and, with them all packed into one bedroom, they'll probably jabber the night away."

"You're all staying here?" Caroline asked Ty.

He nodded. "For now."

"How bad is it? The house?"

"It needs work," Ty admitted.

"So the school is —"

"Now just hush and stop thinking about such things," Martha interrupted. "The important thing to remember here is that everyone got out. You rescued Hannah and Ty rescued you, so all is well, praise God. It's Christmas Eve, Caroline, so let's all just count our blessings."

"Papa, will you put the angel at the top of the tree? None of us can reach it." Eliza handed Ty the angel that Martha had made when Caroline was a girl. It was dressed in a gold silk gown with wings of starched lace and a halo made of tinsel and, as Caroline held Hannah, Ty stretched to his full height and anchored the angel to the top of the tree.

Eliza nudged her brother, who took out his harmonica and began playing "Silent Night." Caroline could not remember a Christmas when she had been happier or felt more blessed as she did on this holy night. But her gratitude for blessings received tripled when, after the last note of the carol had died away, Ty said, "Let's all bow our heads in silent prayer and thank God for the many gifts He has given this family."

After the prayer and everyone's murmured amen, Ty looked up and found Caroline watching him, her eyes so filled with love that there could be no doubt in his mind ever again that they were embarking on a new life together.

"Do we open presents now?" Hannah yawned and stretched as she whispered to Caroline and everyone laughed.

"Not until morning, child," Martha said, lifting the little girl from Caroline's lap. "Come along, children. Henry, I need you, as well."

"What for?" Uncle Henry groused.

Martha cast a none-too-subtle look at Caroline and then Ty, then jerked her head toward the stairway. "Now," she hissed.

"Oh, sure, got to check the window in the children's bedroom. It's been sticking some and . . ." He was still talking as he followed Martha and the children up the stairs.

"You should get back to bed as well," Ty said, but he sat next to Caroline on the settee and pulled her into his arms.

"Can't we just sit here? I love the scent of the fresh evergreen. I promise I'll close my eyes and rest."

"Well, if you're really sure —"

"Stop worrying, Ty. Whatever comes our way, we'll face it — together."

"It's Christmas!" Hannah crowed as she came running down the stairs at dawn.

"Shhh," Caroline heard Eliza caution. "Everyone's still sleeping."

"Aunt Martha's been up for an hour or more. Smell the cinnamon?" Jerome said and he chuckled.

Then all three children turned the corner into the parlor and stopped.

"Good morning, children," Caroline said.

"Merry Christmas," Ty added as he straightened his legs and arms and grimaced at the stiffness.

Hannah's eyes were wide with wonder. "Did you stay up to wait for Father Christmas?" She glanced toward the hearth where a fire blazed.

Caroline pushed away a quilt she was quite sure had not covered them the night before. "We fell asleep," she told Hannah, "but it looks like Father Christmas has come and gone."

"Merry Christmas," Aunt Martha called out as she came down the hall with a tray of sweet rolls and fruit. There was also hot chocolate for the children and coffee for the adults. "Oh, my, it appears Father Christmas brought in several new gifts."

"And made a fire," Ty said with a grin.

"And brought us extra cover," Caroline added.

"And now extra logs for the fire," Henry said as he deposited several pieces of wood in the brass bucket next to the hearth.

"You're not Father Christmas," Hannah said with a giggle.

"Don't be too sure," Ty said and winked at Henry.

"Why don't you three get things started by opening this one?" Uncle Henry suggested, as he picked up from behind the tree a large, oddly shaped present wrapped in brown paper and a red ribbon. "Liza, you read the card."

"To our three favorite children," Eliza read.

"That's us," Hannah confided. "I asked Auntie Martha."

"With love from Aunt Martha and Uncle Henry," Eliza continued.

"Okay, little Miss Hannah, you untie the bow so Jerome can take off the paper."

Hannah pulled both streamers on the bow. The ribbon fell away and Jerome ripped off the paper to reveal a beautiful handmade sled.

"Oh, thank you, Aunt Martha and Uncle Henry," Eliza exclaimed.

"I bet it's faster than the sled Noah Johnstone has," Jerome declared with a grin as he gently slid a finger over the polished runners.

"Look, it has a ship painted on it," Hannah said. "Isn't that pretty?"

"Uncle Henry, you made this?" Caroline asked.

"Tyrone helped. He did the painting."

"Can we try it out now?" Jerome asked.

"Later," Martha said. "That snow we had overnight is not going anywhere."

"Well, then, can we open another present?" Hannah asked and everyone laughed.

"Sure," Ty said as he reached under the tree and gathered three identically wrapped but differently shaped packages. "This is from Mama and me."

Caroline was as anxious to see what Ty had wrapped up for the children as they were. She thought about the gifts she'd been making for each of them, but they would keep. For a birthday perhaps or another special occasion. She could not stop smiling as she realized anew that she and Tyrone would be together for the rest of their lives, watching the children grow up. Perhaps even having a child of their own.

"It's a scrimshaw bookmark," Eliza exclaimed. "It's ivory and, look, it's covered in flowers and hearts, and you used colored inks. I love it," she exclaimed. "Thank you." She hugged Ty and then Caroline.

Jerome knelt next to Caroline's chair and he unwrapped his gift. "A belt buckle with a map of the world on it. I mean, it's the whole world."

"Just don't go traveling until you're older," Caroline said as she cupped his cheek.

"Just on that sled," Jerome answered with a shy grin.

Hannah was unusually quiet as she held the lid of the ditty box Ty had made her in one hand and stared into the empty box. "It's empty," she whispered to Eliza.

"The box is the gift," Eliza whispered back.

"Hannah, let me see," Caroline said. "Oh, no, it's not empty at all. It's full of all the hopes and dreams your Papa and I have for you, but there's plenty of room for you to add your own special treasures. Like those pretty ribbons Papa brought you."

Her scowl deepened. "They got ruined in the fire."

"Not at all, child," Martha protested. "A little smoke is all. I've washed them for you and once they're ironed, you'll see that they'll be as good as new."

Hannah grinned. "I can keep them in my box so they'll be pretty forever and ever."

"Our turn," Eliza announced. "Papa, Aunt Martha helped us make you these gloves."

"I wound the yarn," Hannah said, "and Liza did the knitting."

"And you, son?" Ty asked as he tried on one glove.

"Oh, we could not have done these without Jerome," Martha exclaimed. She took Jerome's hand and held it palm-to-palm with Ty's. "He was our pattern."

"You've grown, son," Ty said, and Caroline saw that it was a compliment that

Jerome took to heart.

"Yes, sir."

"And this is for you, Mama." Eliza handed Caroline a handmade book.

"*The Teacher and the Sea Captain*," Caroline read, "a story by their children." She felt her throat close as tears welled. The book was illustrated with crude but colorful drawings of her with Ty and the three children. "Look, Aunt Martha," she croaked as she slowly turned the pages. "That's you."

"Twenty pounds ago," Martha said. "And is that Henry? What a handsome old man he is," she exclaimed.

Everyone gathered around as Caroline read the story aloud, and it was all Caroline could do to keep her voice steady as the story unfolded of how three children who had lost their mother in a fire came to live in a school. Ty was portrayed as a sort of swashbuckling adventurer who could perform feats of bravery without blinking an eye. Caroline was described as beautiful and loving and, as one line read, "smarter than any teacher in the world."

"But one day," Caroline read, "when the children were all in school, the littlest one slipped up to the attic. She had left something there that she knew was very important for her sister's class report."

Caroline felt her throat tighten and she glanced at Hannah, who smiled up at her. "Keep reading," she said softly. "It has a happy ending."

"Eliza, perhaps you could read the rest," Ty said as he put his arm around Caroline's shoulders. "Mama should save her voice until she's fully recovered."

Thank you, Caroline told him with a look and handed the precious book to Eliza.

The rest of the story was an embellishment of her courage in finding and saving Hannah, and Tyrone's in rescuing the two of them when — in the children's view — the firemen failed to act quickly enough.

"Once they were all together again," Eliza read, "the family closed their eyes and thanked God for keeping them all safe and —"

"— they all lived happily ever after. The end," Hannah announced. "I wrote that part."

Eliza closed the book and handed it back to Caroline. "Do you like it?" she asked.

"I will treasure it always," Caroline said and held out her arms for hugs with all three children.

Henry sniffed back tears and blew his nose. "There are more presents here," he said gruffly, "and they aren't going to open

380

themselves."

Indeed there were gifts for all. To Caroline's delight Eliza had recovered the apron they had been embroidering for Martha and finished it, as well as the tobacco pouch they had made from a piece of chamois and embroidered for Henry. Jerome presented each of his sisters with a set of colored pencils.

"Uncle Henry paid me to help chop wood," he said.

Eliza laughed. "And Aunt Martha paid Hannah and me to help polish the silver for today's dinner." She handed Jerome a present.

"It's from both of us," Hannah said.

Jerome eagerly ripped off the wrapping to discover a stamp album. "How did you know? I've seen this in the shop window and —"

"We saw you looking in the shop window," Hannah said, then giggled. "Because we were already inside the shop."

"Trying to decide what to get you," Eliza explained. "We hid until you left and then the shopkeeper said you had been by several times to look at the album."

"Thanks," Jerome said and gave each sister a hug.

Martha gave Henry a pair of embroidered

suspenders, and he gave her a new knitting bag. "Hope that one's big enough," he said.

"It's lovely," Martha replied as she examined the fine workmanship.

"Papa, don't you have something for Mama?" Hannah asked. "And what did you get, Papa?"

"I — I —" Caroline stuttered.

Ty squeezed her shoulder then knelt next to Hannah. "Sometimes, little one, the best presents aren't wrapped. Your Mama came back to us after being very, very ill and that's the best present I could ever get."

"And imagine how excited I was to open my eyes and find all of you safe," Caroline added. "It was like opening a thousand gifts."

Especially when I knew that I had your father's love.

Hannah considered this for a minute. "I guess, but Papa, you should have gotten her something she could look at. Girls really like presents."

"I'll remember that," Ty said.

This time it was Martha who swiped at tears and then blew her nose. "Well, this mess is not going to get cleaned up without help," she grumbled. "And I need help in the kitchen and dining room."

"I can —" Caroline began, but Martha

stopped her with a look.

"You can get yourself back in bed for the rest of the morning and get some rest. Sleeping out here all night," she huffed then turned accusing eyes to Ty. "What were you thinking?"

Ty lifted Caroline off the settee. "No use arguing with the boss, Caroline."

"I thought you were the boss."

"Not in this house," Henry muttered and everyone laughed.

After her nap Caroline shooed Ty from the room. "I am going to get properly dressed for Christmas dinner, and it would not hurt for you to clean up a bit, as well. That growth of beard, for example."

"All right, I get the message," Ty said. "Just don't overdo. I'll ask Martha to come and help you."

They had just finished their main course of roast goose when they heard the jingle of sleigh bells and then a knock at the front door.

"Company!" Hannah shouted and raced off to see who was calling on Christmas Day. She came back a minute later pulling Thomas Woodstock along with her. The boy's cheeks were bright red, and Caroline did not think that was entirely due to the cold given the way he avoided looking at Eliza. John and Matilda Woodstock followed their son into the dining room.

"Merry Christmas, Caroline, dear," Matilda said. "How well you're looking."

"Merry Christmas to both of you and your family," Caroline replied.

"Reverend Groves announced in church this morning that you'd made a miraculous recovery," John Woodstock said. "We're all so very pleased."

"I'm feeling much better, thank you. Won't you join us?" She glanced at Martha, who shrugged as if adding three more for Christmas dinner was no problem.

"Oh, no, dear. We're calling on friends to extend our best wishes for the holiday and invite everyone to celebrate the dawn of the New Year," Matilda said. "You will come, won't you? Oh, and Mr. and Mrs. Wofford, of course, you're invited, as well. It's going to be a houseful but that's the point of a celebration, isn't it?"

Ty had stood the minute Matilda Woodstock entered the room, and now he placed a protective hand on Caroline's shoulder. "Well, that's really nice of you, Mrs. Woodstock, but we'll need to be sure Mrs. Justice is —"

"We'd be pleased to accept," Caroline

said. "Thank you."

"Now, Caroline —"

"It's a full week away, Mr. Justice. I'm sure I'll be up and around long before that."

"Excellent," Matilda said.

"If you have some time before then, Mr. Justice," John Woodstock said, "stop by the bank. Some of us were talking after church this morning, and I think we have some idea of a space where Mrs. Justice could hold classes until we can get the damage to your home repaired."

"I — that would be wonderful," Ty said. "Thank you."

"Well, everyone is of a single mind here. As Reverend Groves reminded us in his sermon this morning, none of us can know when trouble might come our way. Certainly those of us who have grown up here on this island understand that better than most. We need to take care of each other, Justice."

"We should be going," Matilda said. "We still have so many calls to make. Come along, Thomas."

But Thomas seemed to have something else on his mind. "Uh, a bunch of us are going sledding and I thought maybe — boy, look at that," he murmured as he spotted the sled Henry had made, now resting against the wall of the dining room. "I'll bet that's really fast."

"If it's all right with your parents, Thomas, why don't you stay so you and Jerome can give it a try?" Ty said. "And you too, Eliza," he added after Caroline nudged him.

"What about me?" Hannah demanded.

"I need you and Uncle Henry to help me with the dishes," Martha said. "Then we'll all have dessert after your sister and brother and Thomas get back."

Appeased, Hannah followed Martha and Henry to the kitchen, while Jerome and Eliza hurried to put on their outer clothes. Ty and Caroline escorted the Woodstocks into the foyer.

"Here, son," Ty said, retrieving his new gloves from the parlor and handing them to Jerome. "You can use these since they seem to fit perfectly, but don't get too attached. I want them back."

Jerome grinned as he pulled on the gloves, then the three teens hurried outside.

"Don't go too fast," Ty and Caroline heard Matilda warn the children from the porch steps.

Ty closed the front door and took Caroline's hand. "Now, you have had a very full day and need to get off your feet for a bit."

"I rested earlier."

"And then you exerted yourself by getting

386

dressed and insisting on helping Martha bring out the dinner and —"

"I'm perfectly fine."

Ty cocked an eyebrow.

"Oh, all right." Caroline plopped down on the settee.

"Better," Ty said.

"I'll even close my eyes if that will make you happy. See? Closed tight."

"Good. Keep them that way for a minute."

Caroline heard Ty rummaging around among the discarded wrapping paper. Then she felt him next to her, pressing a small wrapped box into her hands. "Open your eyes, Caroline," he said.

"Oh, Ty, I haven't anything for you."

"You've given me back my life, Caroline. Because of you my children are safe and happy. Because of you, I have learned to love again. Because of you, I have learned to pray again."

Eyes brimming with tears, Caroline fumbled with the blue satin ribbon and opened the box. Inside was an ivory scrimshaw ring, inscribed on its surface with a finely detailed ship sailing into harbor toward a house that looked like their home. And on the inside was engraved, *To Caroline, my safe harbor in any storm.*

"This is what you were working on all

those nights?"

Ty nodded. He had finally found the purpose for that hollowed piece of ivory he had repeatedly rejected. He slid the ring onto her finger. It was a perfect fit, but far more flawless was the way Caroline fit into the curve of his arm.

She curled against him and admired the ring. "It's exquisite, Ty."

"Some day, it will be truly exquisite. I'll buy you a ring worthy of our love — an emerald to match your eyes."

Caroline pushed away and turned to him, her green eyes clear and sparkling for the first time since she had awakened. "Now, you listen to me, Tyrone Justice. I do not need nor do I want fancy jewels or things. I have you and those precious children and that is riches beyond measure for anyone."

Ty couldn't help it. He grinned. The woman was so adorable when she got her back up. "I thought we had decided I would be giving the orders as we set sail on this voyage together, Mrs. Justice. You make an excellent first mate and certainly the most beautiful mate a captain could ever wish for, but —"

"Oh, hush," she said as she snuggled back against him. But she was smiling as she rested her head against his heart and her breathing became peaceful and even.

From outside the window Ty heard the distant squeals of his older children, while from the kitchen came Hannah's giggle underscoring the soft voices of Henry and Martha. It was a world at peace and Ty was more certain than he had ever been that with Caroline — his wife and anchor — at his side, nothing would ever seem impossible again.

Dear Reader,

And so we come back to Nantucket in a different time — 1850 — with women going through their days in corsets and hooped skirts and men of the sea who have lost their way now that whaling is on the wane. It's around the time that Herman Melville wrote his classic novel, *Moby Dick,* and in October of 1846 Maria Mitchell discovered the comet that propelled her to fame as one of America's most renowned astronomers. It's four years after the Great Fire that destroyed much of the waterfront and town — houses, shops, warehouses and candle factories all went up in flames on the night of July 13, 1846. But the people of Nantucket are nothing if not resilient and they came back, rebuilding the homes and shops and finding their way through the troubled times that followed. Their faith remained strong and we can take that lesson from them. Especially if times are challenging for you, dear reader, I hope you will find comfort in the story of Caroline and Tyrone. Please stop by my Web site at www.books-byanna.com to learn more about Nantucket's colorful history and to let me know how you enjoyed this story. (Or you can always write to me at P.O. Box 161, Thiensville, WI

53092.) Until the next time . . . be well, be caring of others and may God's blessing be upon you.

All best,
Anna Schmidt

QUESTIONS FOR DISUSSION

1. Trouble for Tyrone Justice seems to just keep coming. What do you think of Ty's way of meeting his challenges?

2. Caroline Hudson is also struggling. How does her approach to facing her problems differ from Tyrone's?

3. Why does Tyrone feel he is unworthy of God's love?

4. In what ways is Tyrone a good father?

5. How do Caroline's reasons for helping Tyrone's children change over the course of the story?

6. Caroline says that Tyrone reminds her of Job — what parallels do you see between the biblical story of Job and Ty's story?

7. Tyrone says that Caroline is like the Good Samaritan — what parallels do you see between the parable of the Good Samaritan and Caroline's actions?

8. How does the issue of lying come up in the story, and is there ever a time when lying is all right? If so, under what circumstances?

9. The setting of Nantucket for this story is intentional. In what ways is Ty like an island?

10. How do Tyrone and Caroline change over the course of the story, and how do those changes bring them closer?

11. Have you ever faced a period in your life where you were struggling and difficult times seemed to come in waves? If so, how did you meet those challenges?

12. In what concrete ways does your faith sustain you — and in difficult times, how do you sustain your faith?

ABOUT THE AUTHOR

Anna Schmidt is an award-winning author of more than twenty-five works of historical and contemporary fiction. She is a two-time finalist for the coveted RITA® Award from Romance Writers of America as well as four times a finalist for the *RT Book Reviews* Reviewers' Choice Award. The most recent *RT Book Reviews* Reviewers' Choice Nomination was for her 2008 Love Inspired Historical novel, *Seaside Cinderella,* which is the first of a series of four historical novels set on the romantic island of Nantucket. Critics have called Anna "a natural writer, spinning tales reminiscent of old favorites like *Miracle on 34th Street.*" Her characters have been called "realistic" and "endearing" and one reviewer raved, "I love Anna Schmidt's style of writing!"